For Betty,
Blessings!
Carlene

MW00453204

DAUGHTER OF THE KING

Carlene Havel &
Sharon Faucheux

Copyright 2012 Carlene Havel, Sharon Faucheux

ALL RIGHTS RESERVED

Cover art by Joan Alley

Editing by Jacqueline Hopper

This book is a work of fiction and any resemblance to persons, living or dead, or places, events or locales is purely coincidental. The characters are the product of the authors' imagination and used fictitiously.

Warning: The unauthorized reproduction or distribution of this copyrighted work is illegal. No part of this book may be scanned, uploaded or distributed via the Internet or any other means without the permission of Prism Book Group. Please purchase only authorized editions and do not participate in the electronic piracy of copyrighted material. Thank you for respecting the hard work of these authors.

Published by Prism Book Group
First Edition 2012
ISBN 13-978-0615740614 ISBN-10: 0615740618
Published in the United States of America
Contact info: contact@prismbookgroup.com
http://www.prismbookgroup.com

FOREWORD

Daughter of the King tells the Biblical story of King Saul's youngest daughter, Princess Michal. The authors added imaginary conversations and supporting characters, including Tirzah and Sarah.

Names have various spellings in books of the King James Bible. Phaltiel, for instance, is alternately spelled Phalti. David and Abigail's son's name is translated as Daniel in one place and Chileab in another. To avoid confusion, we chose one spelling or name per character and used it consistently.

The Bible does not state whether Bathsheba was a Hittite or a Hebrew woman who married a foreigner. For the purposes of this novel, we theorized she was Hittite, as was her husband, Uriah.

King Saul did not live in Jerusalem. We invoked literary license to relocate his house near the City of David.

Was Jonathan close to David's age or much older? We do not know the answer, but considered the two as contemporaries in the book.

For believers, it is a serious undertaking to write a story based on the Holy Bible. We hope and pray we have done our work in an acceptable manner. Scripture is truth. *Daughter of the King* is fiction.

This is how we think it might have happened.

CHAPTER ONE

"But Saul had given Michal his daughter, David's wife, to Phalti[el] the son of Laish, which was of Gallim." I Samuel 25:44

"YOU'RE NOT TAKING my wife anywhere!" Phaltiel bellowed. He struggled to break free from the soldiers who restrained him.

"Then we will take your widow." The soldier tossed an unconcerned glance in Phaltiel's direction. "It makes no difference to me." He turned to the woman standing nearby. "You will come with us."

"I shall make preparations for a journey of how many days?" Michal struggled to keep her voice calm. The daughter of the king must not show fear.

"We cannot waste time with preparations." Captain Osh sat straight and tall on his horse. "We will leave as soon as—"

"There must be some mistake," Phaltiel's chief steward interrupted. "King Saul himself gave his daughter to my lord Phaltiel."

"King Saul no longer reigns." Osh glared at the steward. "He is as dead as you and I will be if we fail to deliver the woman Michal soon."

Michal addressed her handmaid. "Come, Tirzah, we will gather a few things quickly." She felt the stares of soldiers all the way across the courtyard and braced herself for the thrust of a spear in her back.

"We have endured two days of hard riding, Phaltiel." The authoritative ring of the Captain's voice filled the courtyard. "Feed my men and see to our animals."

Michal breathed deeply to maintain her composure. Was it true her father, King Saul, was dead? Was it possible her dear brother, Jonathan, was now king of Israel? Was there a rebellion? A foreign invasion? Were soldiers, like those in the courtyard, even now rounding up her sister, Merab, and her family? She knew an insurgent ruler could never risk her or her sister's royal blood flowing into the veins of a legitimate heir.

Michal forced down her fear as she walked toward the women's living area. She prayed for courage as she concentrated on keeping her steps steady on the tamped earth of the courtyard.

The clapping of the chief steward's hands broke the tension. Servants grabbed water jars to fill the stone drinking trough for the military animals. Others stoked the kitchen fire and made preparations for the soldiers' meal. Lord Phaltiel's senior wife, Bida, stood watching the activity. Such excitement rarely intruded upon the mundane life of Gallim.

Michal quickened her steps to push through the crowd of Phaltiel's wives, children, and servants streaming into the courtyard. Once indoors, she fought to focus on which of her few possessions she should take.

"Tirzah, fetch the coat. I'll carry it under my cloak. Look through my old robes in Bida's chest, and choose one which clearly identifies me as the king's married daughter. I'll take one additional change of clothing and my sewing box." She looked around her. "There's nothing else in this house I ever want to see again. You can keep everything else."

Tirzah's eyes widened in horror. "You would not leave me behind?"

Michal clasped her servant's slender hand. "There's no reason to drag you into whatever awaits me. If my father is truly dead, these men may well be delivering me to an enemy. Maybe even the Philistines."

"Better to suffer with you than to stay in this Godless house alone." Tirzah's tears spilled onto her cheeks. "Please, my lady, I beg you on my mother's bones, let me go with you."

Michal wavered. Tirzah had been her companion since the two of them were children. "All right. You may come with us. The Captain said it was a two-day ride to wherever they came from. Of course, that may not be true. Try to get us some food to take along. Some dates and goat cheese would be best." Tirzah brightened and brushed away her tears as Michal continued. "Anything you can learn from the soldiers or the other women may be useful. We need to know who has taken King Saul's place and where we are going."

"Yes, my lady. I will do as you say."

Michal straightened. "While you do your duty, I will do mine."

With everyone else outside—their attention fastened on the soldiers in the courtyard—Michal swept quickly through the women's rooms. She gathered the many idols and teraphims, the superstitious god figurines that sat everywhere.

As a girl, she participated in religious activities meant to convince the king's subjects of the royal family's devotion to the Living God. She went mindlessly through the motions of the familiar rituals, paying no attention to their deeper meaning. The devout faith of her husband David made her more thoughtful. Yet it was only when she was thrust into a life of misery that Michal was forced to trust the one God of Israel.

Her family, alienated. Her husband, bargained away years ago. Michal stiffened her resolve against such sorrowful thoughts lest they overtake her. She would concentrate on being grateful the soldiers did not murder her in the sight of Phaltiel and his hateful wives.

Perhaps the soldiers would kill her as soon as they were a little distance from Phaltiel's compound. Or someone could creep near in tonight's darkness and dispatch her and poor Tirzah in their sleep.

Michal shivered at the thought of other possibilities. The prospect of torture frightened her. A quick death would be an answer to prayer. Some conqueror might be planning a public execution of King Saul's family. Even the ultimate humiliation of a forced marriage to an uncircumcised heathen could await her. She gathered her courage to bear whatever she must.

In the beginning of her exile, Michal feared some stranger would bring the information King Saul had successfully tracked down and murdered her beloved husband David. When did she hear the news? Their tenth month in Phaltiel's household, a slave trader stopped to obtain water for his pack animals. From the traveler, Michal's handmaid Sarah heard that David and his loyal followers still hid in wilderness areas, protecting isolated farms from thieves and marauders. Sarah reported to Michal how the man laughed, showing his fine white teeth, when recounting King Saul's irrational fear of his own son-in-law.

Years passed with no new information. Then one day Tirzah was cleaning the hearth in the kitchen when the women from a band of wandering wool merchants came to warm themselves. Hearing familiar words, Tirzah realized the travelers were Judeans. Their country was now being ruled by David, they said. Everyone was prospering under his progressive benevolence. Yes, their king was that same legendary David who, armed only with a slingshot, had in his youth fought and killed the Philistine giant Goliath.

Michal was overjoyed to learn her husband had so far evaded the dark furies of her father, King Saul. She gave thanks that her personal sacrifice to save David was not in vain. Was it possible that he still survived to this day? If so, she was certain some other woman occupied her place in his warm embrace by now.

A startling thought invaded Michal's consciousness as she prepared to go with the soldiers. Perhaps protocol would demand the presence of King David of Judea at a festival given by the new ruler of Israel. Was it possible she might glimpse her adored husband's face once more before her life ended? She must not break down before David's eyes if some heathen ordered her torn to pieces by a wild animal.

Michal took the worthless gods she collected and dumped them on her bed. The crude clay pieces shattered easily when she smacked them against each other. So much for Shapash. One slender figurine snapped in two when she laid it across her knee and applied her full strength to its head and feet. She took her sharpest knife and defaced the other two pieces of wood. The pagans of this house would soon see how powerless their stupid idols were.

The anger Michal held inside for years boiled over as she took particular delight in carving away the ugly features of Bida's favorite idol, Baal. Bida, Phaltiel's first wife, was a thin-haired woman who constantly criticized the other wives, shrewdly playing one against another to maintain her own advantage. Bida was particularly mean to Michal, often referring to her contemptuously as 'Her Royal Lowness'.

Michal thought back to the day she first came to this place in Gallim, as the fifth wife of Lord Phaltiel. Bida met her at the door of the women's quarters with crossed arms, spewing hostility from tiny eyes set almost comically wide apart in the expanse of her broad face. Michal was hungry, thirsty, and exhausted from her journey. Phaltiel had already given her a taste of his beastly nature. She hoped to find some compassion among his women.

"What do you know about growing olives and pressing oil?" Bida demanded without a single word of welcome or greeting. "That is what we do here."

Michal kept her response humble, to show proper deference to the head wife. "I'm sorry, but I know nothing of those things. Perhaps you will be kind enough to teach me."

Bida rolled her eyes toward the women of the household, who stood in a semi-circle around and behind her. "Just what we have been wishing for," she said, "a wife who does not know how to work. No doubt, since you are the daughter of a king, you are accustomed to a life of leisure." The women smirked and giggled. Michal sensed they were less amused than fearful of displeasing Bida. "And I see you have brought along two personal maids," Bida taunted. "They must make things easy for you."

The smell of flour cakes sweetened with honey made Michal aware of her gnawing hunger, but she could go without food. Thirst was another matter. Her dry mouth and parched throat begged for water. "We will do our best to contribute to the continued wealth of this household. I'm sure you will find some useful work Sarah, Tirzah, and I can do."

"You can count on it," Bida snorted. After a pause, she said bitterly, "I understand you have married our lord Phaltiel even though you have never been divorced by your husband who is yet alive."

Michal drew herself to her full height and stared down at Bida for a long moment. Finally she spoke. "I have obeyed the command of my

5

father the king in becoming our lord Phaltiel's wife." *Enough of this foolish game.* "Thank you for your gracious welcome," she continued. "I shall not soon forget it." She looked into the faces of the other women. One by one they dropped their eyes.

Bida took everything of any value from Michal's possessions. She kept the most desirable items for herself, and distributed the remainder among the other wives and servants who happened to be in her favor at the moment. Even though Bida could not possibly have wedged her ample torso into the loosest of Michal's robes and tunics, she kept all of them in her private storage trunk. Sarah and Tirzah were allowed to keep their worst clothing, anything stained, patched, or threadbare, which they shared with their mistress. Phaltiel's women showed no interest in Michal's fabric working tools. Bida handled them warily, but did not ask what they were.

"Royal attendants wear such as this?" Bida tossed a shabby wool coat at Sarah. "Lord Phaltiel's slaves wouldn't dress themselves in this rag."

Sarah stared at the floor and meekly tucked her bottom lip under the top one. She rearranged the coat, neatly folding the patched side underneath the ripped back.

The thought of Sarah threatened to summon emotions Michal could not allow herself to release right now. Sarah had been her wet nurse, taking the newborn princess to her breast along with her own two-week old daughter, Tirzah.

How Michal wished she could slip out of the compound one last time, walk through the terraced rows of olive trees, and sit on the big rock that overlooked the spot where Sarah and the others were buried. Phaltiel was responsible, she thought, him and his nasty drunken brawls.

It did not take Michal long to realize Phaltiel was ruled by the fruit of the vine. Tirzah at first tried to water down his cup when serving him, but Phaltiel loudly demanded stronger wine. Sarah then suggested topping off his goblet at every opportunity. On a good night, their lord and master would drink himself into a stupor before he could summon an unfortunate wife or two to his bed.

CHAPTER TWO

"And Ishbosheth sent, and took her from her husband, even from Phaltiel the son of Laish." II Samuel 3:15

THE MOST DANGEROUS times in Phaltiel's household occurred when the annual harvest of ripe olives was finished. Huge vats were filled to the brim with newly-pressed olive oil in Phaltiel's storehouses. With the hard work done for another year, the celebration began. Generous amounts of new wine were ladled into bowls and consumed at a three-day drunken festival honoring pagan harvest gods. The chief steward conspired to get Phaltiel hopelessly drunk as soon as he could, with his master's full cooperation. Alternately weeping and belligerent, Phaltiel would glut himself on drink and sex. As soon as their master lay passed out on a convenient bed or the floor, the men of the household ran amok.

Michal's old handmaid, Sarah, lay dead in the courtyard the morning after one of these wild new wine orgies, her head crushed against a heavy rock. A foul humor hung over the compound after three days of unbridled intoxication and debauchery. No one, other than Michal and Tirzah, took notice of Sarah's death.

"The old woman drank too much wine and lost her footing in the darkness of the courtyard," was the chief steward's light dismissal.

"Yes," Phaltiel agreed thickly, his hands on the sides of his head. "My greedy servant gorged herself on my new wine and could not keep herself aright." Everyone knew Sarah never touched wine. However, no one dared dispute Phaltiel's pronouncement, particularly on a morning when he complained that the slightest noise made his temples throb.

Michal helped the brokenhearted Tirzah attend to Sarah's burial. Although there was no incense to burn, they dressed the body in the best robe they could spare and used aromatic leaves in place of proper spices and balms. The two women were the only members of the household to observe the seven days of mourning. Tirzah wept at the thought of wild animals disturbing her mother's body. To keep that from happening, they struggled with a large, flat stone, finally rolling it across the mouth of a protective cave.

The little burial cave was an accidental discovery made during the years Michal was responsible for laundry. Initially the dark, cool place was her secret sanctuary. One year she hid food, water, and dirty clothes in the cave before the new wine festival. She and her maids slipped away separately to hide in the cave until the worst of the bacchanalia was over.

The next morning they noisily splashed about, doing the laundry by treading on it in the ankle-deep stream. Afterward, they casually carried the wet garments and stretched them out on large rocks in the courtyard. They pretended to be returning from an early start with domestic chores, and the ruse worked.

Sarah's body rested alone in her cave for three years. Then a fever swept through Phaltiel's compound and Tirzah's frail little girl Zora died. Last year, the tiniest bundle of all came to keep old Sarah company. Tirzah's infant son was born dead after a day and night of difficult labor.

Following Bida's lead, the other wives taunted Tirzah about her stillborn baby and Michal for her failure to become pregnant. If only she would bow down to the pagan gods, the women avowed, Tirzah could have had healthy children. They assured Michal that worshiping Astarte, the goddess of earth and fertility, would certainly remove her curse of unfruitfulness. Tirzah and Michal refused to follow the blasphemous advice. Michal held her head high, attempting not to respond to the women's snide remarks.

When directly challenged, she would merely say, "We worship only the one true God. He has not yet chosen to bless me with sons." She was convinced of the general truth of her statement. Still, she could not understand how the broad expanse of the Living God's divine plan could be affected by whether or not she conceived a child. Regardless of how much she despised Phaltiel, Michal longed to become a mother. Occasionally, she managed to be alone long enough to shed a few solitary tears. The daughter of the king did not cry with self-pity in the presence of other women.

As Michal continued destroying the idols, she envisioned the uproar that would occur when the desecration of the household gods was discovered. How surprised Bida would be to find that the always meek Michal committed such an outrage.

What should she do with the bronze Astarte in her hand? She'd succeeded in making superficial scratches in the figure, but was not yet satisfied with the results.

"Everything is ready, my lady." Tirzah's voice startled Michal. "But I have gathered no information about our destination. The other women know nothing, and the soldiers will not talk."

"As I expected. No matter what happens, we are well out of this place." Michal pulled back a corner of the blanket on her bed. "This is what is left of the meaningless gods they worship."

Tirzah gasped. "We must go before they find out." Then she smiled. "You did well."

"What shall we do with this remaining lump of metal?" Michal pulled the last figurine from the folds of her tunic.

Tirzah paused only a moment. "What about those crocks where the stable boys store dung for the olive tree roots?"

"Excellent!" Michal loved the symbolism of this gesture. "That will be my last act in this house."

"But, my lady," Tirzah counseled, "you have no excuse to go to the stables. You might arouse suspicion. I must deliver Astarte to her new dwelling."

Michal was determined. "No. I will do this myself. Meet me in the courtyard with our bundles."

9

Why did she not think of the huge jars filled with animal dung, stored in a far corner of the stable? Was it three years ago, or four, when she and Tirzah hid there during a particularly frightening celebration of the harvest?

The ever-resourceful Tirzah found a hollow gourd and dipped a little sheep dung in it. "I need a dab of this for the coat," she said, "to discourage anyone from casting sheep's eyes on it." Michal and Tirzah covered their mouths and shook with silent laughter at the thought of sheep dung warding off sheep eyes.

It was absurd now to imagine how anything could be amusing while hiding in that stinking barn, fearful of being raped, beaten or even murdered. There were times when the desperate need for a good laugh overcame the darkest of circumstances.

That must have been four years ago, Michal thought. They hid in the stable not long after she made a beautiful blanket for Tirzah's little daughter Zora. Michal remembered how the other women curiously eyed her nightly work as she combed and carded the wool. They openly stared at her hand-held spindle as she spun the carded wool into yarn. Finally, to their amazement, she knitted the yarn into a blanket.

One of the younger wives, a slight, dark-skinned Canaanite woman who seldom spoke to anyone, shyly asked if Michal would make a blanket for *her* baby. The chief steward became interested, and soon Michal was making yarn and blankets to send to market. Michal persuaded the chief steward she could make more trade goods with Tirzah's help.

Bida complained to anyone who would listen about the chief steward's interference, taking away the head wife's authority to assign work to the women. Nevertheless, the steward had his way. Michal and Tirzah's goods were traded for merchandise everyone in the household enjoyed, such as spices, metal cauldrons, and jewelry— things that put Phaltiel in fine spirits for a day or so.

As she slipped away to the stable, Michal wondered if Bida was worried about losing the necklace and earrings she commandeered the day Michal arrived in Gallim.

"Gold jewelry!" Bida exclaimed as soon as she saw the copper necklace. "Give it to me." Michal avoided looking at Tirzah or Sarah for fear of showing her contemptuous amusement. "Do you have any more?" Bida demanded.

"I have only these earrings made from that same metal." Michal could not resist taking advantage of Bida's ignorance. She owned other jewelry, but the chain and earrings were the only pieces of copper. Bida still wore the earrings from time to time, even though they were tarnished and lost their luster. The chain adorned the senior wife's thick neck every day.

On her way to the stable, Michal avoided the kitchen, where soldiers congregated to consume the meal provided by Phaltiel. She pulled her cloak over the side of her face and stooped to disguise her height. As soon as she reached the barn-like structure, she ducked inside and flattened herself against the wall, waiting for her eyes to adjust to the transition from the brightness outside. Listening intently, she heard only the sound of animals munching on straw. Moving to the dark, low-roofed corner where the dung jars were stored, she selected a container near the wall and pushed Astarte's evil likeness into the goo, head first. She used a small stick to guide the idol deeper into the jar.

Satisfied, she tossed the stick aside and threaded her way through the maze of containers. Michal was about to emerge from the darkness of the smelly corner when she heard men's voices. Stepping back, she crouched behind a high stack of hay.

The murmur of voices became more distinct, drawing closer. Men, two of them. She waited quietly to find out who they were. It was not a matter of friend or foe, merely greater or lesser enemy.

"I served with Lord David when he was the master of King Saul's military operations." It was Joash, a slave who tended the olive groves. He was one of the few men who took no part in the debauchery of Phaltiel's harvest festivals.

"I have no quarrel with Phaltiel. Why should I make off with one of his slaves?" The second voice belonged to the captain in charge of the soldiers.

Michal considered her options. How could she sneak out of the stable? The men stood well inside, but they had a clear view of the entrance. Any movement would cause her long cloak to rustle the straw and attract their attention.

"Captain Osh, Lord Phaltiel has held me as a slave beyond the seven years allowed by the law. Legally, I should be free. I could hide outside the gate," Joash begged. "Your men can pick me up after you have cleared the compound. Please, sir, I am a soldier like you."

Years ago, Sarah taught Michal to keep herself calm by breathing deeply. From habit, she inhaled as much of the foul stable air as she could hold, and regretted it immediately. Just as the slave said, "I am a soldier like you," Michal sneezed resoundingly.

Growing up among palace intrigues taught the princess that boldness would often succeed when stealth failed. She stood, smoothed her clothing, scratched her sandals against the straw, and walked nonchalantly toward the two men.

"On my great-grandfather's bones," Captain Osh swore. "What are *you* doing here?" He clapped his hand over his mouth for a moment and added, "Excuse my language, my lady. This man was just educating me on the subject of growing olives."

Michal smiled at the Captain. "I must be losing my fluency in Hebrew. It sounded to me as if he asked you to smuggle him out of here." She hoped her sarcasm would divert the soldier from questioning her presence in the stable.

"Picking up a few of your essential belongings from the stable, are you?"

Michal doubted this officer was a member of the royal guard, but she knew from the way he talked he was a native of Jerusalem. He might not be devout, but he would not be likely to oppose a blow against idolatry. "If you must know, I destroyed the idols of the false gods the people in this household worship. All but one, a metal Astarte, which I just now buried deep in a crock of dung."

Joash smiled. Captain Osh slapped his thigh, shook his head, and laughed aloud. "Yet another reason to go before Phaltiel can raise the alarm among his neighbors." He chuckled again.

"Why don't you do it?" Michal knew she had no right to challenge Osh.

The Captain sobered immediately. "Do what?"

"Take Joash along," she said.

"I was sent to transport one obviously difficult woman, not everyone who wants to escape from Gallim," Captain Osh said. "Only you will go with my soldiers when we leave."

"Surely you don't expect me to travel without my handmaid." Michal hoped she sounded more confident than she felt.

12

Osh glared at her, his jaw set.

"If Tirzah and Joash come along, I promise not to escape." Michal paused. She could see this soldier was confident she could not get away from his army. So she offered up the only thing over which she had any control, "And I will give you my word I will not take my own life before we reach our destination."

CHAPTER THREE

"And Saul saw and knew that the Lord was with David, and that Michal Saul's daughter loved him." I Samuel 18:28

TIRZAH STRUGGLED TO keep her arm around Michal's belongings while mounting a donkey.

"You there!" Captain Osh said to Joash. "Yes, you, slave. Take the woman's burdens and carry them to the cart outside the gate."

The chief steward stretched his arm in front of Joash's chest to prevent the slave's movement. "Surely there are plenty of soldiers who can serve you, Captain," the steward said.

Osh rode slowly toward the chief steward and stopped an arm's length away. "When I give an order, I expect obedience, not insolence." He beckoned to his armor bearer. "My javelin."

The steward looked nervously around the courtyard and fell to his knees. "I meant no harm, my lord. Spare me, I beg you." No one spoke or moved except for Captain Osh, who took his time inspecting the point of his weapon.

"Please." The steward crumpled into a crouch. "Do this house the honor of taking the slave Joash as the gift of Lord Phaltiel." Seizing the opportunity, Joash scrambled to collect the bundles from Tirzah and hurriedly exited the compound.

Michal walked through the courtyard surrounded by heavily armed soldiers. Outside the gate, other soldiers motioned her into a waiting cart.

The captain brought his horse near the cart where Michal was settling among her few possessions. "I expect you to keep your word," Osh said, gazing back at Phaltiel's stronghold. "Since I brought along your handmaid and risked a riot on behalf of the slave."

"I thank you for your kindness to Tirzah and Joash," Michal answered. "You may be sure I will keep my promise to the Captain of the Royal Guard." She paused before adding, "*If* I ever see him."

Captain Osh snapped his head in her direction and narrowed his eyes. "Do you dare to accuse me of deceit?"

"I have no doubt this is an elite group." Michal looked around. "But I've been around the military enough to recognize war horses when I see them. Your troops are regular army cavalry."

"If the other women of this household are as sharp of tongue as you, I feel sorry for the man Phaltiel." Osh gave a hand motion, and the caravan moved forward. "No more questions"—he smiled ever so slightly—"until this *cavalry unit* reaches its destination." He urged his horse into a gallop and rode to the front of the moving column.

Michal sat facing backward and arranged the hood of her cloak to shade her face from the bright sun. As the cart lumbered along the dusty road, she could see the silvery-green leaves of the olive trees glistening across the low plain beyond Phaltiel's compound. She fixed her eyes on the large rock near the cave where Tirzah's babies were buried next to old Sarah. "Goodbye, dear ones," she whispered as the boulder became less and less distinct in the distance.

Michal pondered who sent these soldiers to fetch her, and why. Common marauders would have looted Phaltiel's household before departing. These well-disciplined men demanded nothing more than food. In a few hours the caravan would reach a crossroads. There they would either turn south toward home, or north into enemy territories.

When the place where she lived for seven difficult years was no longer in sight, Michal made herself as comfortable as she could in the cart. She located her sewing box and took out a small, sharp knife. She ignored the two soldiers who quickly positioned their horses within reach.

Unfolding her ragged wool coat, Michal expertly sliced away the faded border trim that encircled the garment's hemline. Wherever the destination, she was determined to present an appearance worthy of a daughter of a king. She thought how wise Sarah was to suggest the coat as a hiding place for her best jewelry.

The seven gold bangles she withdrew were a gift from her parents on that happy occasion when she became David's wife. She remembered thinking of herself as a woman at barely fourteen. Now she understood why her mother and Sarah clucked over her youthfulness on her wedding day.

Michal ran her fingers over the smoothness of the gold before slipping the bangles, one by one, onto her left arm. Seeing her wedding bracelets gleam in the sunlight swept Michal's thoughts backward. How well she remembered the first time she saw the man who would become her husband.

David had been playing the harp in her father's great hall. King Saul was irritable earlier that day. Only six years old, Michal already knew, as well as everyone else, to stay away from her father when he sank into one of his dark moods. He endured fewer of those mysterious spells back then, but they were always dangerous. No one knew what triggered the king's descent into the depths of despair nor, once stricken, how long he and everyone around him would suffer.

King Saul liked to end dinner with a sweet date cake. The duty of serving the cake belonged to Merab, Michal's older sister. On the day that was burned into Michal's memory, Merab claimed to have a sore toe resulting from an encounter with a thorn.

"Your toe was fine this morning, when you were running through the fields," Michal complained.

"It hurts now," Merab sniffed. "So I'm going to lie down at dinner time. You will have to serve Father's treat."

"That's not fair, Merab! You always try to get your way just because you're older than me." Michal found it difficult to be the baby in the household.

"Of course." Merab grinned. "That's what being older is all about. You have to wait behind me for everything. You can't get married until

I do, and your sons will never have the rank or honors mine will enjoy."

"They might," Michal argued, "if I marry a greater man than your husband. I expect Father will betroth me to royalty, perhaps a prince of Egypt, and I will wear nothing but fine purple robes and different colored jewels every day."

"No," Merab explained confidently, "I'm the eldest daughter. Therefore, Father will secure the best marriage for me. You can then have one of the men who lost the fight for my hand."

"Aren't you both a little young to be talking of marriage?" Their older brother, Jonathan, tousled Michal's hair, to her irritation. She looked forward to being grown. Then she would have a husband and cover her hair like other married women.

"Where did you come from?" Merab demanded.

"I've been out here all afternoon, relishing this fine day. I was practicing my archery and enjoying a little peace until you two came along."

"Jonathan," Michal complained, "Merab claims she has a sore toe and can't serve Father his date cake this evening. The truth is, she's frightened he is falling into one of his moods. So she wants to stay out of sight and make me do her work."

"It's best never to speak of the king's disposition," Jonathan warned. "A good daughter should be eager for any chance to serve her father. As for marriage"—he looked toward the distant mountains—"be content to wait. We will do what we must, all of us."

To everyone's relief, King Saul laughed and joked pleasantly with his sons and the company of government officials and military officers at his table that evening. Many different breads and pastries covered the table, along with pots of honey and a wide variety of fruits.

"The music of this new lad, David, soothes our master," Haggia, a toothless, bent-over kitchen worker observed to the baker's helper, Tabitha.

"Is this David truly the same one who fought and killed the Philistine giant, Goliath?" Tabitha's eyes glowed.

Haggia cackled. "Indeed he is the one. What a great day that was for Israel!" The old woman glanced toward the great room. "If Goliath was a woman, I'd vow he was blinded by young David's beauty."

17

"He would turn any woman's head, no doubt about that," Tabitha agreed. "Well, now, little one..." Tabitha turned toward Michal, who sat near the threshold of the great hall. "Do you want to sample the date cakes before you present one to the king?"

Ordinarily, Michal leapt to Tabitha's side at the hint of a treat. That evening she whispered, "No, thank you." Her eyes never moved from the great room. She studied the young man, David, as he coaxed hauntingly beautiful melodies from his harp. Dark curls encircled the ruddy skin of his chiseled face. Most striking of all were his large, luminous brown eyes framed with dark lashes. How old was he? Fourteen or perhaps fifteen? He was trim, with broad shoulders and well-muscled arms. Until that evening, Michal thought her brother, Jonathan, was the ideal of masculine perfection. But there was something special about David. Michal did not understand the strange excitement she felt when she looked at the handsome young musician.

A few days later, Michal and Tirzah were weaving necklaces for themselves from supple vines, under Sarah's distant but watchful eye. David and Jonathan were in a far corner of the meadow, tossing their javelins at a makeshift target. When the young men passed by, returning to the palace, David smiled at the little girls.

Michal gazed after him, then turned to Tirzah and said, "I hope I marry a man as comely as this David."

THE CART'S LURCHING startled Michal from her reverie and brought her back to the present. She took deep breaths to combat her rising fear. They could not yet have reached the crossroads. Why, then, was the column halting? Was this the moment of execution? She almost laughed with relief when she realized the soldiers were stopping to water their animals at the well located between Phaltiel's compound and the crossroads.

Just as Michal was thinking what a fine idea a drink would be, Tirzah appeared with a skin of cool, sweet water. While Michal took several unladylike gulps, Tirzah leaned close, cupped a hand over her mouth and spoke rapidly. "Your father was killed in battle against the Philistines, along with Jonathan. All of your brothers are dead except Ishbosheth, who is now king. We are being taken to Lord Abner, at Bahurim."

Michal's eyes stung with sudden tears. She loved her brother Jonathan dearly. And the loss of her father, despite all that passed between them, made her heart ache. She sighed and returned the skin of water to her handmaid.

"The slave Joash helped me gather information from the soldiers," Tirzah said. "There's more. Phaltiel's men are following us."

Tirzah jumped as Captain Osh's voice broke across the men and animals still crowding around the well. "Quickly!" he shouted. The men mounted their horses and reformed the column.

Tirzah's information gave Michal much to think about. She never cared for her Uncle Abner. He was a gruff, burly man who spent his life as a military commander. Still, being taken to an Israelite—a kinsman at that—and knowing the kingdom was not in foreign hands made the situation infinitely better than Michal feared.

She hoped the things Tirzah heard were true. What purpose could there be in summoning King Saul's daughter home? Was it possible her brother, now King Ishbosheth, belatedly developed some affection for his siblings? She dismissed that idea immediately, and tried not to dwell on a grim alternative. Given his suspicious nature, it was entirely possible Ishbosheth would eliminate the women who could produce legitimate male rivals for his throne. Of all her brothers, Ishbosheth was most like their father, with his changeable moods and unreasonable hostility.

Michal, like most of her family, always considered Jonathan the only one of her brothers capable of ruling the nation. How could her favorite brother's dear life have been snuffed out so soon? Most of King Saul's children feared their father's dark moods. Jonathan, unlike the others, possessed the courage to challenge the king. Although Michal had been protected from the worst of her father's behavior in her early childhood, she'd heard bizarre stories whispered in the halls of the women's quarters. Once, the king almost killed Jonathan for eating honey. Only the intervention of his military officers kept Saul from using his sword to end Jonathan's young life during that fit of irrational rage. Jonathan's strength stirred the king's jealous wrath in a way the weakness of his other sons never did.

Yes, Michal reflected, King Saul could accept qualities of greatness as long as they appeared in a deeply flawed man. Her Uncle Abner, for example, was an effective soldier. Yet he was irascible, unlikable. Men obeyed Abner because they feared the consequences of insubordination, but they hated him.

No one—not even Jonathan—provoked the king's fury like David. When David came to the royal household as a musician, he was already a national hero because of defeating Goliath. The king developed the same intense love-hate relationship with David that he had with his own children. It seemed those King Saul held in highest esteem when in his right mind were the ones he loathed most violently during his dark spells. As David developed into a brilliant tactician, his military victories alternately pleased and infuriated the king.

On good days, King Saul reacted with irritation to a popular song celebrating David's prowess in battle. On the worst days, merely hearing the tune could plunge the king into a sinister fury. As Michal grew older, her father's dark times overtook him more frequently, and they lasted longer. King Saul raged bitterly against imaginary threats that lurked everywhere. He considered the strong friendship between David and Jonathan to be evidence of disloyalty within his own family.

The king would have been even more jealous if he had noticed his youngest daughter's affection for his enemy. Out of fear, Michal took care to keep her feelings hidden from her father. Yet by the time she was eleven, every woman in the palace knew the princess's heart secretly belonged to David.

CHAPTER FOUR

"Wherefore when Saul saw that he behaved himself very wisely, he was afraid of him. But all Israel and Judah loved David,... And Saul said to David, Behold my elder daughter Merab, her will I give thee to wife: only be thou valiant for me, and fight the Lord's battles. For Saul said, Let not mine hand be upon him, but let the hand of the Philistines be upon him." I Samuel 18:15-17

IN MICHAL'S MIND, her childhood ended not long after Passover, the year she turned twelve. Merab was approaching her fifteenth birthday and anxious to be betrothed. The elder princess begged her mother to press her case for marriage with the king.

Ahinoam was subject to vague maladies and frequently took to her bed for long periods of time. Michal suspected her mother invented excuses to stay out of King Saul's sight as much as she could.

Michal and Merab giggled and fretted over what to wear to serve dinner that evening, frazzling the patience of their servants.

"Both robes are lovely. Just choose one," Sarah demanded.

"Yes," Michal agreed. "Choose, Merab. I have to know what you're wearing so I can put on something that complements it." Michal hoped to wear yellow, but her sister eventually settled on that color for herself. Michal selected a brown, long-sleeved dress, typical of those worn by an unmarried princess on formal occasions.

A huge crowd of military leaders, government officials, and family were present, far more people than the group of close advisors who regularly dined with the king. Everyone was in a jovial mood. King Saul presided over his table in true royal fashion that evening. Michal and Merab joined the household servants, carrying food from the kitchen to the table, removing empty vessels, fetching this and that morsel to offer to their father's most important guests. When they were in the kitchen, the girls compared notes on the snippets of conversation they heard.

"I saw you standing far too long near David." Merab's tone was that of the superior older sister. "Don't make a fool of yourself, especially not with our lord the king watching you."

Michal was indignant. "It wasn't my fault. Jonathan had to look over every raisin cake before he chose one. Then he insisted I bring him a pot of honey to pour over it. I was only doing as I was told when Father happened to be discussing who Israel's greatest soldier is."

"And what did he say?" Merab's high-minded attitude suddenly transformed into eager curiosity.

"He asked Jonathan who was the greatest warrior of Israel," Michal replied.

"What did our brother answer? Tell me everything you heard. Don't make me drag information from you."

"Jonathan said, 'Perhaps Joshua'. Father laughed and said, 'I meant among the living, my son.' Then Jonathan put his hand on David's shoulder and asked, 'Is there any fighting man alive more dedicated to serving Israel than this man, David?' I was sure Father would be angry. Instead, he laughed again and said Jonathan gave the right answer. Then he started going on about how brave David is, yet how he must become ever bolder and more fearless in his service to God, the king, and the nation. Then grumpy old Uncle Abner said, 'Away with you, child.' I didn't hear anything else."

"How unlike our lord the king to be so—"

"Hasten, girls," Haggia said. "It's time to serve fruit."

Merab took a large bowl of pomegranates and went into the great hall. Michal watched her sister walk from the kitchen to the opening in the center of the tables, which were arranged in a U-shape. Guests sat

22

on the floor or half-reclined on cushions around the outside of the tables.

Merab placed the bronze bowl in front of King Saul, who sat at the center of the head table. After Merab returned from serving the king, both she and Michal once more entered the great hall bearing additional pomegranates. Michal walked beside Merab. A few paces in front of their father, the girls bowed their heads while angling in opposite directions. Merab placed her bowl of fruit in reach of the honored guests to the king's right. Immediately afterwards, Michal sat her pomegranate container before the men to King Saul's left. The sisters came to the center of the room, bowed again to the king, and withdrew to the kitchen. They'd practiced repeatedly when they were younger, learning the proper order of service and how to move in perfect harmony. The unison became second nature to them. Minimal effort was required to turn in a flawless performance, not that anyone outside the kitchen appeared to notice.

On occasions when the guest list was extensive enough for both girls to be pressed into service, they lingered after dinner with the kitchen workers. The young princesses sat quietly in a corner and listened to the servants gossip about the important people in the great hall. As a small child, Michal learned people talked freely around her as long as she pretended to have no interest in their conversation. When they were younger, she and her sister sat and played a game that involved arranging the smooth stones Merab carried in a pouch tied around her waist. As they grew older, they worked on the needlework skills their mother insisted they learn.

That evening, like many other evenings before, Michal and Merab sat in their corner of the kitchen, listening to the music that wafted gently from the great hall. Michal's eyes were on the embroidery she was making to grace the hem of a tunic for Jonathan. Merab worked on yet another dress suitable for a married princess, something she must set aside and save for the time when she had a husband. Around the corner, kitchen workers chatted, oblivious to the familiar presence of the mouse-quiet princesses.

"If you want my opinion, our lord the king wants to see David dead," the baker Jacob said.

"Would he kill him with praise?" a young helper asked.

"Listen carefully to the words of praise," Jacob continued. "The king fairly dares the young man to put himself into ever greater peril. Perhaps King Saul wants the Philistines to finish what he started when he hurled his spear at Lord David. "

"Take care!" the kitchen maid, Haggia, warned.

Michal took a long strand of leaf-thin gold and worked it into the design of her embroidery. She trembled to think how near her father came to killing David several times. Within the royal household, such erratic behavior was accepted, even expected, during King Saul's bad moods.

Occasionally, Michal was afraid for David. She was constantly anxious for her brothers, her sister, her mother, and herself as well. She remembered her humiliation a few evenings earlier when the king, in a rage, flung a large bowl of figs at her. She could not guess what provoked the outburst. In accordance with the accepted standards of the royal household, she showed no emotion. She quietly picked up the metal bowl, retrieved the fruit that was scattered on the floor, bowed to her father, and walked back to the kitchen.

No one mentioned what occurred. Without the verifying presence of the ugly bruise on her arm and shoulder the next morning, she might have thought she imagined the entire incident.

Michal longed to please her father, but she was uncertain how to accomplish that objective. She felt both guilty and grateful that she was the target of the king's explosive rages less often than her sister. As Merab's figure became more womanly, their father grew increasingly critical of everything his elder daughter said or did. On many evenings, Michal lay in bed listening to Merab's sobs. She thought how much happier she and her sister would be when they had fine husbands and no longer lived in the palace.

Sounds of cheers coming from the great room interrupted Michal's thoughts. The usually sedate Sarah rushed into the kitchen. "Come with me immediately, girls!" she spoke sharply.

"Why?" Merab asked.

"What happened?" Michal said at the same time.

Sarah laid a hand on the nape of each girl's neck, fairly pulling them to their feet and pushing them out of the room. "We must go right away and share the good news with your mother."

"What news?" Michal asked.

"Mother will be asleep." Merab struggled against Sarah's grasp. "We want to stay."

"Merab is betrothed."

Both girls squealed and giggled, while demanding more information. Sarah pushed and dragged them up the stairs and along the passageway that led to the women's quarters.

"Finally I am to be married!" Merab exulted. "Think of it!"

"Tell us, who is to be the bridegroom?" Michal insisted. "We must know."

"Yes, Sarah." Merab sounded breathless. "Who will be my husband? Is he the son of an important king? A rich nobleman's first son?"

At last they reached Merab and Michal's bedchamber. Sarah sank onto a large cushion and held her bowed head in her hands. "The king has betrothed Merab to David, the son of Jesse," she said without looking up.

Shocked silence sucked the air out of the room. Merab's hand flew to cover her mouth as she half-sat, half-fell onto the bed. Michal stood motionless, unable or unwilling to absorb the hateful information.

"That cannot be," Michal whispered when she found her voice. It was not like Sarah to tell such an appalling, easily disproved lie.

"I have spoken the truth," Sarah said quietly. "The announcement was made just now, in the great hall, before a host of guests."

"But David is not high born," Merab protested. "His father is a farmer, and he freely admits he grew up tending sheep! He cannot be the king's son-in-law. The very idea is ridiculous."

"He himself said almost those very things to your father this evening." Sarah's face was filled with sadness.

Michal did not trust herself to speak. She was angry at Merab for speaking ill of David. Even more, she hated the dawning thought that her sister would be the wife of the man she wanted for herself. She despised her father for choosing David to marry Merab. She was furious with Sarah for bringing the news.

"I won't do it," Merab wailed. "Does Father think I will go and live in that stupid village of Bethlehem where everybody's a farmer or a shepherd? A place no one has ever heard of? He expects me to marry a common soldier who came to the palace with *nothing*, and even wore Jonathan's old clothes. And worst of all, I've heard David's great-

25

grandmother was a *foreigner*, from Moab." Merab crumpled her headdress and tossed it toward Sarah. "No, I will not go through with this marriage!"

The old woman calmly folded the discarded scarf and sighed. "You will obey your father and king, Merab. Surely you have always known he would choose a husband for you. Yours also, Michal, in due time." Sarah stood and chewed her lip. "I will keep everyone away from you tonight. Tomorrow morning, both of you will show how delighted you are with this news, particularly in the presence of our lord the king."

For a long time after Sarah left, both girls were silent and motionless. Michal was stunned to her marrow by Merab's outburst. Nevertheless, she swallowed hard and heard herself say, "David is very handsome, Merab. And brave."

"What difference does that make? He's nothing, a nobody. Sooner or later he will lose favor. Then what? His family has no wealth, no standing, no estate. When I'm an old woman I'll have no home. I'll have to sell my jewelry and live in a tent."

Merab cried herself to sleep that night. After her sister's sobs faded into deep regular breaths, Michal allowed her own tears to flow.

CHAPTER FIVE

"And David said unto Saul, Who am I? and what is my life, or my father's family in Israel, that I should be son in law to the king?" I Samuel 18:18

THE MORNING AFTER the announcement of Merab's betrothal to David, Michal awoke feeling ill. Her head hurt, and she did not want to get out of bed. Merab was already up, dressed, and studying her reflection in the smooth depths of a highly-polished brass disk.

"I don't feel good," Michal said.

"Neither do I." Merab sounded matter-of-fact. "But I will comport myself as befits a daughter of the king. So will you, little sister. We have no choice."

Only then did Michal remember the events of the previous evening. She sighed and struggled to sit up, slowly becoming aware of something wet on her inner thighs. Throwing back the blankets, she stared in shock at the fresh bloodstain on the bedclothes. "I've started my bleeding at last!"

For more than a year, Michal fretted that she had no monthly flow of blood like the other girls her age. She worried she was abnormal. Would she never begin her periods? She feared she would never be able to bear children. Merab went regularly to the women's confinement room for her monthlies. Tirzah started last summer.

Michal lay down again as a wave of nausea swept over her. She stared at the ceiling. She previously longed for this day to come. Now that it had arrived, there was no longer any reason to be a woman. Merab, not she, would be married to David.

The palace's unclean room was a dormitory where the women stayed to avoid contaminating others while their menstrual blood flowed. No man, not even the lowest slave, would dare to enter this place. The women spoke of it as an area of banishment. Nevertheless, Michal found the atmosphere relaxed, almost festive. Only a few women were there when she arrived. Michal recognized Tabitha, the baker's helper, and Lobeth, one of Queen Ahinoam's handmaids. They greeted Michal, and congratulated her on the beginning of her time as a woman.

Michal sank onto one of the soft cushions lining the walls, and covered her eyes with her hand. "Is the bleeding always this unpleasant?"

The other women chuckled.

"No," Tabitha said. "Some months are worse than others. A few women always have a difficult time. Others hardly notice it."

"The first day is usually the hardest. And the flow comes easier after you've had children," Lobeth commented.

The women gave her a supply of the clean rags kept on hand to absorb menstrual blood. Tabitha explained that most of the women sat or lay on the rags, but also demonstrated how to swaddle oneself for walking. Michal found she felt all right as long as she reclined on a cushion, but sitting or standing brought on cramps.

"You are fortunate to have an older sister," Tabitha observed. "I have only brothers. When my first time came along, I didn't know what was happening. I thought I had some horrible disease and was about to die."

"I was ignorant also," Lobeth said. "But my mother explained this would enable me to get married and have children. That was all well and good, until I found out later that it happened *every month*. I understood I would bleed one time and then it would be over and done."

Michal closed her eyes while the women chatted. She wondered what was happening in the rest of the palace with everyone scurrying to prepare for the grand wedding. Soon Merab would marry the only man Michal ever wanted. Would her sister be allowed to walk through the garden with their mother and have a chance meeting with David and King Saul? Michal wondered whether her nausea was because of the bleeding, or came from the thought of her sister someday bearing David's child.

When Michal awoke from a nap later that afternoon, Lobeth offered her broth cooked with leeks and lentils. She began to feel somewhat better after eating and taking a little wine. Soon the confined group was joined by a young woman who played the tambourine and often danced to entertain King Saul's guests. "Ladies," she announced breathlessly, "the king has betrothed his eldest daughter to the magnificent warrior David."

"Truly?" Lobeth gestured toward Michal. "See here, Princess Michal has joined us for her first bleeding."

"Congratulations, my lady," the dancer said.

"Thank you," Michal said. The women's concerned expressions told her they knew her feelings for David and sympathized with her breaking heart. "What good news this is about my sister," she forced herself to say. "With her betrothed and my bleeding begun, my lord the king can now find a husband for me." She shut her eyes and tried to sleep.

Lobeth, Tabitha, and the dancer moved to the far side of the room and spoke in low voices, but Michal's keen hearing caught much of their conversation. They talked of how fortunate Merab was to get such a famous husband, and how she would always be glad she was David's first and therefore most honored wife.

The dancer recounted the conversation between King Saul and David during dinner the night the engagement was announced. "David is a man of great humility. He reminded the king that he is not of noble birth. He said he was unworthy to be a royal son-in-law."

"Perhaps that's true," Lobeth, a widow, observed. "I think he needs an experienced woman, one who could train him in the ways of pleasure."

29

"And did you have anyone in mind? Yourself perhaps?" Tabitha tittered.

"I would be willing to sacrifice myself to provide such a comely young man an education." Lobeth laughed. "Unless I miss my guess," she went on, "David will be the father of many sons."

The dancer giggled. "Let us hope he and Princess Merab have fine, healthy children, and all take their appearance from their father!"

Michal turned her face toward the wall. Merab had King Saul's prominent nose and sharp features atop Ahinoam's squat body. Michal had the opposite combination, their mother's delicately beautiful face and the king's tall, slender build. During the past year, Michal became increasingly aware of the way men reacted to her blossoming beauty. She wondered if David knew who she was or noticed the fairness of her face. Did he share her wish for the two of them to embrace? Did he ever long to come to her and do the secret thing that transpired between a husband and wife?

What difference could it make if he harbored such thoughts? He would marry Merab, according to the king's wishes. Her sister would taste David's full ruddy lips and comb her fingers lovingly through his thick curls. Merab, not she, would be the one to whom he would reveal the marriage secret.

Michal was not sure which emotion was stronger, her wish to die or her hatred for everyone around her.

The next morning Michal was slightly lethargic, but felt much better after a good night's sleep. She asked Lobeth to explain the connection between the monthly bleeding, marriage, and bearing a child. Lobeth seemed to be struck dumb and said, "Ask your mother." Michal doubted she would have the courage to raise such an issue with Ahinoam, and didn't expect a clear answer if she did. She wondered if she could ask Sarah.

Michal completed her period, went through the simple purification ceremony, and emerged with a feeling her life was significantly changed. She was relieved to learn the king and his close military advisors left the palace during her stay in the unclean room. Depending on which rumor Michal believed, Israel's forces went to the border either to mount a defense against a Philistine incursion or to plunder an enemy village.

Michal never considered discussing her feelings for David with anyone, not even Tirzah. What would be the use? Her wishes would carry no weight with the king. Michal watched with envy as her sister soberly went through the preparations for her wedding. Merab no longer giggled and whispered to Michal how eager she was to become a wife.

In a few weeks the men returned from their military adventure, flushed with victory and laden with booty. Not surprisingly, David again distinguished himself by his brave leadership. The palace buzzed with tales of his exploits.

Michal stole glances at him when she dared, trying to visualize him thrusting his spear into a Philistine's chest or slicing off an enemy's head with one powerful swipe of his sword. She'd heard those very things happened. She knew from the whispers among the women that David was fearless and never hesitated to place himself in the thick of a battle among his men. Yet the David she observed around the palace seemed so unassuming. He did not swagger or boast the way most of the younger, unmarried military officers habitually did. How could ruthlessness exist side by side with the sensitivity of the man she knew as a musician and poet?

As his wife, I would study him and gain insight into his mysterious ways, Michal thought. She could not decide whether to be angry or smug, knowing her sister would accept her new husband at face value the way Merab accepted everyone and everything.

The days passed quickly. Merab's attitude of grudging acceptance of her approaching marriage seemed to turn gradually toward cautious eagerness. At times, Michal suspected Merab's growing excitement came from the knowledge she was taking a prize her little sister wanted more than anything else in the kingdom. An uneasy coolness settled between the king's daughters, especially after Merab's spiteful jest that Michal should marry David's armor bearer.

Preparations for the wedding feast began in earnest the week before the marriage ceremony was scheduled to take place. Michal vacillated between quiet depression and barely-controlled anger. It did not escape her attention that the king was in high spirits for weeks. She tried not to attribute her father's fine mood to the fact both of his daughters were displeased.

The day before the royal wedding, Michal helped serve the evening meal. Merab stayed behind in the women's quarters, where she had been the center of attention for days. Michal jealously watched the older women cater to her sister, applying henna to her hands and feet and teasing her about the approaching wedding night.

Michal had hoped David would be at her father's table that night. She wanted to gaze upon him in his unmarried state one last time. However, the dinner crowd was small by palace standards, and David was not present.

A creeping dread gripped Michal as she sensed the change in her father without actually observing an outward sign. It was similar to the apprehension she remembered from walking across the meadow, seeing a dark rain cloud she knew would break before she could find shelter. As the meal progressed, King Saul became quiet. Michal took care to walk softly to avoid attracting her father's attention in any way. The moment her assigned duties were completed, she put her apron away in hopes of retiring to her room. She jumped with fright as her Uncle Abner's voice grated on her ears.

"Where is your sister?" he demanded.

Michal stammered. She never remembered her uncle coming into the kitchen before. It was not according to protocol for him to be there, nor to carry on a conversation with his niece in the presence of the kitchen staff.

"Merab is in the women's quarters, my lord uncle. She is being prepared for marriage." What a stupid thing to say. Everyone in this house was aware tomorrow was Merab and David's wedding day. Probably everyone in the kingdom knew. The servants must think her a dolt.

"Send your sister to my lord the king immediately," Abner ordered. "Your mother is to come with her. To the king's chamber." Her uncle swept away without a backward glance.

Michal looked around at the stunned faces of the kitchen workers. No one spoke. She ran to the women's quarters to find Merab, eager to know the purpose of this urgent meeting.

CHAPTER SIX

"But it came to pass at the time when Merab Saul's daughter should have been given to David, that she was given unto Adriel the Meholathite to wife."
I Samuel 18:19

MERAB SLIPPED INTO the bedroom she and Michal shared, as if in a trance. She slumped into a sitting position on their bed without acknowledging Michal's presence.

"What's the matter? Is Father angry about something?" Michal whispered. She found Merab's behavior frightening. Terror was contagious in King Saul's household. If their father was in one of his dark moods, she could be the next target.

Her sister looked up without expression. She opened her mouth as if to speak, but no words emerged. After a long moment, she sank backward onto the bed.

"Is there a problem with your wedding?" Michal could not fathom what tragedy put her sister into this speechless state. "Was David called away to battle?" A horrific thought pushed aside Michal's concern for her sister. "He hasn't been wounded, or..." She couldn't bring herself to complete the dreaded question. Did King Saul once again hurl his spear at David, this time without missing?

Merab continued to stare at the ceiling. "Father has changed his mind about my marriage," she said softly.

"But all the preparations are made," Michal protested. "Our relatives and many other guests from far away places are already gathered."

"Oh, there will be a wedding. The ceremony will take place as scheduled." Merab pulled herself into a sitting position. Tears moistened her eyes, but none yet escaped. "Instead of David, I will be given to Lord Adriel." A choking sob broke through as Merab said the man's name.

"Adriel? The Meholathite? No, there's some mistake. You heard wrong." Michal's mind refused to process this shocking information. She didn't want her sister to have David, but Merab shouldn't be given to this stern martinet either.

Merab regained her emotionless demeanor. "No mistake. Our lord the king made it perfectly clear this is what will take place tomorrow."

Michal sat beside her sister. She put her arm around Merab's shoulders. The aloofness of the past few months disappeared. Adriel was a strict, humorless soldier older than their father. He often kept company with Uncle Abner at the king's table. Michal tried to think of something to say. "Adriel comes from a good family," she said without conviction.

"Yes," Merab sighed. "And his only wife died childless years ago, so I will always be the senior wife, even if he takes others later."

"No doubt you will have many fine sons." Although Michal knew she was spewing platitudes, she wanted to provide some solace to her sister.

Merab laughed a short, bitter laugh. "No doubt."

They sat hugging each other in silence for a long time. "Can I get anything for you?" Michal asked. "Shall I call Sarah or Tirzah?"

"No." Merab shook her head. "Let me spend my last night as a virgin in peace."

Michal searched for a way to distract her sister. "Where exactly is Meholath? Is it far?"

Merab shrugged. "I don't know. It doesn't matter much, does it?" She paused, then continued. "Remember how, when we were little, we were so sure we would have wonderful husbands? I knew Father would choose for me, but I fooled myself into thinking he would talk

34

privately with me, and at least make certain I felt no strong dislike for my husband-to-be."

Merab stood and began to turn back the blankets. "Do you think people will say David rejected me, the plain princess who is not good enough even for a shepherd from Bethlehem?" Her humiliation was palpable.

"You will be a lovely bride," Michal answered almost too quickly. "And everyone knows this is our father's doing. He decreed you would marry David. Then he changed his mind at the last minute, as he is wont to do. But why?"

"Learn this well, little sister," Merab said, her anger making a rare break through her self-control. "There need not be a reason why."

"This house will be lonely without you, Merab." There was so much more Michal wanted to say. Instead, she climbed into bed. She was ashamed of the relief she felt, knowing her sister would not be married to David.

The next morning Rizpah, one of their mother's handmaids, carefully lined Merab's eyes with a black powder made from burned almond shells. Rizpah was an expert in cosmetics, having learned how to mix and apply makeup from an Egyptian woman. "Lovely!" she exclaimed at her own work. "Now a little rouge on your cheeks, some berry juice on your lips, and you will be as fine a bride as ever there was!" Michal was fascinated by Rizpah's deft transformation of her sister into a fetching bride. "Too bad your veil will all but hide my work," Rizpah clucked. "Now you, little sister." Rizpah motioned Michal closer.

"But I am not the bride," Michal protested. She wanted Rizpah to paint her face as she had Merab's, but feared risking her father's disapproval.

"King's orders," Rizpah said. She grinned broadly. "Perhaps your father wants the men who failed to win Merab to compete now for his baby girl, eh?"

If the king was willing for Rizpah to enhance her face for the wedding celebration, Michal was more than happy to cooperate. Now she could look pretty for David.

After Rizpah swept out the door, Michal admired the reflection of her painted face in the brass disk. "What do you think it is like to be married?" she asked.

Merab hesitated. "I don't know what you mean."

"Yes, you do," Michal persisted. "What is the secret thing a husband does? The thing Haggia says turns a girl into a woman overnight?"

"I'm not sure. Mother said to be prepared for a painful experience. She told me a man is a sword and a woman is the sheath in which the sword rests."

Michal pondered her mother's riddle for several moments. "Do you understand what that means?"

"Not exactly," Merab said. "I think it must mean the secret thing is like being stabbed."

Michal periodically heard sacrificial animals scream as the priests slit their throats. She would not want to be stabbed, even by David. "How does that turn a girl into a woman?"

Merab closed her eyes. "Let us speak of something else."

CHAPTER SEVEN

"And Michal Saul's daughter loved David: and they told Saul, and the thing pleased him. And Saul said, I will give him her, that she may be a snare to him..." I Samuel 18:20-21

MICHAL STOOD NEAR the wall of the great hall, behind the women who gathered at the end of the room closest to the kitchen. Since she was tall enough to look over most of the other women, she could see the crowd of men who talked and laughed among themselves at the opposite end of the hall. David stood in a small group that included her brother Jonathan. To her frustration, the back of Uncle Abner's head blocked Michal's view of David's face. She wanted to search her beloved's fine features. Was he disappointed at being replaced by another bridegroom? Angry? Relieved? Embarrassed? Indifferent? Delighted?

"Michal!" Ahinoam's voice startled her.

"Yes, Mother?"

"Do not stand at the wall like a foreigner. Come up here by me."

Michal dutifully made her way through the crowd to her mother's side. Throughout her life, Michal was reprimanded if she brought attention to herself in public. Consequently, hanging back became a habit. She was surprised by Ahinoam's sudden displeasure at her reticence, but she asked no questions. The queen's motives were seldom revealed.

"Look at me," Ahinoam said. "I want to see if Rizpah did a good job with your makeup."

Michal turned to face her mother. "Beautiful. Beautiful," Ahinoam murmured. "Let me see you smile."

Again, Michal did as she was instructed. Being the focus of her mother's attention was unusual and rather enjoyable, especially since Merab had been the center of household activity for the past few weeks.

"Remember to be joyful today," Ahinoam said as she straightened Michal's tunic. "This is a happy occasion. Your father would have you show how pleased you are that Merab has become a bride."

"Yes, Mother." Michal was glad to have these instructions, since she could seldom predict either of her parents' wishes regarding her behavior.

"Just look at your Uncle Abner over there." Ahinoam grinned and nodded toward the men at the opposite end of the great hall. "He should ask Rizpah to color his locks green. Doesn't he remind you of a palm tree with his shock of wild hair?" Abner could subjugate armies, but he could never control the rebellious hair that stuck straight out from his head at bizarre angles.

Michal giggled at her mother's rare joke. At that moment, Abner glanced over his shoulder toward the women. He nodded to Ahinoam briefly and then took a step to his left, moving in front of Jonathan. Suddenly, Michal was laughing and staring directly at David across the room. She remembered to lower her eyes demurely, but not before she caught David's expression of appreciative surprise. She felt an uncontrollable blush creeping up to the roots of her hair.

Michal stole a furtive look at Ahinoam, knowing her mother could not have missed her boldness. Yet no scolding words were spoken. If Michal did not know better, she would think she pleased her mother well.

"I am going to check on Merab's final preparations," Ahinoam said. She melted into the group of women, leaving Michal to wonder if her mother had been sampling the wine. Remembering her instructions to be happy, Michal smiled and went in search of Tirzah.

The festivities went on for some time. Michal and Tirzah tasted every delicacy and giggled about women whose clothing they judged to be fashionable or dreadful.

"So who shall be married next, I wonder," Tirzah whispered. "Perhaps one of us?"

"I have lost all pleasure in the idea of marriage," Michal said. She thought of the anxious face of her sister Merab as they dressed this morning. No doubt Merab was concerned about being stabbed.

"This is certainly a change!" Tirzah stared at her. "Last year you couldn't wait for Merab to be engaged so your parents could begin to arrange your betrothal. Has your heart grown cold toward someone?"

Michal glanced around. "Let us not speak of this matter. Look over there at that woman in the tunic made for someone half her size!"

That evening, Michal paced restlessly. Having never slept alone before, she missed Merab's familiar presence. The bedchamber seemed so quiet without her sister. There were bare spots where Merab's clothing, mirror, and combs should be. Michal considered going to the place where Sarah and Tirzah slept, but she did not want the other servants to tease her for being a baby. Ahinoam rarely went to sleep early. Perhaps the queen would be willing to accept a visit from her daughter.

While Michal removed the makeup Rizpah so expertly applied, she tried to think of a reason to go to her mother's room. Admitting she was lonely for Merab would only cause Ahinoam to lecture her on the fortitude required of a princess. As she considered complaining too much rich food upset her stomach, Sarah entered the room.

"Your parents would see you, Michal."

Was this because of something unseemly she did at the wedding? It must have been dreadful if she must answer for it immediately. Was she being called to account for her bold smile at David? "I'm not feeling very well."

Sarah did not bother to answer. She stood in the doorway and motioned for Michal to follow her.

No dark shadows of fury were evident on King Saul's face. Nevertheless, Michal was on guard. "Good evening, Father. Mother."

"My little girl." Ahinoam did not sound angry as she caressed Michal's hand.

39

"I have the good news you have been waiting for, my daughter," King Saul announced. He nodded toward Sarah, and the handmaid left the room. "Now that your sister is married, it is time for your betrothal."

"So soon?" Michal regretted her question, and quickly added, "It will be as you wish, Father." She knelt before the king. "May I have your blessing?"

King Saul put his hand on Michal's shoulder. "Are you not curious to know the name of the man I have chosen to be your husband?"

"Your wisdom is vast, Father. I know your choice will be the best for me." Michal cast her eyes down. What difference did it make? Young or old? Rich or poor? Kind or harsh? She would be traded away like a loaf of barley bread to suit the king's purpose. Then she would live out her days in misery, with a secret longing for the only man she could ever love.

"You surprise me, Daughter," the king said. He lifted her chin until their eyes met. "I have heard it said you are eager to be a wife."

"I wish only to please you and Mother," Michal said. She wanted to retreat to her bedchamber to mourn her lost childhood.

"You are betrothed to David, the son of Jesse of Bethlehem. In the next few days, Jesse and I will finalize the terms of the contract and establish the date for the wedding. Meanwhile, you are to ready yourself for marriage."

"As you wish, Father," Michal said. She knew the king was lying. She did not believe for an instant her father would willingly give her the one thing she wanted most, and allow her to become David's wife.

"No delight, Michal?" Ahinoam asked.

"It is a sober thing to become a wife," Michal replied.

"Well said," King Saul declared. Michal felt his eyes appraising her. "You will be a dutiful wife to David, no doubt, without forgetting that you are first, last, and always my daughter. Your foremost loyalty must, in every instance, be to your family. That is, to me. Do you understand what I am telling you, Daughter?"

"Yes, Father." Michal wished she knew the purpose behind the king's cruel game.

Back in her bedchamber, she lay alone and sleepless in the dark, wondering if she was really to be married. If so, to whom? Would her father find pleasure in waiting until the day before her wedding to reveal her future husband's true identity, as happened with Merab? Would she be given to someone as old as Adriel?

CHAPTER EIGHT

"And Saul was yet the more afraid of David; and Saul became David's enemy continually." I Samuel 18:29

A WHEEL BANGED violently into a deep rut and bounced out again. Michal grabbed the side of the cart to avoid being pitched onto the ground. She stretched her arms and shoulders, and then continued to reclaim her jewelry from the old coat. She was counting on the busy work to occupy both her hands and her mind until the head of the column reached the crossroads.

She reached through a fresh cut in the coat, pulled out her garnet ring, and put it on. She held out her hand and spread her fingers. Seven years of storage had done the ring no harm. It looked the same as it did the day she took it off and sewed it underneath a pleat inside the lining of Sarah's ragged old coat.

Moments later the caravan slowed, then stopped. Captain Osh's armor bearer galloped to the end of the column. Michal could not force herself to pretend she was uninterested in what was happening. A soldier brought Tirzah's donkey to the cart and waited while she dismounted.

"We're not moving fast enough," Tirzah said as she settled in beside her mistress. "The captain is leaving my donkey behind because he has become lame. The slave Joash has been told to take the animal to a nearby farm while we move on to Bahurim."

"Bahurim." Michal had not been to that place in a very long time. "I wonder if everyone in the village is still under the command of my Uncle Abner."

"From the talk I heard, I believe Bahurim must still be Lord Abner's stronghold. You have been summoned in King Ishbosheth's name, but your uncle seems to be giving the orders."

King Ishbosheth. How the combination of those two words jangled. Alas, the brother Michal feared most was now in power. "I would love to know the reason for our hurry. It could be solely because of my Uncle Abner's life-long impatience."

Tirzah frowned. "Maybe it's because Lord Phaltiel is still pursuing us. One of his men caught up with the rear guard and offered a bribe for your return."

Michal was immediately concerned. "Who was it? What did he say?"

"I didn't know about it until later," Tirzah answered. "Joash said the soldiers laughed at the emissary and sent him packing."

"You know as well as I that will not stop Phaltiel. If anything, it will make him more determined," Michal breathed. She watched with relief as Captain Osh turned the column toward Bahurim, and away from Philistine territory. She touched the hilt of her knife, silently vowing she would die before returning to Phaltiel's house.

The noise of the cart rumbling along a rough patch of road made normal conversation impossible. Michal broke off a corner of the cheese Tirzah thrust at her, and nibbled at its edges.

It wasn't long before Tirzah began to doze. Despite the reassurance of familiar companionship, Michal regretted Tirzah's proximity. There was a good possibility her handmaid could have slipped away on the donkey. Seated next to Michal in the cart, Tirzah would have no better chance than her mistress to escape if things turned nasty.

Michal tried to relax and sleep, but her busy brain rejected so much as a yawn. The route they were following was consistent with the destination of Bahurim. However, suspicion and paranoia were too deeply ingrained for her to trust even the most convincing outward appearance.

After all, she remembered, there was a time when she and everyone else believed her sister Merab would be married to her own beloved David. Yet it never happened. After Merab became the wife of Adriel, the king commanded Michal to prepare to become David's wife. Still Michal doubted the truth of her father's words. Much as she yearned to belong to David, she did not believe such a wonderful thing could happen. She recalled how carefully she kept a tight grip on the euphoria that threatened to burst forth when King Saul announced her betrothal to David. She was certain her father would betray her at the last minute.

Michal never believed the king would give her to the man she loved until, as if in a dream, she stood in the great public room with David. The wedding ceremony was completed. When the feasting and dancing began, she realized she'd become his wife, truly and forever. And he was her husband. Michal sighed as she relived the sweetness of her happiness and the brevity of her forever.

How long were they together? A little over a year, minus the times David was called away on military duty. Just when she thought she could not bear another day of separation from her beloved, she would hear a noise in the street, or a shout in the courtyard. Michal's heart would race, and she would run to meet her returning husband. The sight of him filled her with unspeakable joy. He smiled at her as he leapt lightly from his horse. Without removing his eyes from her face, he tossed his reins into the waiting hands of his armor bearer. Her heart almost burst with delight as he swept her inside their house and into his arms. "Did you miss me, Princess?"

"Oh, yes, even more than last time." She laughed as he kissed her.

"I missed you, too," he said between kisses. "I thought about you every moment I was away. Look, I brought you something pretty. Though not half as beautiful as you."

Michal rubbed the garnet ring on her finger. Their home seemed so empty when he was gone. It was almost as if she and their household staff only came to life when David walked in the door. His exuberance affected everyone around him.

"Sarah, my dear! Is there any of your special lamb stew in the house?" The answer was always yes, because Sarah, like everyone else, did everything she could to please him. The appreciation he expressed for even the smallest service translated into a powerful energy that made the household hum with activity.

"You should join the army, Sarah," David teased. "We would never have to fight another battle. The Philistines would smell your stew and willingly give themselves up in exchange for one taste of it." After all these years, Michal could still close her eyes and hear his hearty voice, see the smile that involved not just his mouth, but his whole face. If she could tolerate the pain, she might allow herself to remember the way her heart raced when he touched her.

What did David say or do that made their household ring with laughter? She could not remember specific words. It was more a feeling, an atmosphere of happy anticipation. When he was home, otherwise routine events became exciting, delightful, exhilarating. Michal acknowledged that some of this joy resulted from her being so in love with her husband, but the effect stretched beyond her.

Charismatic. That was Jonathan's word for the all-encompassing sphere of warmth in which her husband lived. All who knew him enjoyed David's company and respected his counsel, even King Saul on his good days. Yet each time the king was in a dark mood, fear of his son-in-law seemed to intensify—giving Michal increasing concern for David's safety.

"You are besotted with your husband," the king accused her, striding into a palace room where Michal talked quietly with her mother and the visibly pregnant Merab.

"Of course I am, my lord." Ahinoam's quick hand motion warned her daughters to remain silent.

The king ignored his wife. He bent near Michal's face and spoke menacingly. "I will not tolerate your husband's treason, Daughter. You will be a lovely young widow, much sought after by men who know how to be loyal." King Saul glared at her in silence for a long moment, then turned on his heel and left. The clatter of his sandals against the passageway stones faded away, while his humorless laughter floated faintly on the air.

"So, Merab, have you located a good midwife?" Ahinoam asked, as if the king's intrusion was nothing out of the ordinary. "Oh, I *do* wish those children in the garden would play more quietly."

Michal was shaken by the incident. She feared her father's moods while growing up, but as a child she did not fully recognize his absolute power of life and death. Michal and David spent that evening together, as they always did when they had the opportunity. They sat on the rooftop talking, enjoying the warmth of each other's closeness, and watching the twilight deepen into darker shades of night. Michal loved the view of the valley below, the mountains in the distance, and the clear, star-dusted sky above. She loved the times when David was at home and missed him when he dined with the king, or was away on military business.

"I went to the palace to see my mother today," Michal spoke quietly. "My father threatened you again. He called you a traitor. He frightens me, David."

David nuzzled her hair and said, "You don't need to worry about me, Princess."

"I believe he's capable of committing murder when he flies into one of his rages." Michal fought to keep her voice from trembling.

"And so he is. You should stay out of his way as much as possible." David grazed her forearm with the back of his fingers. "I don't want anything to happen to you."

Michal studied her husband's calm features. "*Me*? I'm far down his list of threats. You are the focus of his fear and hate. Jonathan, too, but not as much as you."

"You're right that Jonathan is in jeopardy," David agreed.

"And you, my love," Michal insisted. "You most of all. Why can't you see that?"

"You're shivering in this night air. Do you want to go inside?"

His attitude exasperated her. Why wouldn't her husband admit he was in danger? "I'm shaking because I'm afraid."

David put his arm around her and pulled her close to him. "You have no need to fear, my darling. I'll take care of you. I'll be your own private shepherd."

"Who will be *your* shepherd, husband?"

"The Lord is my shepherd. He will protect me from danger." David looked toward the starlit sky.

"Does He love you more than anyone, the way I do?" Michal asked, snuggling against him.

"I think He loves each one of us the same, beyond what we can imagine. However, He's not finished with me yet. I believe there are things God plans to do through me, Michal. Marvelous things."

"What things?" He'd stirred her curiosity before, when he talked in general terms about a bright future.

"Someday you'll see, when the foretold events begin to take place." David stroked her hair and kissed her. "A more immediate concern is that we should get ourselves a son."

Michal felt excitement course through her. "You talk like a foreigner," she whispered as she slid her hand inside his robe.

CHAPTER NINE

"Saul also sent messengers unto David's house, to watch him, and to slay him in the morning: and Michal David's wife told him, saying, If thou save not thy life to night, to morrow thou shalt be slain." I Samuel 19:11

DARKNESS FELL. SOLDIERS with torches led the way. The pace slowed, but the column did not stop. Michal longed to get out of the small cart, stretch her cramping legs, and quench the thirst that left her mouth as dry as desert sand. When a light drizzle began to fall, Tirzah roused, yawned, and drew her shawl more tightly around her shoulders. The two women used the remnant of the old coat and rearranged their meager belongings to shelter themselves from the rain.

Damp, chilly nights always reminded Michal of the last time she saw David. She would never know what awakened her in the middle of that horrible night. Perhaps an unfamiliar noise, or maybe a guardian angel tapped her on the shoulder? She remembered opening her eyes and being filled with a sense of dread. David slept peacefully at her side while her heart pounded in response to some undefined evil.

Unable to return to sleep, Michal rose and walked barefoot to the table where she kept fresh water. Earlier that evening a three-quarter moon flooded the courtyard with light. Clouds must have gathered, for the bedroom was noticeably darker. Michal felt for the clay water jar and was about to lift it to her lips when her keen hearing picked up sounds from the street below. She tiptoed to the window and peered between the slatted shutters. Four men stood in the street. Even in the shadows, she recognized the men as members of the king's private guard. She could hardly breathe. *These men are here to murder David!*

When her shaky legs regained the strength to walk, Michal crept back into bed. She put her hand lightly over her husband's mouth and whispered into his ear, "David, wake up."

He kissed her hand before gently moving it from his mouth.

"There are men outside," she whispered. "Four of them. They are armed with javelins and swords." When a moment of silence passed, she said, "My father means to kill you this time for sure. You have to get away."

David raised himself onto an elbow. Michal stroked the side of his face. "Please, leave now and hide until my father is himself again. I beg you to do this, David. For me, if not for yourself."

He eased out of bed and peered through the shutters. Meanwhile, Michal stepped out onto the balcony that overlooked their home's inner courtyard. Seeing no one there, she returned to the bedroom and felt around on the floor to locate David's sandals. She gathered his shoes as David pulled her to her feet and led her outside.

Michal and David crept silently down the stone steps into the courtyard. The air was heavy with mist and smelled crisp with new-fallen rain. Drifting clouds occasionally obscured the moon and stars.

They slipped into the kitchen, past the hissing embers of the still-warm cooking fire. Michal's hands trembled as she filled a leather pouch with food. "Where will you go this time?" she whispered. They were far enough from the men in the street to talk normally, but fear kept her voice quiet.

David slipped on his sandals. "I don't know. When I find a safe place, I'll get word to Jonathan. You can trust your brother."

"Why don't you kill my father and have done with this madness? You know you could do it."

"I could, but I won't." David pulled her into his arms and held her close to him. "We are not heathens, Michal. We are God's people. I will never lift a weapon against our king, and I will defend him to the death against anyone who would do him harm."

"My father doesn't deserve your loyalty." Michal fought to hold back the tears she knew her husband would not wish to see at this moment.

"My loyalty is to our God," David whispered as he stroked her hair. "Your father is God's anointed king." He kissed her forehead. "I'll go out the kitchen window."

Their house sat on the side of a hill, with the courtyard sloping downward to the kitchen. Beyond the kitchen, the terrain dropped away sharply into a deep, stream-carved valley. "After I get my footing, you can hand me the food bag and lock the shutters behind me," David whispered.

"How long will you be gone?" She turned her face up to his.

"Too long." In the dim light she could see his smile. He clasped her to him again. "Come with me, Michal."

"What?"

"I'll take good care of you. I promise I'll protect you."

Michal wavered. She hated the thought of another separation, but could he run for his life and take care of her at the same time? Could she bear to watch her father's men tear David apart, knowing her slowness was the cause of his capture? After a moment, she said, "I don't have my sandals."

"You're right, of course. Forests and deserts are not fit places for a princess." He kissed her one last deep, searching kiss then slowly released her. "Don't give up on me," he whispered into her hair. Then he turned and leapt lightly out the window.

"God be with you, my husband," she breathed. Michal struggled against the impulse to follow David. It would only take an instant to run and get her shoes. But he would move faster and hide better without her.

As she walked stealthily back to her bedroom, Michal wished there was something she could do to make David's escape successful. If only she had Jonathan's military skills. She could see the shapes of

50

objects in the courtyard now, which meant dawn would soon break. David needed time to make his way down the steep cliff behind their house. The men must not see her husband before he reached the cover of the trees at the bottom of the valley. But what could she do?

Going back to bed was futile. Michal was far too upset to sleep. She peered through the slats of the shutters again. The brutish men were still in sight, lounging against the front of the house across the street, no doubt waiting for dawn. Oh, to be a skilled archer! She imagined the pleasure of launching four swift arrows from her upstairs window, striking down the king's men before they had a chance to pursue her beloved husband.

She glanced at the bed where not long ago she snuggled comfortably against David's warmth. He slipped from the bed so carefully the blankets continued to hold his shape. She paced. Suddenly, something her mother said that afternoon floated back to her.

"My husband Adriel has no respect for a man who is not a soldier," Merab said, "and even less for a woman who could never become one. Every day he finds a new way to remind me how worthless I am."

Ahinoam patted Merab's hand. "Women fight as many wars as our men do. Smiles, tears, and a clever wit can be more powerful than a javelin, my daughter. Hone your skills in the weapons of women, just as you see your brother Jonathan practice his archery. Do this, and you will win your share of desperate battles."

Michal tossed a pillow aside, wondering what defense a smile would be against an armed soldier. She longed for a sharp sword and the power to wield it. Looking into the street once more, she felt helpless. Daylight was approaching. Soon anyone who looked down from the vantage point of her kitchen would have a clear view of the valley below. She thought again of her mother's words, and a fully formed plan sprang into her mind.

Michal ran quietly down the stone steps, crossing the courtyard to the gardener's shed. Behind a collection of broken clay pots, she found the wooden idol she sought. "Perfect," she whispered. David's nephew bought the idol at a festival, thinking it was a toy. Sarah had shrieked at the ugly figure with its oversized head sitting in her kitchen. To calm Sarah, Tirzah tossed the idol into the shed.

Next, Michal ducked into the larder to locate the pouch where Sarah kept bitter herbs. As she reached the stone steps, she stumbled over an exposed root near her favorite Rose of Sharon bush and almost fell. At the last moment, she caught herself, looked around to make sure she was alone, and hurried to her bedroom. She snatched the throw rug from the floor. Fortunately, she chose black when she selected the bedroom rug from among the goatskins at the market.

Michal twisted clothing into long rolls. She then stuffed the rolls under the bed's blanket to make it appear David was still lying there. She put the wooden idol's head on David's pillow, facing the wall, cut a slit in the goatskin rug, and pulled a strip of black goat fur across the back of the idol's head to give the appearance of hair. Finally, she tucked the blanket so only a thin strip of black wool was exposed.

For anyone standing very near the bed, the deception would be obvious. From a distance, however, an observer might think the bed was occupied by a man who'd turned his face to the wall and pulled the covers halfway over his head. Michal then tossed a pile of linen rags on the floor next the bed, in the same spot where the curly black goatskin so recently protected her feet from the bare floor.

She chose her best linen garment to wear that morning, and laid it near the bedroom's entrance along with a pair of sandals. Next, she took care to enhance her face with her cosmetics. When all other preparations were made, she mixed the bitter herbs in her water jar.

Michal held her nose and swallowed the herb and water mixture in one gulp. She spent a few minutes worrying that the foul-tasting herb concoction might not have its usual effect. Then, without warning, she felt her stomach twist violently. She gagged, and threw up on the pile of linen rags by the bed. Smiling, she rinsed her mouth with water, and spat on the rags. The night was chilly and damp, but the early morning air heated up rapidly. Michal knew the slightly unpleasant smell inside the bedroom would soon ripen into a first-class stench.

The first light of dawn shot rosy streaks through the low clouds as Michal stepped onto the balcony wearing her favorite dress. She spotted Sarah crossing the courtyard, heading for the kitchen.

"Good morning, Sarah," Michal called brightly. "My dear husband has been ill all night. Please make a clear broth for his breakfast."

The surprised look on Sarah's face pleased Michal. The room the old woman shared with Tirzah was closer to the kitchen than the other sleeping chambers. If light-sleeping Sarah was not awakened by this morning's furtive activity, it was unlikely the gardener or other household members who slept in rooms encircling the courtyard were aware of David's escape.

Michal descended the stone steps from the balcony. She forced herself not to look toward the slight movement near the gated courtyard entrance. "Zebulon," she called to the gardener as he emerged from his room. "Would you and Eli fetch some grapes and yogurt from the market as soon as possible? Our master is very sick this morning. Perhaps yogurt will settle his stomach, and you know how he loves grapes."

Zebulon was an ancient soldier who had no living family. David took him on as their gardener, even though the old man did not know a fig tree from a thistle bush. Zebulon scowled at the mention of the market.

One more detail, Michal thought, and she would be ready for her unwelcome visitors. While Sarah would play her part best without knowing what was going on, Michal needed to enlist her handmaid's complicity. "Tirzah," she shouted from the center of the courtyard.

Tirzah emerged from her room, rubbing her eyes. "Yes, my lady?" She ambled toward Michal. "Is something wrong?"

Michal kept her back to the gate and used hand motions both to beckon Tirzah and to warn her to remain silent. As soon as they stood near each other, Michal spoke quickly and quietly. "Some men are here to take David. He's gone, but they don't know that. The longer we keep them from finding out he has left the house, the better chance he will have of making good his escape." Michal grasped Tirzah's arm. "No, don't look toward the gate. The story will be that David is desperately ill. Your job is to pretend you're scared to death you'll catch what he has. We have to keep these men distracted in any possible way."

Michal continued, almost whispering. "Go as if to clean my bedroom. Watch. When the time is right, try to create fear about the seriousness of David's illness. Let's see how much courage these big, strong men have."

Tirzah nodded and hurried up the stone steps. All traces of sleepiness vanished from her round face. Michal lingered to pluck a few flowers, thanking God her handmaid had a fanciful imagination and would know what to do.

The gardener Zebulon and his young helper Eli were ready to leave for the market. Eli carried a woven basket and a soft skin. Michal took silver from the leather pouch around her waist. "Buy lots of grapes, and only a little yogurt," she instructed Zebulon. "And please return as quickly as you can."

Little Eli opened his mouth as if to question, but the gardener stopped him with his gruff, "Come, son." Then Zebulon muttered, loudly enough for Michal to hear, "When you take orders from a woman, don't expect them to make sense."

Michal followed them to the gate. "Bring us almonds as well, if you find them."

As soon as Zebulon and Eli disappeared down the street, four armed men rattled the iron gate at the first floor entrance into the courtyard.

Michal opened her eyes wide and smiled. "Good morning, gentlemen. What brings you to my humble dwelling this fine morning?" She brought the fresh flowers she'd gathered to her nose and took a deep breath. "Do you not think these fresh blossoms are magnificent?"

Two of the men returned Michal's smile—and not solely in appreciation of the flowers, she thought. A grim-faced man spoke. "We are here under orders of our lord King Saul and his servant Doeg. We would see your husband, the Lord David, immediately."

"Do come inside then." Michal let her gaze linger on the two men who'd smiled at her earlier. "I trust my father the king is well?" she asked as she led the men to a table that sat in the courtyard under the shade of a tall sycamore tree.

The grim-faced man grunted a noncommittal response.

"Good," Michal continued. "Then my dear father has not come down with the same illness that overtook my husband, Lord David, last night. Would you honor this house by taking some refreshment? Some wine and cheese, perhaps? Or in a little while some grapes from the market?" She paused to let the men consider the idea of having something to eat and drink in cool comfort, then added brightly, "Perhaps you would prefer to see my poor, sick husband immediately and be on your way to other business?"

The men looked at their leader expectantly. He licked his lips and hesitated.

Suddenly the courtyard reverberated with Tirzah's shrieks. She tore down the stone steps leading from the bedroom balcony. "He has the fever! Fish fever!" she screamed. At the bottom of the steps, Tirzah stumbled across the Rose of Sharon root and fell into the courtyard, exposing a generous expanse of shapely leg well above her ankle.

Two men sprang to the hysterical Tirzah's aid.

"I will not return to that chamber," Tirzah wailed. "My aunt's master died from just such a fever. He ate a yellow speckled fish, exactly like the one our Lord David had last night, and in three days' time he was dead."

"Nonsense, Tirzah," Michal said, taking care to make her voice quiver.

"And my poor aunt cleaned up after him. In another three days, she too was dead because she had been in his room and touched his bedclothes. I will not go back up there, my lady." Tirzah lifted terror-filled eyes toward the upstairs bedroom. "Not even if you beat me senseless."

Michal opened her eyes as wide as she could, hoping to appear frightened. "Sarah is making my husband a breakfast of broth, Tirzah. You must serve it to him."

"You are his wife," Tirzah spat angrily. "*You* serve our lord his breakfast. It is not worth my life to do so."

"I have guests to attend to." Michal hoped the flimsiness of her excuse was obvious.

"I will take Lord David his broth." Everyone turned to see Sarah standing outside the kitchen, hands perched on her wide hips, disgust written on her lined face. She glared first at Tirzah, then at Michal. "If God in His wisdom chooses to strike this old woman dead for serving my master, then so be it." With those words, she swept back into the kitchen.

Michal tossed her head and smiled at the leader of the soldiers. "You must excuse my servant Sarah," she said. "The woman is so old-fashioned. What may we serve you, gentlemen?"

"Lord David is obviously not going anywhere while we sit in his courtyard," the grim-faced man said. "There's no reason to refuse all hospitality."

CHAPTER TEN

"And when Saul sent messengers to take David, she said, He is sick. And Saul sent the messengers again to see David, saying, Bring him up to me in the bed, that I may slay him." I Samuel 19:14-15

THE MEN ATE, drank, and talked at Michal's table all morning. After taking the clear broth to David and Michal's bedroom, the old woman sat on the bottom stone step, held her apron over her face, and sobbed.

"Lord David would take no nourishment," Sarah said as she passed the table where Michal and Tirzah busily poured more wine. "Look." Sarah held out the full bowl of clear broth.

It was nearly noon when Sarah emerged from the kitchen with a pot of steaming soup. "Perhaps my lord will eat now."

"Men take their strength from wine," the grim-faced soldier announced. "I will give him a drink." He grabbed the skin of wine from Tirzah's hands. The women stood back as he took a meandering path to the stone staircase on unsteady legs. At the top of the stairs he turned and smiled. "I shall return soon, my friends." With a wave of his hand, he disappeared into the bedroom.

56

Michal glanced down at her almost-nonexistent midday shadow. She was grateful to have delayed these men in their mission to capture her husband. There had been plenty of time for David to get away.

The guard bolted from the upstairs bedroom. "On my grandfather's bones!" he yelled. "What a stink hole."

The women exchanged glances as the man clattered down the stairs. "Come." He motioned to his companions. "We must report this illness to our master Doeg."

"Shall we not take Lord David with us?" The shortest fellow emptied his cup of wine.

"No." The man's speech was no longer slurred. "No. Lord David, he cannot get out of bed. He burns with fever."

Michal was astonished at the guard's words. He spoke as if he'd investigated the situation in her bedroom. Yet in doing so, he would have discovered the dummy. She immediately spoke up. "Wise decision, sir. You are quite right that my husband is too weak and feverish to get out of bed." Sarah and Tirzah nodded their heads in solemn agreement.

The moment the men were out of sight, Michal sank to the ground, limp with relief. Sarah brought clean jars from the kitchen. "I made a vow before Tirzah was born never to touch wine myself," she said, "but it would be an honor to pour a toast to your gallantry, ladies."

"What made him think the piece of wood was Lord David?" Tirzah asked.

"The drinking probably helped," Michal said. "I'm more inclined to believe he was embarrassed to admit he ran out of the room as soon as the smell assaulted his nose. I think he just repeated what I said without bothering to confirm it."

"The king will be angry when this hoax is discovered," Tirzah observed as she and Michal sipped wine.

"True enough," Sarah agreed. "But you two may have saved Lord David's life by your wit this morning."

Michal nibbled a bite of cheese. "You did your part, too, Sarah. Those were convincing sobs when you came back from delivering breakfast."

"I was laughing," Sarah admitted. "When I saw the idol in the bed, I realized at last what was going on. The thought of you two little girls holding those four men hostage with your theatrics overcame me with amusement."

"You cannot call us little girls." Tirzah raised her wine as if to toast. "Today, Michal and I have proven we are women. And women of Israel, no less."

An undercurrent of fear ran beneath the surface of their giddiness. The king would be furious when he discovered his daughter outmaneuvered him. Those who once lived in the royal household knew only too well how vindictive King Saul could be.

Late that afternoon, a group of twelve men shoved their way past old Zebulon into the courtyard. Leading them was Doeg, the Edomite. Michal remembered Doeg well from her days at the palace. Although his official title was chief shepherd, insiders knew he was a ruffian who did King Saul's dirty work. Her mother, Ahinoam, always took pains to avoid this man's venom.

"Greetings, sir." Michal stood straight and did not shrink from Doeg's menacing look.

"Where is your husband?" His words were brusque.

"Lord David is too ill to rise from his bed."

"Then my men will carry the bed into our lord King Saul's presence with your husband in it. *Where is he?*"

Despite the fury in Doeg's voice, Michal refused to tremble. "The bedroom is at the top of those stone steps."

Six men climbed the staircase, while Doeg and the others waited in the courtyard with folded arms. Then a voice rang out from inside the bedroom. "He's gone."

"What?" After standing motionless for a moment, Doeg bounded up the steps two at a time. "What's that you say?"

Accompanied by shouted oaths, the wooden figurine sailed through the air. It bounced and skidded across the courtyard's paving stones. The bedclothes, the goatskin rug, and the rolled up clothing soon followed. Finally, the bed itself came hurtling over the balcony rail.

Doeg descended the steps and came to stand near Michal. His gravelly voice was quiet and low, in contrast to his seething features. "So, your innocent face conceals a lying tongue. When I have killed Lord David—and I will—be assured the king has promised you to a man who will teach you to be truthful."

Despite her best efforts, Michal trembled. Nevertheless, she did not avert her eyes from Doeg's. I am the daughter of the king, she reminded herself. I will not let this bully stare me down.

After Doeg and his men left, the women cleaned the courtyard and the bedroom. Old Zebulon honed his sword on the whetstone he normally used to sharpen gardening tools. Then he asked permission to send Eli to Bethlehem to gather cuttings for the household garden. Michal agreed to Zebulon's request, although she knew plant shoots were available in the city market not far from her house.

"It's a strange coincidence that the cuttings you want are available only in Judea, and in my husband's home town of Bethlehem," Michal said. "Am I better off not knowing the true purpose of the boy's mission?"

"Well said, my lady," Zebulon responded. Michal noticed a new note of respect in the old man's manner toward her.

At twilight, Michal sat alone on her rooftop. It was a clear, cool, cloudless evening. Although exhausted, she dreaded sleeping alone. She studied the contours of the distant mountains, wondering if her husband was on one of those craggy crests. She looked up at the stars as the darkness deepened. Those same stars were shining on her beloved, somewhere. A dove cooed softly. There was a dry, rustling sound as a light breeze breathed through the leaves of the sycamore tree in the courtyard. Michal hoped David knew what he was talking about when he said God would be his shepherd, for only the Almighty One could protect him from a determined savage like Doeg.

After sitting and staring at the mountains for a long time, Michal reluctantly retired to her patched-up bed. She could not put the events of the day out of her mind. She didn't bother to light the clay oil lamp beside her water jar. She lay awake and wondered what she would say when the king demanded an explanation for her behavior. Love for David was her motive, but she knew such an answer would be unacceptable. Everyone in the royal household knew King Saul counted his daughter's affection for her husband as betrayal. Fear was something her father would understand, Michal thought. He was afraid of the most harmless actions. During his bad times, the king could interpret the most polite greeting as a veiled threat of assassination.

She turned to face the empty space where David should be. What would her mother do if forced into this kind of situation? In spite of her apprehension, the improbable notion of her mother boldly facing a dangerous man like Doeg made Michal smile. Ahinoam's ways were sly, not confrontational. Her approach would be to cower in silence until the danger was past. Nevertheless, her mother did have ways of getting by the king.

Tears, Michal thought. *My father hates to see my mother cry, and she knows only too well how to turn that to her advantage.*

The next morning, Michal dressed herself carefully in a long-sleeved, blue linen tunic suitable for a married princess to wear on a formal occasion. She dabbed olive oil on her lips and cheeks to make them shine, and put a fine line of charcoal dust around her eyelids. She put on her best earrings, and all her gold bangles. She slipped on the garnet ring David recently gave her, along with the gold and silver rings she wore every day. As a final touch, she draped a fine chain over her linen headdress, adjusting it so the beaten gold discs attached to the chain and overlapped each other just above her eyebrows. She expected a summons to the palace and wanted to look as regal as possible. Perhaps looking her best would bolster her courage when she had to face her father.

Sarah found several bouquets of flowers and a pot of honey outside the street-side entrance that led through a passageway into the courtyard.

"Where do you suppose these things came from?" Michal wondered aloud.

Sarah shook her head. "Tributes to your bravery, I suppose."

"How could people outside the palace and our household possibly know of the events of yesterday?" Michal countered.

Sarah shrugged and busied herself in the kitchen.

Michal sat in the courtyard and waited. She tried to knit, but her hands would not cooperate. Delaying the discovery of her husband's escape seemed like a game when she was stuffing David's likeness under the bed clothing. However, after an encounter with Doeg, and a fitful night's sleep, the situation felt anything but playful.

Tirzah chatted about this and that, but Michal could not concentrate on her handmaid's words. It was almost a relief when the contingent of royal guards arrived at mid-morning and their leader announced the king required his daughter's presence at once.

Guardsmen surrounded Michal. One soldier marched on her left, another to her right. There were three men behind her, three more in front, and one guardsman leading the moving square of humanity. She emerged from the courtyard to find the women of her neighborhood standing across the street, arms folded. As Michal passed them, one said loudly, "Good morning, Princess Michal!"

"Good morning," she responded, doing her best to sound brave.

"God be with you, my lady," a young mother called from an upstairs window.

"And with your husband, the good Lord David," a matron with folded arms added defiantly. The guardsmen ignored the women, and kept a brisk pace. Michal began to regret wearing her best sandals. They were pretty, but the straps were new and stiff. Before long, she could feel several spots on her feet and ankles being rubbed raw.

The road to the palace wound through narrow streets near the marketplace. All along the way, people shouted encouragement as they watched the procession of royal guardsmen herding the princess toward the palace. Along many stretches of road, young girls sang the popular song that praised David's military prowess. *Saul has slain his thousands, and David his ten thousands*, resounded from house to house. A small boy dashed between the soldiers to hand Michal a welcomed jar of cool water to drink. A guard shouted a curse at the boy, but did not confiscate the water. With growing apprehension, she slowed her steps and sipped the water.

Crowds of observers grew larger. Near the market, there were as many men as women watching from the sides of the road. As the streets narrowed into the oldest section of the city, Michal rounded a corner and saw a flock of at least a hundred sheep coming toward her. The guard leader ordered the shepherds to let him pass. The young men nodded their heads obediently, but the task was hopeless. Swimming in sheep, the guardsmen and Michal's progress slowed, and then stopped. *My husband would have his flock under better control*, she thought.

The swearing, sweating guard leader threaded his way through the bleating animals and motioned his men to follow. As the group stretched out single file, people along the street emerged from their houses and joined the melee. An old man yelled at the guardsmen that the noise was disturbing his sick child. Meanwhile, a woman wearing a plain tunic appeared next to Michal. "Your husband is safe," she said, and faded into the crowd before the princess could see her face.

CHAPTER ELEVEN

".. And Doeg the Edomite turned, and he fell upon the priests, and slew...both men and women, children and sucklings, and oxen, and asses, and sheep, with the edge of the sword." I Samuel 22:18,19

KING SAUL RECLINED against the purple cushions that lined the raised platform at the end of his ceremonial chamber with his advisors on a lower tier, flanking the king on both sides. Michal had been in this room many times. How many petitioners, supplicants, and accused criminals once crouched in exactly the same place where she herself now kneeled? Were they as careful as she to keep a respectful distance from the front of the royal platform?

The king glowered at her. "You have deceived me, Daughter," he roared. "Why did you help my enemy escape?"

"I was afraid, my king," Michal spoke softly. "My husband is strong. He could easily have killed me if I refused to help him. What chance would a weak woman have against a soldier of my lord the king?" She tilted her face upward to look at her father. The blisters on her feet burned painfully, and the king's face was a thundercloud. It was not difficult to produce the tears that oozed slowly, one by one, down her cheeks. "I would never willingly do harm to you, my father and my king." She longed to assure her father that David, too, was a loyal subject. But she knew any favorable mention of David would incite King Saul's fury.

The king stared at Michal for what seemed to be a very long time. When he spoke, the angry edge was gone from his voice. "You have become so like your mother, Michal. You have those same beautiful eyes. How well I remember the night you were born. Your mother wept, saying she had disappointed me with a second daughter. That seems so long ago now. Those were good days. God was with me then. That was before He turned his back on me and the love of my people turned to bitterness. Before my own family turned treacherous. I have made this nation strong, but where is the man who shows me loyalty? All of you conspire against me." He met the eyes of the men around him. "Do you think I don't know? Am I a fool?" the king screamed. "You, Jonathan, my own flesh and blood, in league with that son of Jesse. All of you want me dead, so you can move forward with your own evil plans." King Saul gestured toward Michal, shouting, "Take her away!" Guardsmen stepped immediately to either side of Michal.

"My king," Abner began. Michal dared not glance toward her uncle.

"Silence!" Saul commanded. "Take her to her mother. They are like twin vipers, gnawing at my flesh."

Michal never knew whether it was the king's idea or someone else's suggestion that she not be allowed to return to her home. After a week, Sarah and Tirzah quietly moved into the royal residence to join her. Michal was grateful for their comforting presence in a household that seemed increasingly hostile. She quickly adopted her mother's tactic of avoiding King Saul, never knowing whether he would be jovial or furious.

Private conversations were difficult to arrange. There was always the danger that someone listened near a door or behind a curtain, waiting to gain favor by reporting a secret learned through eavesdropping. The courtyard garden was lovely, but its low walls and hedges afforded far too many hiding places to risk talking there.

Michal took to walking through the long meadow behind the palace each morning. She and Tirzah would stroll down to the brook, dangle their feet in the cool water, and reluctantly return to the oppressively paranoid atmosphere of King Saul's house.

One bright, sunlit morning, Michal and Tirzah were enjoying their daily walk along the edge of the brook. Suddenly their old gardener stepped from behind a tree.

"Zebulon!" His name escaped her lips before Michal remembered to look around and check for observers.

The old man grinned. "Greetings, my ladies."

"What brings you here?" Michal asked apprehensively, hoping her old employee was not the bearer of bad news.

"Prince Jonathan wishes to speak to you, at a place he calls the forbidden stone."

"Thank you, Zebulon. I know you are taking a big risk by delivering a message to me."

"Lord David has always been a kind master," was Zebulon's reply.

Michal and Merab named a broad, flat outcropping of rock the forbidden stone years ago. As children they were told not to wander beyond the brook. However, they loved to go a little past their limit to sun themselves on that rock.

Michal quickly made her way up the opposite bank of the brook, through a thicket of trees, to the forbidden stone. She was glad to see her brother waiting alone.

Jonathan embraced Michal. "I hope you are well, little sister."

"Yes, considering." She searched his face. "Do you have news of David? Is my husband all right? You look so tired. What's wrong?"

"By God's grace, my friend David is alive and well."

"How long can he keep evading the king's killers?" Michal asked as she settled beside her brother on the flat rock. "There's a rumor being whispered through the palace that a group of holy men were murdered for giving David food and shelter. Please tell me that didn't happen."

Jonathan shook his head. "I'm afraid this story is true, and more gruesome than you've heard. After the holy men of Nob showed kindness to David, that beast Doeg went into the city and butchered them. Then he murdered their wives and children as well, even helpless babies. When he ran out of human victims, he slaughtered the priests' animals."

Michal shuddered. "How can our father permit such sacrilege?"

"The man we know as our father is rarely with us these days," Jonathan said. "Michal, you did a very brave thing, covering for David until he could make good his escape."

"I wish I were a man with a sharp sword and a strong arm." Michal thrust her fist into the air. "I'd kill any man that so much as cast a threatening look at David."

Jonathan grinned. "I'm sure you would be a dedicated bodyguard. But I'm equally convinced Lord David is grateful you are not a man."

Michal laughed for the first time in many days. "Well, you know what I mean. I wish I could protect him."

Jonathan looked away. "Most of the king's troops pursue David without enthusiasm, knowing he's done nothing wrong. A good number have defected and gone into hiding with him. This man Doeg is different." Jonathan scratched at the stone with his knife blade. "He's brutal, ruthless. He kills for pleasure. If I can somehow stop Doeg, David will have a chance to live."

"Maybe our father will recover, and he will welcome David home. He has forgiven me, after all."

"Don't fool yourself, Michal. Father will deal with you in his own good time. He has made it known you will remarry as soon as he gets word of David's death. I think he views that as the beginning of your punishment for loving your husband more than your father."

"No!"

"It may even be that the king has already made a rash promise. Doeg seems to be convinced if he can kill David, you will be his reward."

"I'd rather die." Michal was near tears at the thought of belonging to anyone but David.

"You would be better off dead than under the heel of that monster." Jonathan leaned his head back until his face pointed directly to the sky. "I'm sorry I've upset you. These are difficult times." He stood abruptly. "I'll get information to you as often as I can. I have to get back now, before I am missed."

"Thank you, Jonathan. I know how dangerous this is for you. I'm glad you're my brother. David is fortunate to have so loyal a friend."

"I hope I can be half the friend to him that he has been to me," Jonathan said. "Your husband has saved my life more than once in the heat of battle, and I have done the same for him. There's a special bond between men who have fought side by side in mortal combat. I don't know that anyone can understand it unless they've been through the same intense experience." He hugged her, and slipped into the trees.

"Jonathan," she called after her brother, "don't forget to tell David I love him."

Michal was bitterly disappointed when her monthly bleeding came upon her. Her time was more than a week past due, and she hoped with all her heart to be carrying David's child. Her disappointment was magnified by the sure knowledge that the word of her retreat to the unclean room would be the subject of whispered conversations throughout the women's section of the palace. Her mother would hear the news, and before long King Saul would be assured his daughter was not pregnant.

Michal missed David's company, the intimacies whispered in the darkness of their rooftop, the warmth of his body against hers. She ached for the tenderness she had never known from anyone but her husband.

When the menstrual bleeding stopped and she was cleansed, the princess returned to her room to find new clothing being arranged on her bed by Miriam, one of Ahinoam's servant women. Michal examined the dress. It was too bright for her taste, and not quite modest enough for a married woman. "Why are you here?" she asked. "Whose clothing is this? Where is Tirzah?"

Miriam averted her eyes. "Your handmaid Tirzah has gone to your home in the city. I am to serve you in her absence. This dress is a gift from our lord the king. He commands you to wear it when you sing for his guests at dinner tomorrow evening."

Michal grasped Miriam's shoulder and spun the servant toward her. "How long will Tirzah be gone? Why did she go?"

"She left by order of our lord the king," Miriam's voice was fearful. "I know nothing more."

"And Sarah?" Michal dreaded the answer.

"She, too, has been sent home."

"I understand," Michal said, although at the moment she understood nothing. She released her grip on the young woman, dropping her hand to her side. "Thank you, Miriam. I will call for you if I need anything."

She sat by the window where she and her sister looked down on the palace garden so many times. If David were here, he would hold her hand, look into her eyes, and make her troubles melt away. He always had a solution to any problem.

How she missed Merab. Her sister would have scoffed at Michal's spoken thoughts until she formed them into the straightforward logic Merab's literal mind could accept. If Tirzah could be there she would offer no advice, but at least she would have listened and loyally guarded her secrets.

Isolated, with no one to confide in, Michal kept her thoughts to herself. How she longed to talk to someone she could trust not to report every word of conversation to her father. Would it be possible to steal a few minutes with Jonathan? Was he in the palace or on duty? She'd never before felt so alone.

Michal stared out the window, seeing nothing, until the shadows began to creep across the garden, obscuring the lively colors of the flowering hedges but heightening the heavy sweetness of their fragrance. Not daring to risk endangering her brother by contacting him directly, she decided to attempt a talk with her mother.

"Queen Ahinoam is not well enough to receive a guest," the handmaid Lobeth said without raising her eyes from the embroidery in her lap.

"Not even her daughter?" Michal made no move to leave. She knew better than to suggest this was an emergency. Such a plea would immediately have intensified her mother's real or imagined ailment.

Lobeth looked up at last. "I'll check. Wait here, please."

After a few minutes, Lobeth returned. "Not too long. She is not a well woman."

Michal was always struck by the contrast between the outer chamber and Ahinoam's bedroom. The first room was sparsely decorated with a few dust-colored cushions that matched the brown walls, and a single large vase that usually sat empty. Inside her mother's private room, rich red and gold fabrics covered three walls. The remaining wall, lined with windows, was stained deep purple. Mounds of red, gold, and purple cushions covered the floor, except for a small square in the center of the room. There a low gold leaf table held a water jar, an oil lamp, and an ornate incense burner. Copper trays were kept filled with fresh fruit or some seasonal delicacy.

Tonight the trays held plump shiny dates, pitted and stuffed with almond paste. The garden's main fountain sent the soothing sounds of gurgling water through the open window, while slatted wooden shutters maintained the illusion of privacy.

"Good evening, Mother." Michal kissed Ahinoam. "I hope you are well."

The queen's tone was wary. "I am never particularly well, my daughter. The least noise disturbs my sleep. I am awake at least half of most nights. And you?"

Michal looked into her mother's mercurial eyes that shifted colors, sometimes green, sometimes almost yellow, but always shot through with amber fire. Some said these were the most beautiful eyes in the land. For Michal, seeing Ahinoam's face was like gazing into the polished metal of a mirror. "I am sick of heart, my mother. I fear for David's life."

"There is nothing to be gained by worrying about what you cannot control." Ahinoam eased from her sitting position to recline on a nearby cushion.

"What will happen to me if—" Michal swallowed hard, "—if Father is successful in making me a widow?"

Ahinoam sighed. "Surely you have learned by now that I know nothing of your father's plans in any matter, not even when our children are involved."

"The king may not speak directly of his intentions, but you have your ways of learning things."

The suggestion of a smile crossed Ahinoam's still-beautiful face then quickly disappeared. She gestured toward the tray of fruit. "Would you like a date? These are particularly succulent."

"No, thank you." The thought of food did not appeal to Michal.

"Ah." The arching of Ahinoam's eyebrows dismissed Michal's refusal. "What life does a woman have if she is not married?"

"I *am* married, mother. To David."

"Of course you are, my dear. I merely remind you when a king's young daughter becomes a widow, he naturally seeks another husband for her."

"I do not want another husband. Alive or dead I can never belong to anyone but David."

"You must think this way because of your affection for David." Ahinoam seemed genuinely mystified by such a notion.

"Weren't you ever in love with father?"

"Certainly. It is a woman's duty to love her husband."

"I'm not talking about duty," Michal responded. "I'm talking about a man who makes your heart leap with joy when he looks at you, or smiles at you, or touches your hand. Someone for whose happiness you would give your very life. That kind of love, Mother."

"Do take some dates."

Michal exhaled and reached across her mother's body to the copper tray. Ahinoam caught her arm, pulled her near, and spoke softly into her ear. "The king speaks constantly of the advantage he will gain by giving you in marriage. Getting rid of David is important, because the king needs to trade your hand to gain a military alliance. When he strikes a deal with someone, you will be that man's wife, either willingly or in chains. Do you think Merab wanted to marry Adriel? You have lived for a year with a husband you adore. Few women ever have that much. Be content with your memories." Ahinoam relaxed her hold on Michal's arm. Her tone became conversational again. "I wonder where they are from."

"What?" Michal was still trying to take in what her mother said about the king's plans.

"These dates. I wonder if they're from Ethiopia."

"No doubt. I must go now. Thank you, dear mother. I hope you feel better tomorrow."

Ahinoam stretched out on her cushion. "Yes. God willing, perhaps I will walk in the meadow with you."

CHAPTER TWELVE

"I will lift up mine eyes unto the hills, from whence cometh my help. My help cometh from the Lord, which made heaven and earth. He will not suffer thy foot to be moved: he that keepeth thee will not slumber." Psalm 121, 1-3

MICHAL WISHED MERAB would come to the palace for a visit so she and her sister could sit and talk like old times. Ahinoam dashed that hope when she reported that Merab was having difficulty in the final stages of her pregnancy, and was not able to travel. So Michal knitted, did needlework, walked up and down the meadow alone, and thought. She spent so much time alone she was almost grateful when the king would summon her to sing. Yet strangers among the guests—men who appraised her with cold eyes—would make her welcome a return to solitude.

Merab and Michal occasionally sang duets when they were children. The elder girl's clear, sweet soprano was a lovely counterpoint to Michal's throaty contralto. Though Michal did not have David's exceptional musical gifts, her husband taught her to accompany herself passably on the harp. Her song selections these days were sad, haunting melodies that reflected the state of her emotions.

One still evening, Michal sat in her dark bedroom looking out the window toward the Holy Mountain, its top obscured by a thick cloud. She wondered if the cloud was a signal the Living God was at home on His mountain, as some people believed. David assured Michal that God chose their nation to belong exclusively to Him. Great men such as Moses and the modern day prophet Samuel spoke with the God of Israel concerning nationwide policy or future turning points of history. That kind of significant communication seemed completely unconnected to her, a broken-hearted girl with no one to turn to for help.

"Great Living God," Michal whispered, "If You are on Your mountain tonight, please hear me. Show me how to protect my dear husband David."

As she slept that night, Michal had a dream unlike any other. She and a man were walking together in the palace garden. In her dream she was certain she knew the man well and was completely comfortable with him, although she never saw his face. After she awakened, she could not think who he was. Despite her clear recollection that the two of them carried on a conversation, she was sure she did not hear the sound of the man's voice.

"Did you mean what you said when you told your mother you would give your life for David?" she understood the man to question.

"Yes," Michal thought.

"Then do it."

She pondered. "I would gladly die for him. But I don't understand how to do that in a way that helps him."

"Not death," was the answer. "Sacrifice is the way."

"Should I take an animal to the temple to be sacrificed?" Michal wondered.

Suddenly she and the man were in the courtyard of Michal and David's house. The wooden idol came flying over the bedroom balcony, while Michal and the man stood laughing. Someone very much like Ahinoam was with them, and she laughed also.

"Yes," Michal heard Ahinoam think aloud, "my daughter has become skilled in the use of women's weapons."

"This is the way," the man conveyed to Michal. "A different kind of sacrifice. Arm yourself from the arsenal of your mind."

Michal opened her eyes and stared into the darkness of her room. Her dreams normally receded quickly, if she could remember them at all. Always before, in a wakened state, she easily recognized the unreality of what she experienced. Yet this memory remained intact and fresh in her mind, with no dreamlike quality. Against all logic, she was sure the events she recalled truly happened. She sat up and thought through every detail. She could not rid herself of the feeling there was meaning in the dream, something she was expected to decipher. But what? After a long period of restlessness, she went back to sleep.

Michal's first thought upon awakening the next morning was the dream. She relived it again as she dressed, and once more as she walked through the meadow. She tried to put the dream out of her mind and think about David. She hoped he was safe in some remote sanctuary.

A single arrow flew through the air and fell a short distance from Michal. She looked in the direction of the arrow, and judged the point of origin to be the forbidden stone. *Jonathan!* She smiled and set out across the stream.

"I am thinking of a plan," Michal heard herself telling Jonathan, as they sat on the great, flat stone.

He looked skeptical. "I'm ready to listen to anything. The situation is desperate and getting worse every day. Doeg is an animal."

"Father is obsessed with the idea he needs a northern ally. He believes the best way to seal the alliance is to marry me to a war lord."

"How did you come by that piece of information?" Jonathan's voice conveyed a mixture of surprise and respect.

Michal ignored her brother's question. "What if someone, meaning you of course, could convince Father to go ahead and make an agreement to marry me off without waiting for David to be caught?" Michal could almost see Jonathan's mind working. "That destroys Doeg's need to kill David to win me. It satisfies father's obsession to make an alliance, and"—she took a deep breath—"punishes me by separating me forever from the husband I love."

"You have some good points. But you know David as well as I do," Jonathan said. "He would never let such a betrayal pass unanswered. He would find you. If he couldn't raise an army, he would go by himself. He would reclaim you or die in the attempt."

Michal agreed. "What you say is true. However, Father would not want to flaunt his treachery toward David before the people. Convince the king to wed me in secret. Then your job would be to make sure Doeg knows I will never be his." She closed her eyes. "And to convince David that I am dead."

"You do not know what you are saying, little sister," Jonathan protested. "You would be unhappy all of your days."

"Let us not think of me at this moment," Michal insisted. "Let us concentrate on whether or not this plan would save David's life. And if so, will you help me carry it out?"

Jonathan held the sides of his face with the palms of his hands as he stared down at the forbidden stone. When he said nothing for several minutes, Michal knew her brother found no flaw in her scheme.

"Is there no other way?" Jonathan asked at last. "Shall I lie to my best friend? Must both of your hearts be broken to spare him?"

"He knows I would never give this up." Michal removed the ring David put on her hand on their wedding day. One last time, she ran the tip of her finger around the gold grapevine motif that encircled the wide silver band. Then she thrust the ring toward her brother.

"Are you sure, Michal?" Jonathan's eyes pierced hers. "Once these events are set in motion, there will be no turning back. Think for a while before we do anything."

"There is no time to think," Michal said. "Please, Jonathan, I beg you to help me fight for David the only way I know."

Her brother took the ring and dropped it into a small leather pouch. Then he stood up slowly. "Our father spoke the truth when he said his daughters were better men than his sons. If you were my brother, I would kneel at your feet and call you king."

Michal forced a smile. "Perhaps someday when you rule this nation, you will remember your little sister and call her out of exile."

"The crown will sit on the head of one more worthy than I." Jonathan stepped down from the rock. "The army will be going to the desert on a mission tomorrow. Perhaps I can put this plan in motion as soon as that. God be with you, Princess Michal, most noble daughter of the king." He kissed her hand, and then he disappeared into the thick trees. Michal wondered what he meant when he said someone more worthy than he would rule. Surely Jonathan did not think himself inferior to one of their brothers.

The enormity of the commitment she'd made settled over Michal like a mantle. Jonathan was right. Once her ideas were transplanted into the mind of the king, they would assume a life of their own. Events would sweep her along toward an unknown fate. She would have no control, and no refuge.

She looked toward the Holy Mountain. One of David's favorite songs played through her mind. *I will lift up mine eyes unto the hills, from whence cometh my help. My help cometh from the Lord, which made heaven and earth.* She could not bring the rest of the words to mind, but what she could remember gave her some measure of comfort.

As she lay in her bed that evening, Michal wondered how she could endure marriage to another man. Day-to-day life would be empty without her husband. Yet the torture would come at night. She came to David as an ignorant, inexperienced virgin, full of curiosity about the secret thing that passed between a husband and wife. A second marriage would hold no mystery, and certainly no joy. She shuddered to think that before long she would lie in bed with someone other than the man she loved. The thought was deeply repulsive. Yet she could think of no other option if she wanted David to survive.

She allowed herself to sink into the memory of her wedding night. That time of new marriage was a precious recollection, one that never faded. Michal saw David many times when he was in the company of her male relatives. She heard him sing. She looked at him, and she heard him speak. Yet she was never alone with David—nor with any man to whom she was not closely related—until the day of her marriage. Perhaps Ahinoam spoke wisely when she advised her daughter to be sustained by her remembrances.

On the evening of the day they were married, David smiled at her in the quietness of his house. He held her close to him. "My own beautiful wife," he whispered. "I thought this dream would never come true."

"I, too, have hoped and dreamed I would someday be yours," she said boldly.

"Have you, my precious one?" He searched her face with his luminous brown eyes. "You aren't disappointed at being given to an upstart sheep herder?"

"Today, I count myself the most fortunate woman in all of Israel," she said.

She heard the sound of his breathing, and felt the beating of his heart. He guided her face upward with his hands. The first soft kiss warmed her like strong wine. As he kissed her again, Michal felt as if her legs would collapse beneath her. Maybe they had, for he swept her into his arms.

David carried her up the stone steps and into their bedroom. He laid her on the bed gently. In one deft motion he was beside her, propped up on one elbow, caressing her with his free hand. Michal remembered her sister Merab's prediction made that very afternoon. "Don't be surprised if he makes you feel like a city to be ransacked. For a soldier, taking a wife is merely another conquest."

"You don't have to be afraid of me, Michal," David whispered.

"I'm not afraid," she said, looking away from him.

"No?" He turned her face back to his. "Then why are you trembling like a newborn lamb?"

"Because you're going to stab me," she whimpered. The tension and fatigue of the preparations for her wedding left her nerves raw. Until the wedding ceremony concluded, Michal was terrified her father would have one of his sudden changes of mind and give her to someone other than David. Furthermore, the old women in the palace frightened her half to death with their stories of painful wedding nights and bloody bedding.

"*Stab* you? My darling Michal, I want to take care of you, protect you." He looked puzzled. "Whatever gave you the idea I would take a knife to you?"

"When Merab was to be married, our mother told her that a man uses a sword to turn a girl into a woman. Or something like that. The old women told me I will be a bloody mess by morning." She swallowed hard, regretting the mention of her sister's name. "Because that's how people get babies."

David smiled and sat cross-legged on the bed. He patted the spot next to him, and Michal sat there. Lifting a bowl of grapes from beside the bed, he offered her some before taking a few himself. "First of all," he said, "I will not force you to do anything you don't want to do. Second, if anything hurts, all you have to do is ask me to stop. Are we in agreement?"

Michal nodded yes. She knew her husband had every right to treat her as his possession. Yet he spoke with her as if they were equal partners conspiring together, or children playing a game. The kissing was deliciously exciting, and she wanted him to kiss her again. But she dared not ask.

"All right," he said. "Let's start at the beginning. You do know that men and women are different? Our bodies are not identical?"

"I know that men do not have monthly bleeding," she said proudly. "You don't have breasts like we do. And we don't have beards."

"You're right." He seemed amused. "But there's more." He held a grape near her lips. She opened her mouth, and he gently fed her. "I suggest we remove our clothing. Then we'll compare what you have to what I have and see how it all fits together."

Michal hesitated. Was she supposed to voice her agreement, or merely keep quiet and do what he said? For years she was insatiably curious to know what it was that made men and women different. Should she say so?

"I'll snuff out the lamp," he said.

Michal shivered with excitement as David slipped off first her tunic, then his. She was fascinated to find hair growing on his muscular chest. He guided her hands downward and said, "This is what the old women called a sword."

David's delicious nearness inflamed Michal's desire. She touched him cautiously, surprised at how different he was from her. "Amazing," she whispered.

"That part of me fits inside of you, here." His touch set her on fire. Yet her logic refused to accept what he said.

"That will never work!" she blurted without thinking.

David said, "It has been working for thousands of years, ever since Adam and Eve. I can't think why we would be an exception."

"We don't match," she said, certain he would divorce her when he discovered what she said was true. "It won't fit."

"I assure you, Michal." He drew her close against him. "We will find a way."

CHAPTER THIRTEEN

"And her husband went with her along weeping behind her to Bahurim. Then said Abner unto him, Go, return. And he returned." II Samuel 3:16

MICHAL AWAKENED THE morning after her marriage to David, full of energy and happy to be alive. She turned her head to see her new husband silently looking her over. "Good morning, my sweet wife." David smiled in a way that always melted her heart.

She said the first words that came into her mind. "David, you are wonderful."

He took her hand and kissed each finger. "Is it possible so lovely a creature as you could care for a simple man like me?" He kissed the palm of her hand. "God has done some mighty miracles on my behalf. You may be the greatest of them all. Certainly the most enjoyable." He yawned and smiled. "What do you want to do today, Princess?" he asked. "I have no duty for a while. We will do whatever you choose."

"I would like for you to sing to me."

"Of course." David seemed pleased. "Anything else?"

"Last night..." she began. She was not certain how to put her thoughts into words.

"Last night?" he prompted.

"Last night we did the secret thing." Michal felt the blush begin to creep up her neck. "I was wondering…" She stopped again.

"You were wondering?"

"After our child is born, will we do the secret thing again?"

David appeared to be holding back an answer. His lips formed a small circle. Then he flung himself onto his back and exploded with laughter.

"What is so funny?" Michal demanded crossly.

David sat up. "Michal," he began. Laughter overtook him again. He kept trying to speak, but each attempt ended in another cascade of mirth. "My dear little wife," he managed to say at last, "you are not automatically pregnant because we have slept together once." He punctuated his statement with another laugh, and wiped his eyes. "And as strict as the laws given by Moses can be, the only limitation is that we will abstain during your time of bleeding and just before I go into battle."

"Well, I didn't know." Michal was chagrined that he found her question so amusing.

"Of course you didn't," he said soothingly. "Are you saying you want to repeat last night's pleasure?"

Michal burned with embarrassment. "It might be nice to… to… uh… I mean, it *was* very pleasant."

"My sweetheart can deal with the concept easier than the words," David observed. He drew her arms around his neck and kissed her lightly. "I hope I never disappoint you in any way. As for what you call the 'secret thing', I expect to give you as much as you want." He looked upward. "If I am dreaming, Lord, please let me sleep on."

Michal's curiosity got the better of her. "How did you know what to do last night? Do you have another wife I don't know about?"

"No." David nuzzled her hair. "I have no other wife. Before I came to the palace, I lived out in the pastures with my father's flock. Animals are not secretive about getting their young the way we humans are. Since I began to serve the king, I have lived constantly among soldiers. Add six older brothers who love to boast, and you can see I have had a thorough education. A little rough, maybe, and until yesterday strictly theoretical."

"I love you, David," Michal declared. "I always have, and I always will."

"Out of bed, my lady," he said. "We'll get dressed and have some breakfast. I'll take my harp, and we'll ride up into the hills where the red anemones are in full bloom. I know a little brook where we can sit and listen to the birds sing."

The days that followed were the happiest of Michal's life. David held nothing back from her. She asked her husband searching questions about his family, God, war, poetry, and life. His thoughtful answers reflected a determination to deceive neither her nor himself.

"Why didn't I realize you would be as intelligent as you are beautiful?" he asked one evening as they sat on their rooftop watching the sunset.

Michal said nothing. She never knew any man to grant the possibility a woman could have a share of wisdom.

"One of the best things about my friendship with Jonathan is that we make each other think," he said, as much to himself as to her. "You're his sister, made from the same blood and bone. How could there not be a fine wit hiding behind those incredibly beautiful, mysterious eyes of yours?"

"I used to wish I could study, like my brothers. Of course, that would have been impossible." Michal glanced at him. "I've never admitted that to anyone before."

"Your secrets are safe with me. I like knowing things that no one else knows about you." David rubbed her back lightly. "I always thought I would like to design and build things. Houses, maybe even large public buildings. But that was out of the question for the youngest son of a family that farms and tends flocks of sheep."

"And so you chose to become a soldier."

"I cannot say that I chose," he said. "After the business with Goliath, the king took me into his service. A military career was more or less unavoidable from then on."

"Were you afraid of the giant?"

David leaned back and tilted his head toward the darkening sky. "Not really. The only emotion I remember is anger."

"Didn't you realize he could kill you? Or slice off an arm and disable you for life?"

"I was aware of those possibilities." David seemed lost in thought for a moment. "How could I not be, with the king's armor bearer and my older brothers arguing about who would be responsible for my

80

death and who should break the news to my father? I even heard them bickering over who would provide the donkey to take my body home, since I walked into the camp on foot."

"But you fought the giant anyway. Why?" she asked. "What was it about Goliath that made you angry?"

"I guess the giant's blasphemy was a good part of the reason. It was bad enough when he belittled our army. Then he started hurling insults at our God. The king and his battle staff did nothing but wring their hands. I was furious not only with the Philistine, but with your father and his advisors as well. I decided if our soldiers wouldn't do something about the giant, this shepherd boy would. I was confident God would take care of the results if I had the courage to make the effort."

"I hope you are never that upset with me." Michal snuggled closer to David.

"I can't imagine you would ever speak against the Holy One of Israel," he said as he put his arm around her. His tone turned playful. "Anyway, I wouldn't use a slingshot on you. You strike me as the kind of woman I would prefer to stab. Assuming that would work"

"Stop teasing me!" Michal pretended to be upset. "How was I supposed to know?" Both of them laughed.

"Let's go inside," David whispered. "I think it's time to polish my sword."

"You talk like a foreigner." Michal giggled as they left the rooftop.

"I THOUGHT WE would go on that way for the rest of our lives," she said.

Tirzah's voice shocked Michal from her reverie. "So did I. Every bone in my body aches from riding so long in this stupid cart. I thought you were asleep."

"I was remembering, half-dreaming." Michal rubbed her eyes. "Thinking of my David."

Tirzah nodded. "Those were good times."

"They were indeed." Michal sighed and took in the scenery around them. "What you heard was correct, Tirzah. This is the road to Bahurim." Michal's fatigue gave way to anxious concern.

Lord Abner's house was situated on the crest of the hill on which Bahurim was built. Captain Osh dismounted and stopped the cart at the front entrance. Michal was shocked to realize the old man standing in front of the house with folded arms was Uncle Abner. She might not have recognized him, except for his hair. The locks that were once brown were now white. Yet the cowlicks that made the man's hair stick out from his head like the blossom of a thistle were unmistakable.

"Good job, Captain Osh," Abner said. "We will leave tomorrow at daybreak for Hebron. We take twenty men, no more."

"Yes, sir. We will be ready. One more item, if I may."

"Well, what is it? Speak up." Abner's impatience showed in his voice.

"Princess Michal's husband, that is to say, the man Phaltiel has followed us all the way from Gallim with a handful of men. Their party has proceeded into the village and they are even now on their way here. Do you want me to kill them or take them prisoner?" The man tossed out the question of whether Phaltiel should live or die as casually as someone else might ask whether to take a glass of wine or not.

"Let him come," Abner said after a moment. "A few men are no threat. But remain here with your troops until he arrives. If he listens to reason, I'll avoid making an enemy of his father. If not..." Abner pointed away from his house. "Take them outside the village first so there will be no witnesses."

Michal filled the ensuing silence by saying "Greetings, Uncle Abner. I trust you are well."

"A blind man could see that I'm not well at all. In fact, I am worn out, sick, and near death." Abner still stood tall and straight, but the man Michal remembered as fleshy was now reed-thin. The skin of his face stretched tightly across sunken cheeks. His clothing hung loosely around the bones of his once-powerful arms and shoulders.

"What news can you tell me of our family?" She yearned to hear the years had been kind to those she loved.

"Other than myself and Ishbosheth, there are no men left," Abner said without preparing her. "King Saul and your other brothers died at the Battle of Mount Gilboa where we fought the Philistines."

"My mother? And my sister? Have you seen them?" she asked.

"Your mother died in her sleep not long after you were sent to Gallim," Abner said without emotion. "Merab, last year. It may be that a few children remain, none old enough for you to have known them."

Michal felt weak with sorrow and was grateful for Tirzah's comforting hand on her arm. She heard the thud of horses' hooves on the packed earthen road that led to Abner's house. "Go inside," Abner barked. Michal knew the words were directed at Tirzah and herself, but she could not move. She shivered as Phaltiel and his men drew near.

A stone's throw from the house, Phaltiel gave a signal and his party stopped where they were. He dismounted, threw a baleful look in Michal's direction, and led his horse the last few yards to where Abner stood. "Lord Abner, what have I done to bring your evil down upon my house?"

"Go home, Phaltiel," Abner said.

"I will gladly go home if you'll give me my wife, Michal." Phaltiel was on the verge of tears. "She is mine. King Saul himself gave her to me. I want her."

"David, the Son of Jesse, married Michal before you. He is still alive, and he has never divorced her. Legally, she belongs to him."

Michal silently thanked God for her uncle's unyielding nature. She knew what Phaltiel could not, that nothing would keep this old soldier from accomplishing his mission.

"Her first husband deserted her," Phaltiel insisted. "I have fed and clothed the princess for almost seven years. She gives me more pleasure than all of my other wives combined." His voice broke as he choked out the words, "I love her."

Michal could hardly believe her ears. How could Phaltiel dare to speak of love, after the way he mistreated her? The steward must have brought a plentiful supply of wine along to keep Phaltiel in a drunken stupor.

"Ridiculous," Abner snorted. "King David of Judea demands to have Michal returned to him. So it shall be. Return home to Gallim, and count yourself fortunate to leave Bahurim alive." He inclined his head slightly toward Captain Osh. "Most outsiders who dare to ride into this village bearing arms never live to see another sunrise." Abner glared at Phaltiel. The silence seemed endless to Michal. She hoped her uncle was about to send Phaltiel to his death. Finally, the chief steward dismounted and walked to where his master stood.

"Come, my lord," he said as if to a child. "Let's go home."

Phaltiel hesitated. Then he broke into great, heaving sobs. The steward helped his weeping master onto his horse. Without a backward look, the servant led Phaltiel's mount to the group from Gallim. Then the steward swung his leg over his own horse's back, turned in the direction from which they came, and retreated.

Abner and Captain Osh looked at each other quizzically. "Tomorrow at dawn then," the captain said crisply. He swung himself onto his horse and led his men down the same road where Phaltiel and his men now appeared small in the dusty distance.

Abner turned toward the women huddled in the doorway. "What is wrong with that man, Phaltiel?" he asked. "Has he no dignity?"

"He's drunk," was Michal's terse assessment.

Abner looked down the road. "Not merely a fool, but a drunken fool at that." He turned back to Michal. "Rizpah will show you where you will sleep and get you something to eat. Be ready to leave by daybreak."

Michal glanced around to make sure there was no one other than Tirzah within earshot. She doubted Abner would answer her question in the presence of his servants. "My uncle, is it true Lord David has asked for me?"

Abner exhaled noisily. "You mean *King* David. Yes. He refused to negotiate with me. Then he practically threw me out of his palace and told me to leave Judea and never come back, unless you were with me."

Michal was rooted to the spot where she stood. "Why?" she managed to ask. What would David do with her?

"How should I know?" Abner did not appear to be the least bit curious. "Your husband is a powerful man. He will not allow me to speak with him on a matter of grave importance until I bring you to him. And so I will do as he commands."

"Powerful?" Michal asked incredulously. "Helpless little Judea?"

"You have been away a long time," Abner replied. "King Saul fought a bitter war against the Judeans after David became their king. We lost every major battle. As a result, our nation has become weaker and weaker, while David has grown progressively stronger." He continued, as if speaking to himself. "Once every five hundred years or so, someone like this son of Jesse comes along. He is not like other men. Successful commanders know how to force men to obey them.

Something I cannot understand in David makes men *want* to do his bidding. Soldiers willingly give him more loyalty than a man like me could ever command. At various times he has been my student, my rival, and my enemy. I regret that I will not live long enough to serve him as my king."

"If you were in David's place, what would be your purpose in sending for your remarried wife?" Michal's mind refused to function.

Abner spoke matter-of-factly. "For my part, the overriding concern would be to avenge my honor. I would either have such a woman publicly stoned, or I myself would plunge a dagger into her faithless heart."

CHAPTER FOURTEEN

"And he said...Thou shalt not see my face, except thou first bring Michal Saul's daughter, when thou comest..." II Samuel 3:13

THEY WERE UNABLE to leave for Judea the next morning. Abner had fallen dangerously ill. Michal overheard one of the servants say he would never rise from his bed again. Rizpah, once a handmaid in the palace of King Saul, stayed with Abner through the long nights, retreating to the women's quarters each morning looking pinched and drawn. Then, after a few hours of sleep, she would return to Abner's bedside. Members of the household were preoccupied with their master's health, and they ignored his visitors.

Michal strolled in Abner's pleasant garden, grieving for her now-lost family. She allowed her thoughts of David to go on without interruption. She prayed to have a chance to see him, maybe even talk to him. Would he be pleased to see her, or angry that he had been deceived?

Though Michal never stopped thinking of herself as David's wife, she did not dare to hope he would feel the same way. She harbored a fleeting fantasy he might take her into his service in some capacity, but dismissed the thought immediately. The only skill she possessed was the ability to spin, dye, and knit yarn. What would that be to a powerful man, now a king?

Although David was a mighty man of war, Michal knew only his tender side. She could not bring herself to believe he truly wanted to kill her. Still, even kings could not always do as they wished. Regardless of what commoners might believe, the daughter of the king realized a ruler frequently made political concessions. As a child, she was aware her father sometimes formed distasteful alliances. King Saul often made decisions he regretted under the influence of the men who surrounded, flattered, and advised him. Many acts were carried out not for their own value, but solely for the impression they made on the king's subjects or his enemies.

After three days, Michal learned that Abner was able to sit up and take a little nourishment. That same afternoon a servant girl brought word that Lord Abner expected her to be ready to leave for Hebron at dawn the following day.

That evening, Michal slept fitfully for a while before she gave up and rose from her bed. She put on a blue linen dress—one she had not worn in years. It was looser than she remembered, and slightly faded. Nevertheless, she hoped she would make a reasonable public appearance. She put on her best jewelry. Tirzah obtained some makeup from Rizpah. Michal used it sparingly before awakening Tirzah to prepare for the journey.

Michal sat in the flickering light of the oil lamp and waited to hear the first stirrings of Abner's household. As was her habit, she prayed a morning prayer. She asked the Living God to allow her to speak to her husband long enough to explain the circumstances of her marriage to Phaltiel. Since there was no longer any reason to ask God's favor on Merab, Michal prayed her sister's child survived and was being cared for. She wept to think that she would never see Merab's face again.

Her bittersweet recollections made Michal fling off the blue dress and change into the shabby tunic she wore when doing household duties in Phaltiel's compound. She washed the makeup from her tear-stained face before putting her jewelry into a leather pouch. Her father was no longer king. What would be the point of representing herself as royalty?

In the courtyard, Michal and Tirzah waited near the exit gate. "You expect to take along your handmaid?" Abner rasped.

"Yes, my lord," Michal replied calmly. "A lady cannot travel without a maid."

"No." He pointed at Tirzah. "Go inside at once."

Tirzah hung her head and obeyed Abner's order. Michal pulled the hood of her traveling cloak forward. She longed to draw on Tirzah's strength for the unknown trials this day might hold. Nevertheless, she stepped on the stool a soldier placed on the ground, and mounted the horse whose reins another soldier held. The horse seemed much taller than the donkeys Michal customarily rode. She avoided looking down and tried to sit as straight as her uncle.

When the sun peeked over the hills around Bahurim, Michal noticed Abner's face was ashen. She knew a less determined man would not attempt this trip. Although he looked like a cadaver, he made no reference to his health. Instead, the old soldier continued to command his men as always.

Captain Osh led the column forward. The soldiers followed him, two abreast, five pairs in front of Michal and Abner, and five pairs riding behind them. Michal rode in silence until the column left Bahurim. She checked the sun's position and determined they were going south. That would be the general direction of Hebron, which she concluded must now be the capital city of Judea. She decided to attempt a conversation with Abner if only to ease the growing terror inside her.

"My lord uncle," she began respectfully, "is my brother, King Ishbosheth, well?"

She thought perhaps Abner was ignoring her question, because there was no immediate response. After a long pause, her uncle turned his face in her direction.

"Ishbosheth is a fool. He isn't fit to be king. If we don't stop him, he will be the ruin of the nation."

Such venomous words, so openly spoken, shocked Michal into silence. She pondered the purpose of her uncle's visit to Judea. Clearly, Abner was not being sent to do business on behalf of King Ishbosheth. That meant he was undertaking an alliance with King David on his own initiative. No doubt Ishbosheth would consider such a move outright treason. Michal knew she would suffer the same punishment as her uncle if this treachery came to light. She rode along in silence, worrying about the reception they would receive at their destination.

"Greetings, brothers. What brings you to the land of Judea?" The youthfulness of the soldier at the border crossing took Michal by surprise.

"We come in peace," Captain Osh said. "Lord Abner was instructed to fetch King David's wife, Princess Michal. We have the lady with us. If you will allow us to pass, we will deliver her to your king at Hebron."

Michal gazed at the mountainous landscape behind the Judean. Her traveling cloak hid much of her face, but did not prevent the soldier and his companions from casting curious glances in her direction. "Some of my men will accompany you, to assure your safe passage," the fellow said. "Simon!"

An even younger man emerged from the brushy undergrowth. He was mounted on a fine war horse, carried a short sword, a bow, and a quiver of arrows. He was completely without armor. "Follow me," he said confidently.

Simon led Abner's party along a road into the mountains. A contingent of ten or twelve additional Judean soldiers followed them at a discreet distance.

"Bunch of undisciplined kids," someone behind Michal muttered sourly.

"Young perhaps," Abner commented, his eyes straight ahead. "But disciplined enough to beat us like a worn out drum each time we met them in battle."

Michal was entranced by the lush beauty of the countryside. The people in the scattered farms along the way were smiling and cheerful. Their steps were lively. Children in colorful clothing fearlessly exchanged greetings with the soldiers. Homes were in good repair, surrounded by well-manicured gardens filled with vegetables and grains. Sturdy flocks of sheep grazed on lush hillsides. Michal couldn't help but compare the spirited sights of Judea to the gaunt faces and drab colors she saw in Bahurim.

As the caravan drew ever nearer to Hebron, Michal could no longer push away the question of what David would do with her. Her body pulsed with a mixture of fear and delight. She was only a short distance from the man who had held her heart captive for more than half her life. She willed herself to concentrate on the delightful prospect she might glimpse David's face, and refused to consider other dark possibilities.

The lead Judean soldier turned and shouted, "Not much further now. I'll ride ahead and announce your arrival." He whistled and flicked his reins, pressing his horse into a full gallop. Michal lost sight of him as he swung around a bend in the road, with the wind billowing in his loose tunic, and his dark hair flowing behind him.

Michal could hear a faint murmur of conversation from the Judean rear guard, but could not make out their words. The Israelites rode without speaking. The regular thud of the horses' hooves on the packed dirt of the road and the occasional trill of birds were the only other sounds.

She stole a glance at Abner. He sat ramrod straight on the back of his horse. The pallor of his face and the firm set of his jaw were the only clues to the state of his health. Michal felt a rush of admiration for her uncle, and wondered once again why he felt compelled to make this journey.

As the group pressed on, Michal searched each bend in the road for signs they were approaching a center of population. She considered the possibility the Judean had misjudged the distance when she caught sight of a city through a gap in two hills. Rounding a sharp turn in the road, the soldiers ahead of Michal and Abner stopped. She looked past their backs to see a small group of Judeans on horseback facing them, blocking their passage.

Abner went to the head of his column to confer with the Judeans. Suddenly Michal recognized the handsome man in the center of the group. Even from a distance, and after the passage of years, she knew it was David himself riding the magnificent white stallion. Her heart pounded as her eyes fastened on her dear husband's face. His ruddy complexion glowed bronze in the sunlight. When he fixed his deep brown eyes on Michal, she made no attempt to resist returning his gaze.

David left Abner talking and guided his horse through the ranks to where Michal waited. He was as she remembered him, though perhaps a little heavier, with the hint of character lines beginning to form at the corners of his beautiful eyes. Within a moment, he was so near she could have reached out and touched him. She thought her heart would burst with delight.

"Michal, is it really you?" he asked.

"My husband," she whispered.

David took the reins of her horse in his hands. "Lord Abner, my brother Eliab will lead your party on to my house," he said without taking his eyes from Michal's face. "Michal, would you like to ride up into the hills where the red flowers are in bloom? There's a little brook where we can sit and listen to the birds sing. It's not as beautiful as the place where we used to go when we were first married, but I think you might like it. Will you go with me?"

There was so much Michal wanted to say to him, but a weak "Yes" was all that came from her lips.

"My lord." Abner rode near David, his voice brimming with frustration. "We have traveled a long distance."

"You can negotiate with my brother Eliab. He speaks for me." David leaned forward and clapped Abner on the shoulder. "Tomorrow we will have a great feast for you and your men, to celebrate our pledge to fight each other no more. Right now"—he removed his hand from Abner and looked back at Michal—"I have other business. Surely you can understand."

Without waiting for a response, David rode away, up and over a small hill, leading Michal's horse behind him.

CHAPTER FIFTEEN

"My beloved spake, and said unto me, Rise up, my love, my fair one, and come away. For, lo, the winter is past, the rain is over and gone; The flowers appear on the earth; the time of the singing of birds is come, and the voice of the turtle is heard in our land;" Song of Solomon 2:10-12

DAVID REMOVED HIS long scarlet drape and spread it on the ground before helping Michal dismount. She drew in her breath at the pleasure of feeling his hands on her body. The sensation of being lifted from her horse by David's powerful grip was intoxicating. Her best hope was to kneel before him in a public chamber and beg for mercy. She was completely unprepared for the delicious excitement of being alone in the fragrant woods with him. How desperately she wanted to put a hand on his arm or his face, but she dared not.

David turned to where his horse was grazing. "I brought some refreshments." He tossed a pouch on the makeshift blanket and reclined under a blossoming almond tree. He propped himself up on one elbow and gestured for Michal to sit opposite him. She removed her traveling cloak and sat cross-legged.

He is my husband and we are alone, she thought. There is no reason for my head to be covered. She pulled off her headdress and shook out the waves of her waist-length hair. She hoped David would pull her into his arms and kiss her, but he did not.

"Can you forgive me?" he asked.

"I? Forgive *you*? For what?" Michal was baffled by such a strange request.

"My last words to you were not to give up on me. Then I gave up on you. I thought you were dead, that I had lost you forever."

"I wanted you to believe I was dead," Michal said slowly. "I hope you will allow me to explain." She felt unwelcome tears forming.

David nodded, "I know everything."

"What do you mean? How could you know?"

"Two years ago, my men took a prisoner who claimed to have been a royal guard serving in King Saul's household. He said he had information that would be of interest to me. At first I was skeptical. I thought the man was trying to improve his lot as a prisoner by making up a wild story. But the more I questioned him, the more I believed his story could possibly contain some truth. He claimed to have ridden with a detachment that spirited you away from the palace one dark night. He said they took you to a secret rendezvous, where you were married to a man whose name he did not know, and that the guardsmen were threatened with death if they ever disclosed what they knew." David offered her a drink. "This water is from the sweetest well in Judea. Try it."

Michal accepted the skin and drank. "Excellent," she agreed. "I remember that night you described only too well. So the prisoner persuaded you I was yet alive?"

"Not completely. He merely planted the seed of doubt. I decided to send a message to Ishbosheth and demand he turn you over to me. The weak words of his denial convinced me he was withholding information." David plucked a nearby wildflower and studied it. "I sent spies and told them to leave no stone unturned until they found out what happened to you. Your sister Merab was the one who brought everything together. She knew the entire story of what you did and why. You are as brave as you are beautiful, Michal. I owe you my life."

Was that why David brought her here? To say thank you? Then what? "I did what any wife would do for her husband in the same circumstances."

"You must associate with a different group of wives than I do," David said with a short laugh. "Would you do such a thing for Phaltiel?"

"No. But he is not my true husband, not in my heart." She wanted to steer the conversation in another direction, and not waste precious moments thinking about Phaltiel in David's presence. "It is a sober thought that I will never see my family again. Uncle Abner told me both my mother and father are dead. As are all of my brothers except Ishbosheth." The tears she could not contain began to slide down her cheeks. "Then my sister Merab, just last year. I don't know how."

"I'm sorry." David tossed the wildflower aside. "Have you not been in contact with your family?"

"Not for the seven years I've been at Gallim. I'm grateful Tirzah has been with me. Dear old Sarah was there, too, until her death. I hope to learn the circumstances of my parents' and brothers' deaths. Perhaps someday I can make a pilgrimage to the place where they are buried."

"King Saul and Prince Jonathan died bravely in battle, as you would expect. I don't know about your mother." After a long moment he said, "Tell me about your life in Gallim."

"There isn't much to tell." Michal ached for the comfort of David's arms. "The household business is olive growing. I help with the harvest and pressing oil from the olives once a year. Otherwise, I spend my days spinning and dying yarn, and knitting. Tirzah helps me." Did she dare beg him not to send her back to Gallim?

"Did my spy report accurately that you have no children?"

"Yes." Michal hated this admission.

David absently plucked a nearby wildflower. "Do you ever regret what you did for me?"

"Never. Not for one moment." *Does he not know I love him more than my own life?* "Of course, I have often been homesick. And I have desperately missed my loved ones. But if it was all to be done over again, there is no question I would make the same choice."

"So," he asked, "are you content in Gallim?"

"No," she said quietly. "Phaltiel's household is filled with jealousy, greed, and selfishness. They worship idols. God has given me the resources to go on despite my situation. What peace I have found has come from Him." She reached out, but stopped herself from touching his arm. "Can you understand what I mean?"

"Yes, I think I can." There was a far away look in his eyes. "My life as a fugitive was hard. Yet alone in the desert, with no one to turn to but God, I felt a nearness to Him. There is nothing that compares to that inner peace. I find it's challenging to maintain intimacy with Him in a palace where everyone is concerned with politics, money, and power." David rested his warm brown eyes on her face. "What of this man, this Phaltiel? Is he kind to you?"

"He is kind to no one, not even himself."

"Are you—" A look of pain crossed David's face. "That is, do you care for him?"

"I once tried to do so, but without success." She folded her hands and stared at them. "When he's drunk, which is most of the time, he is either maudlin or sadistic. I can never predict which it will be, but he is disgusting either way. When he's not drunk, he's the most boring man you can imagine. His conversation consists of planning his next meal—what he will eat, how it will be prepared, and the wine he will consume with it."

David shifted from half-reclining into a sitting position. "After Jonathan convinced me I was a widower, I took two wives." He sipped water from the skin. "First Abigail, who has my sister's name and then Ahinoam, who happens to have the same name as your mother. They have never done anything that would give me cause to put them away from me." He drew a deep breath, exhaled, and rubbed his hair. "Over the years, I have made four alliances that involved marriage." His voice took on a note of pride. "I have a son with each of these six wives." David took another sip of water, then added, "And one sweet little daughter. My children are the delight of my life."

Michal said nothing for a moment. She expected David would remarry and father children, but six wives? More even than Phaltiel. Hearing this information from her husband's lips was excruciating. "Your wives. Do they care for you?"

"Some more than others. Each in her own way." He picked up a pebble and tossed it. "One regards me as a hero. One is grateful I rescued her from a desperate situation. All are enamored with my wealth and one with my power. There is only one woman, a beautiful high-born lady, who loved me when I was a penniless shepherd boy with nothing but myself to offer her."

Could she dare have hope? Did he remember their passionate love as tenderly as she did?

"Michal." He leaned forward and took her hand in his. "I won't force you." He put his free hand on her shoulder. "But I ask you, will you come back to me and be my wife again?"

For a moment, she could not speak. Was this a dream? She dared not lift her eyes to meet his. "I love you, David. My heart has not given up on you, and it never will."

"Does that mean you will stay with me?"

"Yes, if that is truly what you want, after all that has happened." At last she trusted herself to look at him.

David's smile dazzled her. He pulled a length of fine gold chain from inside his tunic. On the chain was the ring he gave her the day they were married. David removed the ring and slipped it on Michal's finger. The warmth of his body lingered on the metal. Then he took her into his arms. Michal closed her eyes and rested her head against his broad chest. Joy, relief, and desire overwhelmed her.

David caressed her cheek as he said, "We need never speak of Gallim or Phaltiel again." Their first kiss ignited the fire Michal feared would never burn again.

"Uncle Abner predicted you would either have me stoned or plunge a dagger into my heart," she whispered.

"I don't happen to have a dagger with me." David kissed her ear and eased her down on the blanket. "But I did bring my sword." He pressed his body close to hers.

"Here? Now?" Michal's delight overrode her reticence.

"Why not here and now? We have so much catching up to do."

CHAPTER SIXTEEN

"So Abner came to David to Hebron, and twenty men with him. And David made Abner and the men that were with him a feast." II Samuel 3:20

THE SILENT SERVANT girl stole sidelong glances at Michal as they walked through the broad hallway leading to the women's quarters. Michal barely restrained herself from clinging to David, begging him not to leave her to face his wives alone. She kept reliving the hostile reception she received when she first arrived at Gallim. That was almost seven years ago, but the sting of Phaltiel's waspish women felt as fresh as yesterday.

"Princess Michal, welcome!" The woman who stepped up quickly to embrace her was a full head shorter than Michal, but similarly slender. Almond-shaped brown eyes dominated her sweet face. "I am Abigail. We learned only a short while ago that today would be the day of your arrival. But we have been working for months to prepare for your coming."

Michal hardly knew how to respond. However, something about Abigail's air of quiet confidence appealed to Michal at once. "My lord David spoke of you, Abigail."

"How kind of him!" The woman smiled, obviously pleased. "Everyone is excited to meet our senior wife at last, but we know you must be tired from your travels. Let me show you to your chamber."

As Abigail's words sank in, Michal realized for the first time that she was senior among the women. The idea of assuming the responsibilities that went with that title was daunting. She had been treated as either a servant or a baby in her father's household, depending on the prevailing moods of her parents. Her own house and staff were tiny compared to this extensive palace. Even then, Sarah was responsible for running the household. Certainly, Bida's chaotic mishandling of Phaltiel's wives would not serve as a model. And seven years of being the object of others' scorn obliterated her self-confidence.

Abigail ushered Michal into a sunlit room at the end of the corridor. The walls were hung with striped linen. Well-stuffed cushions of darker green, blue, and turquoise lined the walls. "This is lovely," Michal said. "But I should not displace the rightful owner."

"That's not the case at all." Abigail straightened a cushion. "David started designing this new addition as soon as he learned you were yet alive. I'm glad you like it. These doors lead to your private room, and those to the rooftop."

Michal was surprised to realize where she stood was merely a reception area. The bedchamber itself was much larger, and lavishly appointed. Green tiles of every shade formed an intricate geometric pattern around the bottom half of the walls. The walls above the tiles were covered with the same pale green fabric as the reception room. The late afternoon light sifted through the slatted shutters of windows that ran the full length of one wall. After years of sharing her little corner of a common area with Tirzah, the prospect of her own private space filled with beauty took Michal's breath away.

"Someone has left her things here." Michal pointed to a garment hanging from a peg on the wall.

"I made you a headdress," Abigail said. "The Judean fashion is a little different from the styles I hear they wear in Jerusalem, plainer. I wouldn't blame you if you don't want to wear it. But it's meant to make you feel welcome."

"Thank you. I'm sure I will enjoy it," Michal said warily. She looked around the room, trying not to remind herself that she and Abigail were rivals for David's affection.

"There's fresh water in the pitcher," Abigail said. "Shall I wash the dust of the road from your feet?"

"Thank you, no. I will attend to that myself," Michal said, suspicious that Abigail merely pretended to be so kind and humble.

"Of course." Abigail's voice was mild. "I'll go now. If you want anything, please let me know your wishes. The other women are anxious to meet you and convey their welcome when you are rested from your journey and ready for us to greet you properly." She turned to go, and then looked back at Michal. "Our lord the king has told us how you saved his life. We are all your admirers."

Michal watched Abigail retreat down the wide corridor and thought of David's characterization of his wives. Which one was Abigail? Did she need protection, or did she find powerful men appealing?

David, my husband again, at last, she thought gratefully. *And yet, never again totally mine.*

She tested the softness of her bed with one hand. It felt so inviting she lay across it fully dressed, not bothering to remove the blanket. She decided to rest for a moment or two.

Michal awoke with a start. For an instant, she did not know where she was. With the realization she was in her own bedchamber in the house of King David, she felt a wave of relief. Judea was not Israel, but what would there be for her in her homeland now? Ishbosheth, her one remaining brother, no doubt wished she was dead and out of his way. Uncle Abner had not hesitated to give her up to the Judeans despite the knowledge she could be killed.

For the first time since she said goodbye to David at their kitchen window so many years ago, Michal felt safe. She was amazed at how much her life had changed over the span of only a few days. She sat up and surveyed her bedchamber in the dim light of early dawn. She was not in imminent danger, and she was reunited with David as his wife. She never expected to have such good fortune again.

Michal thought about how to settle in to her changed environment. She trusted David without question. Her natural caution required everyone else to earn her confidence. She wanted to live in harmony with the other wives. Feelings of jealousy were natural, but she hoped not to let them show. Though her father married only one wife, Michal remembered the decorum with which her mother bore

King Saul's habit of taking concubines. Ahinoam simply ignored the semi-illicit relationships. When children resulted, as they sometimes did, the queen treated them graciously without ever acknowledging their parentage.

Michal removed her sandals and slipped quietly from the bed. She bathed with water from a pottery basin and changed into a clean linen garment. The tunic she chose was a few inches longer than normal, making it the perfect length for a woman of Michal's height. Again struck by the thoughtful planning that seemed to precede her arrival, she cracked open a heavy door that connected her bedroom with its ante chamber. The only sound was the regular breathing of the young servant girl curled up on a mat. Michal closed the door softly, since it was apparent the household was still asleep.

She went to the wide double doors that led directly from her bedchamber to the rooftop stairway, and smiled with pleasure. Did David include this architectural detail merely because they both loved observing their surroundings from a high perch? Or was it perhaps in memory of their first house?

Her view in one direction was the road that ran from the distant hills to the Hebron city gate. If she looked the other way, she saw the wide expanse of the square interior courtyard around which the house was built. Michal drank in the beauty of David's gardens in the first light of dawn. Neatly-trimmed fruit trees shaded the courtyard. Stone benches and tables sat here and there among flowering hedges. In a bare spot near the center of the courtyard, wooden swords and toy shields lay haphazardly beside two sleeping goats.

Michal's morning prayer was filled with thanksgiving for being welcomed by her generous husband. Even though her bigamous marriage occurred under duress, she knew most men would have rejected an unfaithful wife. She then asked God to allow her to know Merab's child. And she earnestly pleaded to conceive a son with David.

After giving God thanks, she threw open all of the doors and shutters, bathing herself and the space around her in the morning sunlight. The servant girl who slept in the reception area awakened and fetched fresh water, honey cakes, and a plate of hulled almonds. Michal learned the girl's name was Salome. She was assigned to Michal's service by Abigail.

"I am to let my lady Abigail know when you are ready to receive her," Salome reported.

"I am at her disposal," Michal replied. There was a surreal quality to waking gradually and being asked rather than told what she would do next. She went to the window again, and ran her fingers along the low, cool exterior wall.

Was this really to be her new home? Was she forever beyond the reach of Phaltiel's drunken moods? Never again to face the dreaded summons to his bed? Would she never have to hear Bida's angry shouting? Was there no need to constantly search for a safe place to hide during the next season of new wine?

The sight of David walking briskly across the courtyard with Abner caught Michal's attention. She automatically stepped behind a row of trellises that allowed her to watch the men unobserved. They appeared to be engrossed in deep conversation. Michal did not doubt her uncle had urgent business with David, and she was certain Abner was not here with King Ishbosheth's blessing. She knew her brother to be a selfish, unyielding man. Every soldier in Israel could die before King Ishbosheth would humble himself before David—a man King Saul's son would always regard as an upstart. She watched her husband and uncle disappear through a set of massive double doors that opened into the street-side sector of the house.

"May I intrude upon you, my lady?" Michal jumped at the unexpected question. "I'm sorry," Abigail said. "I didn't mean to startle you."

"It's all right," Michal said, smoothing her hair. "You aren't intruding, Abigail. I welcome your company."

"You are too kind." Abigail's smile lit her face with pleasure. "Shall we discuss the plans for the feast our lord the king will give in your kinsman's honor?"

"Of course," Michal replied warily. Was Abigail waiting for an invitation to sit down? "Please." Michal waved toward the luxurious cushions carefully arranged along the wall. She wondered what she and Abigail could possibly have to talk about in regard to the upcoming banquet.

CHAPTER SEVENTEEN

"Now these were the sons of David, which were born unto him in Hebron; the firstborn Amnon, of Ahinoam the Jezreelitess; the second Daniel, of Abigail the Carmelitess: The third, Absalom the son of Maachah the daughter of Talmai king of Geshur: the fourth, Adonijah the son of Haggith: The fifth, Shephatiah of Abital: the sixth, Ithream by Eglah his wife." I Chronicles 3:1-4

MICHAL SAT ON a stone bench in the Hebron palace courtyard. Abner sat across from her, sipping wine from a silver chalice. Nearby, King David stood talking quietly with Captain Osh. Judean dignitaries and military leaders, along with the soldiers who accompanied Michal to Hebron from Bahurim, mingled among the trees and flowering hedges of the courtyard.

"You look tired, my uncle." Michal searched for words to reach out to this man she never liked, but who might well be the only remaining blood relative she would ever again engage in conversation.

"Yes." Abner's nod emphasized his unruly white hair. "But I've done what I came here to do. Anyway, what soldier should expect to live to be as old as I am?"

"A cautious one, I would suppose," Michal said. "A man who chooses his battles with care."

"Or one who was preserved for one last errand on behalf of his God and country."

Michal measured her uncle's words. It must be the wine, she thought. He sounded more like a man with a few social graces than the taciturn, withdrawn Abner she was accustomed to. "I never thought of you as a believer in God," Michal said, pushing back the stray lock of hair threatening to escape from her headdress. She suspected her uncle would reveal more if she did not follow his hints with direct questions.

"Do you think me to be unbelieving because a soldier's success is measured by how many men he kills? I say striking down an enemy who would otherwise threaten me, or my family, or my king, is different from the murder forbidden by the Law of Moses. King Saul was of the same opinion." The trace of a rueful smile passed fleetingly across Abner's wasted features. "Whether or not God agrees has given me a few sleepless nights."

Michal could not restrain herself from asking the question that nagged at her since arriving at Bahurim. "And delivering your niece to a man you thought would execute her, is that inside or outside the law?"

The old man paused, as if to gather his thoughts. When he spoke, his voice was quiet, not the stinging retort she expected. "Michal, try not to judge me too harshly. When your husband was in danger, you did what you had to do to save him. While some might say you were brave, your father saw you as a traitor." He raised his hand, one finger extended. "Whether you were right or wrong to help your husband escape King Saul depends entirely on one's perspective." Abner turned his head and coughed so violently Michal thought he might collapse. Then he continued, his voice weaker than before. "The situation I face now is not all that different. Ishbosheth cannot rule. If we do not remove him from the throne, some heathen army may well take it from him. Then what? Should I stand by idly and let the people of God go back into bondage, as we were for hundreds of years in Egypt?"

"You raise an interesting point, Uncle." It had been a long time since she'd had a chance to exchange ideas with another thinker. Michal found herself thoroughly enjoying this debate of current events. "But I believe you have sidestepped my question."

"Not at all." Abner hunched forward, elbows resting on his bony knees. "What do you think happened to that detachment of guardsmen? The men you deceived into thinking David was too sick to appear before King Saul?"

"I have no idea. I never gave it much thought, Uncle. But back to the—" Michal began.

Abner waved a hand to stop her words. "What if I told you Doeg killed every one of them?" His eyes burned into hers. "If you had known in advance that would be the outcome, would you have given up your delaying game, and allowed David to be captured?"

"No," Michal said, as the impact of what Abner revealed sank in. "Saving David was uppermost. He was more important to me than the guardsmen, or myself for that matter. Please tell me those young men weren't executed for believing my ruse."

"I will spare you the horrible details of what Doeg did to them, but they paid with their lives." Abner gave himself over to a series of racking coughs. When he could talk again, he continued. "You had to concentrate on your objective. So it is with me. King David would not do business with me or any other Israelite until we turned you over. And so, in pursuit of a higher goal, we met his condition."

"It sounds like such a simple decision when you put it that way."

"Would you put yourself above the independence of our nation?" Abner's sunken eyes searched her face.

"No, I would not. If I thought that way, I would be guilty of the betrayal my father so often suspected me of committing."

"You see?" Abner coughed again at length. "Likewise, I am not the ogre you think me to be. While I'm defending myself needlessly, let me ask you how long you think you would have survived if Osh had not taken you from Gallim?"

"I was there almost seven years," Michal began.

"Ah, yes, years when no one of any importance knew or cared that you existed. But as soon as King David demanded your return, you became a political problem for your big brother." Abner's eyes glowed feverishly. "I sent Osh to pull you out of Gallim on King Ishbosheth's authority. I had strict orders to bring you directly to him. Had I obeyed that command, you would have died much like your sister Merab."

"One of your servants told me Merab died giving birth," Michal countered. "And as you can see, I am not with child."

"And neither was your sister," Abner hissed. "Not visibly, at least."

"You confuse me, Uncle."

"Merab was murdered in her own bedroom, by King Ishbosheth's henchmen. Afterward, the king publicly announced with great sadness that his dearly beloved little sister passed away while being delivered of a child."

"How can you be certain of this?" Michal challenged.

"One of Merab's sons was an eye witness. Your sister was warned that Ishbosheth's men were approaching. She managed to slip her handmaid out with the baby and the toddler. Merab stuffed rags into her four-year-old's mouth, hid him behind a curtain, and told him not to move or cry out no matter what happened. Fortunately, he followed her instructions. Your sister told the killers her husband took their sons away for a visit with a relative, when in fact Adriel had only their two oldest boys with him. Merab would not tell the soldiers where to find her boys knowing, of course, that Ishbosheth wanted to kill all of his nephews. The soldiers tortured her in an attempt to find out where her sons were. They went too far, and Merab died by their hands. Based on the handmaid's report and the little boy's description, I learned more than I believe you want to know."

Michal felt shaken. "Poor Merab. I mourned for her before, but now even more. I hope her sons brought her happiness." She closed her eyes for a moment, and took a few deep breaths. "How many children did she have, and where are they now? It sounds as if they are in grave danger."

"Adriel has their five sons hidden in a safe place." Abner arched his eyebrows "At any rate, they are safer than they were in Meholath. Even Ishbosheth isn't stupid enough to venture too far into the mountains."

"What will my brother do to you when he finds out you've brought me to Judea and made a truce with King David?"

Abner sat up straight and snorted like the old war horse he was. "I have done more than agree to a cease-fire, my niece. I have pledged my personal allegiance to David, and I have offered him your father's crown. Ishbosheth will certainly shout treason and command my execution. If things go as I've planned, he will no longer have the power to enforce his orders. If not…" The old man finished his thought with a shrug.

"David? King of Israel? Could it be?" Michal whispered.

"It *must* be," Abner rasped fiercely. "I have the support of every elder in the nation." He gestured toward David's back. "Surely you know he was secretly anointed years ago by the Prophet Samuel to be your father's successor?"

"I have heard talk of prophesies but nothing specific. Certainly nothing about a special blessing from that great man of God, Samuel."

"The lore has been around for years, since before David conquered that Philistine giant, Goliath. His brother Eliab gave me more details yesterday. It's an amazing story, probably worth the trip to Judea just to learn that slice of history." Abner looked back at Michal. "I know now that's why your father feared him so. He couldn't help but hear rumors of Lord David's destiny."

"I can scarcely take all this in," Michal confessed.

Abner nodded his head in affirmation. "This turn of events clearly demonstrates the power of the God of Israel."

"Truly?" Michal was fascinated.

"Through Samuel, God announced that a poverty-stricken shepherd boy from an obscure little village would ascend to rule a great nation. That is impossible. The whole idea is absurd, unthinkable. And yet, it's all happening precisely as Samuel foretold."

"So you believe it has always been God's plan for David to reign?"

"And if so, why wait until now to cast my lot with him?" Abner correctly anticipated her question. He smiled. "I admit my judgment may be influenced by a bitter argument I had with Ishbosheth recently. Above all else, my love for our country drives me. The conviction that we cannot let Ishbosheth destroy Israel with his incompetence troubles my thoughts the same way the gut sickness gnaws at my vitals day and night."

"I am sorry for your illness, Uncle. It saddens me to see you in pain."

The old man stared at her for a moment. "Thank you, Michal. I believe you actually mean that. You and Rizpah will be the only sincere mourners at my funeral."

"I'm sure there will be many others," Michal said, although she could not think who any of those *others* might be. "I did not know until we reached Bahurim that Rizpah..." Michal searched for her next words. "Was living there."

Abner narrowed his eyes. "Are you, like your mother, too refined to say the word concubine?"

She was flustered. "I could not know, not for certain, that is."

"Ishbosheth refused to allow me to make Rizpah my wife," Abner said. "I should have defied him and gone ahead, instead of shaming her as I have. She is a good woman with a kind heart."

"What is it to Ishbosheth if you take another wife? What difference could it make that she happens to be my mother's former handmaid?"

"Rizpah herself doesn't concern him, but the king doesn't want her sons under my protection."

"What would my brother care for the sons of Rizpah?" Michal sensed the answer almost before she heard Abner's words.

"Our gracious king," Abner spat scornfully, "must keep a careful eye on his two half-brothers, even if they are illegitimate. Surely you always knew Rizpah was your father's concubine."

"No, Uncle. No, I had no idea."

"You know now," he said before giving in to another coughing spasm. For a few moments he could not speak. "There were other women, of course, and several children. They are all gone now, except for Rizpah's two boys. Some died in battle, the rest under mysterious circumstances. There are rumors that Jonathan's boy, Mephibosheth, is alive and in hiding somewhere. I have searched but found no trace of him."

"Then dear Jonathan had the son he always hoped for. So little remains of our family," Michal said sadly. "Only you are left of our elders. Ishbosheth and myself from our generation. Other than Merab's and Rizpah's sons, do I have any other nieces or nephews?" She mourned to think Abner would not be among the living for long.

Abner pursed his lips. "There could possibly be another youngster or two your brother hasn't wiped out, but I doubt it. When Ishbosheth sees a handsome young relative, he senses a rival for his power. The ironic thing is that Ishbosheth will be the last king in his line. So, in terms of royal succession, it doesn't matter which of his relatives lives or dies."

"It matters to me. If there is anyone in our family left, I want to know them. Doesn't it sadden you to think of having no kinsmen?"

"I'm too near death to worry about kinsmen," Abner declared. "I have only a little strength left. I must conserve it to do what I can for our country. That is my contribution to the well-being of the children in coming generations."

David's hand suddenly rested on her shoulder as Abigail suggested everyone go inside for dinner.

CHAPTER EIGHTEEN

"So Joab and Abishai his brother slew Abner, because he had slain their brother Asahel...And the king said unto his servants, Know ye not that there is a prince and a great man fallen this day in Israel?" II Samuel 3:30, 38

MICHAL KNEW SOMETHING was wrong the instant she saw David's face the next afternoon. His grim expression, ripped clothing, and ashes sprinkled in his hair told her the king was in mourning. She could not move as she saw her husband walk slowly toward her, followed by a weeping Abigail and a solemn Ahinoam.

Michal wanted to shout 'Who died?' but her voice failed her. What could bring her husband to her in such a state of obvious grief? Was it a royal son? Or one of the king's remaining brothers?

David folded her into his arms and held her tightly. When he spoke, his voice was sorrowful. "Abner sleeps with his fathers."

"That's not possible." Michal pulled back from David's embrace and protested, "I talked to him this morning, just before he left to go back to Bahurim."

"I know. It happened quickly."

Part of Michal realized her uncle was dead. Still, she fought against acceptance. "He has been so sick, but I thought he was improving."

"It was not the sickness," David said as he looked away for a moment, and then turned back to her. "Lord Abner was murdered."

Michal's eyes rounded in disbelief. "Murdered? How?"

David drew her into his arms again. "It's a blood feud. Some years ago, Lord Abner killed a man named Asahel. This morning, Asahel's brothers took their vengeance by ending your uncle's life."

Michal's legs gave way. Had it not been for David's support, she would have collapsed on the floor. A part of her recognized the sobbing she heard as coming from her own throat. David slipped one arm under her knees, the other around her back, and carried her to her bedchamber. He gently put her down while Abigail and Ahinoam arranged cushions beneath her for support. David sank beside her. Michal buried her head in his chest and cried as if her heart would break.

"Just let all the tears come out," he murmured, stroking her hair.

For what seemed like a long time, the four of them did not speak. Ahinoam's eyes drooped shut, while Abigail sat doing needlework. Michal's weeping and the breeze rustling the trees outside the windows were the only sounds to be heard. Finally, the tears subsided and David relaxed his embrace. Without understanding why it mattered, Michal sat up and tried to stop crying. Abigail put away her sewing to remove Michal's sandals, and Ahinoam awoke and offered her fresh water.

"I hope you know I had nothing to do with this. I admired Abner. He lived a long and honorable life before God," David said.

Michal nodded her agreement, not yet feeling capable of speech.

David took her hand. "I will be gone for a while, making arrangements for your uncle's funeral. Will you be all right?"

"Yes," she whispered.

"Abigail and Bird will be here if you need anything." Michal realized her husband's eyes were awash with unshed tears. David stood and turned toward Abigail. "I know she's in good hands. I'll be back as soon as I can."

"Tirzah!" Michal exclaimed. She suddenly remembered her dear friend was at Bahurim. Without Abner's protection, the village could soon fall victim to Ishbosheth's revenge.

"Lord Abner's men will be in Bahurim before King Ishbosheth knows what has happened," David assured her. "Those who are willing will take refuge in Judea, and Tirzah is sure to come with them. I have no doubt Captain Osh will deliver Abner's people here safely."

There was an awkward silence after King David's departure. After straightening the cushions several times, Abigail said, "We can go, if you would prefer to be alone."

"No, please." Michal's voice sounded strange to her own ears. "I don't want to be by myself."

"Would you like something to eat?" Ahinoam's tone begged for an assenting answer.

Michal shook her head. "Thank you, no."

"You must have loved your uncle very much," Abigail commented as she took up her sewing again.

"He was around often when I was a child, but I hardly knew him." Michal's words came slowly. In spite of her resolve, she began to cry again. "It's not Uncle Abner so much." A sob broke forth. "But he was the last remaining member of my family that I know. Knew. Except my brother Ishbosheth, who hates me. There are children I will probably never see. I've lost everyone. My sister, my brothers, my parents. Everyone."

Abigail hugged Michal. "I'm so sorry. Losing those you love can only be understood by someone who has suffered that same pain."

Was it Abigail's kindness that caused the tears to flow freely again? After a few struggling moments, Michal took a deep breath, and used both hands to smooth back her hair. "Their passing happened over a span of years, but I've just learned of their deaths. It's overwhelming." She felt the crush of loneliness mingle with her sadness, but a natural reticence kept Michal from exploring those feelings with women she met for the first time two days earlier.

"You did not know what was happening with your family?" Ahinoam asked. When Abigail shot her a warning glance, Ahinoam quickly added, "You must have lived very far from them."

"More than distance separated our family," Michal said. "It's difficult to explain." She was not comfortable disclosing her innermost feelings. Yet she longed for companionship and a sharing that transcended superficial conversation. "Like every blessing, royalty can also be a curse. I believe my father loved his children as well as he could. Eventually his duty as the king took precedence over our family. As I was taken away to Gallim, his last words to me were that he no longer considered me his daughter." Michal's shoulders shook with sobs as she buried her face in her hands.

"What kind of father would do such a thing?" Ahinoam demanded in an angry voice.

Abigail cut in smoothly, "Perhaps it would lighten the sadness of this morning to think on better times. Tell us, what is your happiest memory?"

Michal dried her tears on a soft handkerchief. She found Abigail's approach lacking in subtlety, but she appreciated the effort to lessen the atmosphere of grief. "The best time of my life began the day I was married to David. He was my heart's desire since I was a little girl. I could hardly believe my good fortune when I became his wife." Michal smiled despite her sorrowful mood. "I was young and quite naïve. He amazed me with his kindness and patience. I've never known another man like him. The time that followed our wedding was golden. I relived our few short months together over and over during the next seven years. Those memories and our strong God sustained me during many long, bitter days in Gallim. I never expected to leave that house." She looked around her. "Sometimes I fear I will awaken and find I have not."

"Did you know our husband when he fought and killed the giant Goliath?" Ahinoam leaned forward eagerly.

"No, that was before my father took David into his service." Michal felt a calmness returning. "But enough about me. Tell me about yourselves." She nodded to Abigail. "We should get to know each other."

"My family is from the Jezreel Valley," Ahinoam said in her country girl accent. "I am the youngest of six boys and three girls. My father's ancestors thought the valley was good farm land. Everybody around us seemed to think it was a fine place to wage war. My mother told me every time they had a crop about ready to harvest, soldiers would trample it. If men weren't fighting on our land, they were riding through the fields with chariots and carts, going to battle somewhere else in the valley."

A servant slipped into the bedchamber bearing a large, round tray laden with fruit, bread, and cheese. She set the food on a low table near the room's entrance and silently withdrew. Ahinoam immediately moved across the room to inspect the tray while continuing to speak. "As my brothers grew older, mother made them dig a pit in the back yard. When an army was close by, the boys knew to hide in the pit. My parents pulled a covering of planks over it and piled hay on top of the boards." Ahinoam burst forth with a high-pitched laugh that was both hearty and piercing. "Once a bunch of war horses got into the hay and ate almost the whole stack. My mother handed out wine and cheese to distract the soldiers while father scooted the planks closer together over the pit where the boys were."

Michal's thoughts strayed as she studied the two women. What would it feel like to become family with them and the rest of David's wives? Until now, Abigail ran the household. How would she accept relinquishing her position of authority?

She cannot dread that transition any worse than I, Michal reflected. Ahinoam, the one she heard David call *Bird*, held a certain status because she was the mother of David's eldest son. It was clear that she was Abigail's confidante and good friend as well. Was the bond between the two women one of affection or convenience?

Abigail was pretty enough, with her regular features and sweet smile. Her straight brown hair was tied back in a plain, practical style. She moved with a natural grace and dignity, yet was the kind of woman someone could meet one day and not remember the next. The younger Ahinoam had thick, glossy hair and dark eyes. Despite her stout build, Ahinoam's mobile face had a singular loveliness that commanded attention.

Interesting that she has my mother's name, Michal thought. *She actually looks a little like her.*

"So after they burned the house for the third time, my father decided his sons would be soldiers instead of farmers," Michal heard Ahinoam saying. "When I was almost fifteen, I was engaged to Nepheg. He was a soldier and a good friend of my youngest brother. Nepheg was killed in battle six months before we were to be married. My brothers went to their commander, who happened to be David, to complain that none of Nepheg's male relatives would take another wife. David said Abigail was pestering him to bring home another wife to help with the chores, so that was that."

"I didn't pester." Abigail sounded slightly defensive.

Ahinoam grinned. "I'm just repeating what my bothers told me."

"Life at Ziklag was hard." Abigail directed her explanation Michal's way. "We were not well-established the way we are here. I must admit I did need help. I was happy when David married Bird."

"Bird?" Michal worked up the courage to ask.

Both Ahinoam and Abigail laughed aloud. "I got that nickname when I was pregnant with my son Amnon," Ahinoam said. "When Abigail was expecting she never had morning sickness. Me, I was queasy the whole time. The only food I would stand was roasted pigeon breast. Everybody said I was going to turn into a bird because I ate so many of them. David started calling me Bird, and pretty soon everybody else did too. You may as well use that name for me, Michal. Nobody calls me Ahinoam any more."

"But it is such a beautiful name," Michal said as tears sprang to her eyes again. "My mother was called Ahinoam."

CHAPTER NINETEEN

"And when the servants of David were come to Abigail to Carmel, they spake unto her, saying, David sent us unto thee, to take thee to him to wife. And she arose, and bowed herself on her face to the earth, and said, Behold let thine handmaid be a servant to wash the feet of the servants of my lord. And Abigail hasted, and arose, and rode upon an ass, with five damsels of hers that went after her; and she went after the messengers of David, and became his wife." I Samuel 25:40-42

"I'M FROM CARMEL," Abigail said. "High country, near the seashore. My father owned large land holdings and vast herds of sheep. I was the eldest daughter and had five older brothers and two younger sisters. We were all healthy, well-fed, and happy."

Abigail leaned against the wall, and adjusted a cushion behind her back. She put her needlework aside and continued her story with a faraway look in her eye, as if she had forgotten Michal and Bird were in the room. "My parents were strict, but loving. My brothers worked with our father, learning to farm and raise sheep. Mother taught her girls how to manage the household. It was she who oversaw the kitchen, supervised the servants, and kept the larders stocked. What we didn't make, my mother struck deals to buy from merchants. She

115

believed in hard work, honesty, and thrift. Nothing was wasted. I don't know how she arranged to have spare time, but she did. In those hours, we sat together and talked while she taught me and my little sisters to weave."

"Abigail does beautiful work with colored yarns," Bird chimed in.

Abigail smiled at Bird and continued. "My favorite times were when we would go to Jerusalem for Passover in a caravan with other Carmelites. The children were allowed to walk if we wished, or ride in carts when we were tired. We played and sang songs along the way. The men told stories that kept us spellbound around the campfires. The year I was nine years old, a deadly sickness swept over the mountain. Half of our servants fell ill, then my father, my youngest sister, and four of my brothers. Mother and I nursed everyone as best we could. Then I came down with the sickness. I don't know how long I was ill. I remember rousing slightly from time to time, and have vague recollections of my mother trickling soup down my throat or wiping my feverish forehead with cool water."

Abigail seemed near tears, but hardened her tone and went on, "Everyone seemed surprised when I awoke one morning and said I was hungry. My father snatched me into his arms and wept like an old woman. I didn't understand why he was crying at the time, but soon I learned I was my parents' only surviving child."

"How sad," Michal said. She marveled at the undercurrent of heartbreak beneath the surface of lives that seemed perfectly placid. Perhaps Abigail could empathize with her own difficult past.

"Nothing was ever the same again." Abigail stood, walked to the doors that opened onto the courtyard, and leaned against the doorpost. "My mother never caught the sickness, but she was damaged more than anyone." Abigail gently tapped the side of her forehead. "She told my father he should take another wife, a young woman who could return the laughter of children to our house." She shook her head. "He said he didn't have the heart for another wife, let alone more children. I missed my brothers and sisters terribly. I felt so alone without them."

Michal willed herself not to let the tears flow again, even though her heart ached to think of a little girl losing all her siblings.

"In my childish way, I was able to go on," Abigail continued. "My parents went through the motions of living, but they could not set aside their heartbreak. Mother sat under a tree and cried most days. I did what I could to pick up her household chores. My father turned what energy he had into finding me a suitable husband as soon as possible."

"Suitable indeed!" Bird interjected.

Abigail turned her face toward the courtyard. "Father wanted to do what was best for me. If he had been as he was before the illness, I know he would have made different choices." She sighed. "I was ten years old when he betrothed me to a repulsive old neighbor named Nabal. My father's entire fortune was to be my dowry. Mother died that winter, of a broken heart I believe. When my father's health began to fail, he pressed Nabal to take me as his wife immediately. I heard him promise my father he would not consummate the marriage until my bleeding began." Her voice became almost inaudible. "But Nabal was not an honorable man."

Michal watched the other woman's graceful movements as Abigail stepped back into the lounging area of the bedchamber and came to sit between Bird and Michal. She leaned against a brightly colored cushion. "My father passed quietly from this life to the next in his sleep one night. Nabal had sole possession of me and my father's wealth." Her eyes rested on Michal's face. "And there was no family for me to turn to. I did my best to please my husband, but it was not possible. Immature as I was, I could see that Nabal's affairs were in disarray. I devoted myself to the only task I knew, which was managing the household. Nothing was organized. My husband would make a rule, then curse or strike a servant who tried to obey it. For fourteen years, my life consisted of going behind Nabal's back to apologize for his behavior, and putting up with his scorn for my failure to give him children. And then one day…"

Michal's mind strayed as Abigail's story continued. Fourteen years, she thought. Twice as long as my time in Phaltiel's house. Perhaps Abigail's sympathy was genuine.

"When I learned that Nabal had insulted David, I was frightened," Abigail was saying. "I gathered the supplies my husband denied David's men and set out, hoping once again to make amends. My servants and I met David not far from our farm. Sure enough, he was on his way to kill Nabal." She smiled knowingly. "You know how David is when his hot temper overtakes him."

Bird and Michal nodded their heads in agreement.

"I offered David the supplies I brought and anything else he and his men needed. That was their due, since they protected our shepherds and flocks. I tried to convince him not to kill Nabal in revenge, assuring him the satisfaction of taking one foolish, surly man's life would not be worth the guilt he would then carry around forever. To my surprise he discussed the matter with me, instead of pushing me out of the way and pressing on. As we talked, I told David I believed him to be a man of destiny. Even though he would be justified in seeking revenge, killing Nabal was beneath the great warrior who slew Goliath.

"David's anger cooled, and he thought better of his plans. I was astonished when he thanked me not just for the supplies but also for what he called my 'sage advice'." Abigail sighed. "I took my time returning home, knowing Nabal would never believe I saved his life."

Abigail rubbed the back of her neck with one hand. "When I got home, Nabal was having a drunken party with some of his so-called friends. They were slothful men who hung around with Nabal for the free liquor he dispensed. I waited until the next morning to confess what I did. Nabal was furious. His face bright red, he cursed and raised his arm as if to strike me. Then he fell back onto his bed, clutched at his chest, and said he couldn't breathe. A healing servant, a midwife, and I did what we could, but in a few days Nabal was dead." She raked her bottom teeth across her top lip. "I was terrified about my future. Nabal had a worthless servant who let it be known he planned to force me into a marriage in order to gain possession of Nabal's flocks and land. Most of the wealth was my father's, of course, but that didn't mean I could control anything of value. It was only a matter of time before the servant, one of Nabal's kinsmen or some other unscrupulous man would come for me."

Before continuing, Abigail shifted onto her back on Michal's luxurious cushions. She folded her hands across her abdomen and stared up at the ceiling. "I prayed as I've never prayed before," she said. "Although I didn't know what to ask for other than God's help. The next morning, as I feared, one of my handmaids reported that some strange men wanted to see me. I went to greet them, scared to death I would be abducted. What a relief it was to realize my visitors were some of David's men. I assumed they needed more supplies. It took a while for them to convince me they were there on behalf of their master, Lord David, who wanted me to be his wife. It was clearly an invitation, not a demand." She stood again, and began to pace the floor.

"I have never been impulsive. But that day, I seized my one chance to live life as a wife instead of a slave. As soon as David's servants left, I told a few trusted handmaids I was leaving the house for good within the hour. They begged to go with me. How could I refuse? I told the women they could go along, provided they told no one else what was happening. Each of us saddled our donkey, and took one small bundle each—our clothes, a little food, a few shekels. Nothing else. We sneaked out of the stable one at a time, leading the donkeys. We walked until we were well away from the house." Abigail smiled triumphantly. "Then we jumped on the donkeys and rode those poor beasts mercilessly."

She shifted her back against the cushion nearest Michal and Bird, and continued her story. "For the first time ever I was without luxuries, but it was the happiest time of my life." Abigail rested her hand lightly on Michal's arm. "I could see how painful David's memories were. There seemed to be so little I could do to ease his burden. When he spoke of you, Michal, his hearty laugh would leave him and he would go into the wilderness alone for hours." Abigail pulled back her hand and locked her arms under her knees. "One by one my maids came and asked my blessing on their marriage. I asked David to take an additional wife, not only to relieve me of some of the household chores, but also to bring children into our home." She chuckled slightly. "By then I was twenty-six and certain I would never be blessed with a child."

"Would anyone else like some bread?" Bird asked, breaking off a generous portion for herself.

Michal shook her head.

"No, thank you. It wasn't long," Abigail said, "before David brought Bird home. That was just before we moved to Philistine territory."

"You lived with the Philistines?" Michal was surprised.

"Yes," Bird said, before Abigail could react. "We lived at Ziklag a little over a year. That was an adventure, I'll tell you for sure. You don't know the meaning of the word heathen until you've lived among the Philistine foreigners for a while."

"You were actually in their midst?" *How utterly unthinkable!*

"Only Hebrews lived in Ziklag proper," Abigail assured her. "But Philistines were all around us. We traded goods with their women, and our men were loosely attached to their army. Our contact was limited, but neither group treated the other as an enemy."

"I wouldn't say that," Bird objected. "What about the time they burned Ziklag to the ground and took us prisoner?"

"Those were Amalekites, Bird, not Philistines." Abigail's voice was gentle.

"What's the difference?" Bird insisted. "They're all foreigners. Worthless heathen dogs, every one of them."

"You two were captured by Amalekites?" Michal shuddered. "How horrible! How did you manage to get away from them?"

Bird broke into a huge grin and stated the obvious, "Michal, you don't know the story of the Amalekite raid on Ziklag!"

CHAPTER TWENTY

"So David and his men came to the city, and, behold, it was burned with fire; and their wives, and their sons, and their daughters, were taken captives. ...but David encouraged himself in the Lord his God. ...And David recovered all that the Amalekites had carried away: and David rescued his two wives." I Samuel 30:3, 6, 18

"OUR MEN LEFT with the Philistine Army, headed north toward Jezreel," Bird said. "I guess they wanted to wreck some poor farmer's fields with yet another battle in my home valley. It was the first time after our marriage that David had gone to war, leaving Abigail and me alone in the house. I was just about to go to the well for water, when Abigail yelled, 'Ahinoam, come here immediately!'"

Bird smiled. "I thought how Abigail had been so nice to me as long as David was home, and now all of a sudden she's ordering me around. I took my time responding, just to show I could be independent. When I got inside the house, Abigail was shaking. She grabbed me and said she saw a group of strange men sneaking into the city. 'Probably Philistines looking to trade for lambskins or produce,' I said. I was so skinny back then." Bird sighed and patted her waist with both hands, causing her ample belly to jiggle.

"Anyway, Abigail reminded me the Philistine army was up north, along with our men. Ziklag was just a bunch of dwellings, really. We didn't have a city wall, or any fortifications to speak of. Still, I was sure nobody was going to attempt any mischief in David's stronghold. Little did I know!"

"Michal, can I get you anything?" Abigail asked. "Some fresh water, perhaps?"

"I'm fine." She managed to smile in appreciation for the thoughtfulness of her companion. "But I am interested in the rest of the Ziklag story."

"Of course." Bird rolled her big brown eyes in Abigail's direction. "The first thing Abigail had to do was get everything organized." Both women smiled. "She told me to go on to the well and pass the word there might be dangerous foreigners about. Which, what else would there be in the middle of Philistine country? Anyhow, I did what Abigail said. I told the women I ran into to let their neighbors know what Abigail saw—or thought she saw—and whatever happened not to panic. Now all this time, I was as calm as a desert night. I kind of wondered if Abigail was trying to stir things up so she would look important."

"Bird!" Abigail exclaimed.

"Well, I didn't really know you then, Abigail. So anyway," Bird continued, "I went back to the house. As soon as I got inside, off in the distance I heard the most horrible scream. May I never hear such a sound again as long as I live. All of a sudden, I realized this was real, and we were in serious danger. There was dead silence for about five heartbeats, and then I heard all kinds of yelling, men's voices as well as women's. 'God help us,' I shouted, 'we're under attack!' I was a mess," Bird confessed. "I started crying and looking for a place to hide. But Abigail, she was a rock. She made me put on my most comfortable shoes, and an extra layer of clothes as quick as I could." Bird chuckled. "She had bloodied some rags with pigeon blood, and swaddled me up like it was my time of bleeding."

Bird's eyes glistened. "We didn't have time to hide any of our belongings before those hideous foreigners broke in and grabbed us. You wouldn't believe how foul they smelled! They stank like they'd never had a bath in their lives. They pushed everybody out of their houses and herded us into a pasture. A few guards stood around us, while the main group of foreigners took their time going through every house. I saw that it wouldn't have mattered if we hid things. They took it all. They tore through everything—breaking pottery, pulling the stuffing out of our bedding. It was horrible. I watched in terror until Abigail sidled up to me and said, 'Ahinoam, I know you're scared, but you have to hush crying and start acting like the wife of Lord David. Help me get everyone ready before the rest of the Amalekites come back for us.' While the foreigners looted Ziklag, Abigail put us to work." Bird nodded affirmatively.

"Abigail made sure there was a helper assigned to each mother with more than one baby. Several women had extra clothes that we twisted up to make slings for carrying the little children. We shared what food we had, eating some and keeping the rest hidden away for later. The older wives got together and worked out our ground rules. A few of them were captives before. No one was to be separated from the others or to willingly go anywhere alone. We were to be absolutely defiant, but in a sneaky way. No taunting, no spitting, but also no cooperation. We were supposed to act like we didn't understand *anything* the foreigners told us. And movement of the group away from Ziklag was to be as slow as we could make it. We decided to break plants and twigs and leave as much of a trail as we could without getting caught at it."

Bird shook her head again. "Little children and mothers with babies were always to be surrounded by older girls and boys, then the senior wives. The old women who were still hearty made up the outer rim of every group." Poking Abigail with an elbow, Bird continued. "Do you remember how creative people were? One woman used henna to paint splotches on her pretty teenaged daughter, to make it look like the girl had some kind of skin disease." A sad shadow passed across Bird's pretty face. "With everything set up as best we could, we sat in the pasture while Ziklag burned to the ground. To keep ourselves from mourning, we sang a psalm."

Bird began to sing softly. "The Lord is my light and my salvation." Michal and Abigail joined in. "Whom shall I fear? The Lord is the strength of my life; of whom shall I be afraid?" Abigail stopped after drifting wildly off tune, but Bird and Michal sang all the way through the song, ending with, "Wait, I say, on the Lord."

"You know all the words!" Bird seemed surprised.

"Yes. I thought about that psalm often when I was at Gallim. There was a rock by a stream where I could occasionally go and be alone." Michal stopped herself. This was no time to allow her former life to intrude. "I still don't know how you got away from the Amalekites."

"David rescued us," Abigail said in her matter-of-fact way.

Bird picked up her story, ignoring Abigail's comment. "It was late in the afternoon before the foreign dogs had all their stolen loot packed. It was hard to tell who was in charge, but after a lot of loud talking, they must have decided to wait until morning to start on the journey south. We slept sitting up, huddled together against the cold night air, taking turns with one woman always awake. I don't know what we thought we would do if the foreigners started something, but we kept watch anyway. One day was gone, and we hadn't left our home base yet. The old women said that was a good sign. I figured we would be on the road at daybreak, but the foreigners were a lazy bunch. Or maybe it was the amount of stolen wine they put away the night before. Anyway, by the time they were ready to go and got us moving, it was almost noon. So we started walking, while the foreigners rode horses and camels. In the evening the foreigners cooked and ate meat right in front of us, and gave us nothing. Not that we wanted to eat, or even smell any of their food. They would rub their full bellies and laugh, making sport of us."

"I'm surprised they didn't do much worse things to you," Michal ventured.

"Well..." Bird rolled her eyes. "There was obvious fussing among the foreigners. Zillah, one of our people who understood a little of their language told us there was a big row going on over who got what, especially who owned the women. One group wanted to have a great big orgy then and there. The others wanted to keep the virgins intact so they could get more money when they sold them into slavery."

"God forbid," Michal whispered.

"It gets worse," Bird insisted. "The men who wanted to sell the girls also claimed they could get a good price for the babies from the followers of Molech. That pack of foreign dogs kept saying Molech's women liked to buy babies and use them as human sacrifices, instead of burning their own young ones alive. Zillah told Abigail one of the men kept saying sell the babies and virgins, cast lots for any women

124

they wanted for themselves, and kill the rest. Then they could move faster and raid more towns."

Abigail loosened her hair and began to twist it into a braid. "Zillah should have kept those things to herself..."

"Why?" Bird asked. "It wasn't like we thought those Philistines were going to be nice to us."

"Amalekites," Abigail said softly.

"What's the difference?" Bird asked. "Anyway," she rushed on breathlessly, "while they bickered over how to divide us up, neither group would take responsibility for feeding us. At the end of the fourth day, we only had enough of the food we brought for the children and nursing mothers. Everyone else got one good drink of water and a few raisins. That afternoon, we camped in a big pasture surrounded by woods. By then I was filthy, starving, and scared sick. I hope I'm never that miserable again in my life. I started crying. Abigail tried to comfort me, saying David would find a way to rescue us. I told her what a fool she was. The men wouldn't be back from the north country for weeks, and we were already out of time. I was sure we were doomed." Bird grinned at Abigail. "She held my hand and told me I didn't really know David if I thought he wouldn't come for us."

"Yes," Abigail agreed. "That's exactly what I said. I knew he could save us."

Bird rolled her eyes. "Meanwhile, the foreigners had obviously come to terms with each other. That night, they laughed and slapped each other on the back while they ate their food in our sight. They danced around and had a drunken party like you've never seen. We kept asking Zillah what they were saying, but she wouldn't tell us. I had an awful feeling I was going to die that night. I watched the sun going down and all I could think was that my life was over and I would give anything for one last decent meal. I don't know why it mattered whether I died full or hungry, but those were my thoughts at the time."

"It's strange what we think about in desperate situations," Michal said.

Abigail stopped fussing with her hair and patted Michal's hand. "We've all had them."

Bird seemed to be enjoying her own story. She paused only a moment, then went on. "All of a sudden, Abigail said, 'Ahinoam, how many men are guarding us?' I said, 'About twenty. Why?' She didn't look up, but she had a big grin on her face. She crawled over and talked with some of the other senior wives. Then she stood up and stretched, and said she simply must have a bath. I was shocked when she asked who else wanted to go down to the river and bathe. If that wasn't wild enough, about ten other women said what a good idea that was."

Bird smirked at Abigail. "Now, here all this time we have been sticking together like burrs on a donkey's tail, being careful to have nothing to do with the strangers. Then Abigail strolls up to one of the foreigners all sweet-like and uses sign language to get across that she wants to go down to the stream and get a bath. I thought, 'You little harlot!'"

"Bird!" Abigail admonished gently.

"I'm just telling this story the way it happened," Bird said, holding her hands palms up. "How was I to know? So anyway, the foreigners seemed only too happy to head off to the river to see the Hebrew women bathe. Only three guards stayed behind. Then Joab's wife told us to form tight family groups and leave a pathway wide enough for a lot of people to go between the families. I decided the constant fear and hunger had driven everybody but me crazy, and I wasn't all that sure about myself. But I was too weak to argue. I just did what I was told. We all did. I guess obedience was a habit by then."

Bird poked Abigail with an elbow. "Remember? The last piece of sun had just gone behind a hill when the women came back. 'You didn't even bother to wet your hair,' I said to Abigail when she sat down beside me. She was still grinning like a farmer the day after a big rain. She told me not to react, but to take a good look at the guard nearest us. When I did," Bird smiled as her voice quivered with emotion, "I saw my brother Elaboam standing there wearing the clothes of a foreigner. I looked around and recognized all of the guards as David's men, standing around us, armed, protecting us. Anyhow, at first I didn't believe what my own eyes saw." She wiped a tear. "I'm sorry. This part always makes me cry."

Going to the food tray again, Ahinoam picked at it briefly. "Why don't we move this where we can reach it?" she asked. Without waiting for a response, she relocated the tray to the floor near Abigail's feet and helped herself to more cheese. "Just as it started to get dark, our men thundered through the area where we were gathered and attacked the foreigners. There was nothing but confusion, yelling, and dust around the heathens' campfires. I saw our husband right in the middle of the fight, swinging that sword, cutting down filthy foreigners left and right. Lord, what a beautiful sight!"

CHAPTER TWENTY-ONE

"And David said to Joab, and to all the people that were with him, Rend your clothes, and gird you with sackcloth, and mourn before Abner. And King David himself followed the bier. And they buried Abner in Hebron: and the king lifted up his voice, and wept at the grave of Abner; and all the people wept." II Samuel 3:31, 32

ABNER'S FUNERAL WAS a blur for Michal. She remembered Abigail walking on her right and Bird on her left for support during the procession. Someone sang a sad song with a haunting melody. She glimpsed David, his head often bowed in sorrow, walking alone behind the ceremonial cart and bier where the body rested. Michal recalled thinking how strange it was that her husband knew her uncle better than she. Women she did not recognize embraced her and murmured condolences.

She saw no dry eyes when David finished his brief, eloquent eulogy. It was comforting to find the old soldier was wrong to think his passing would not be mourned. She briefly wondered what would become of Rizpah, now that Abner was gone.

At Michal's request, Abigail pointed out Joab, David's nephew and top military commander. It was common knowledge Abner killed

Joab's brother Asahel. Therefore, Joab acted within the law when he took Abner's life.

Relief mixed with her sadness as Michal realized this particular blood feud was over. Abner had no remaining sons or brothers to seek revenge against Joab, and only a male of the same blood as Abner could claim the legal right of reprisal.

Nevertheless, Michal stared hard at Joab, feeling anger well up within her. Did he know or care that Abner would have died soon enough without human intervention? It was too bad her uncle wasn't the man he'd been ten years ago. In those days, he would have been no easy target, even for a strong-looking man like Joab.

Guests mingled in the courtyard of David's house after the funeral was over. Abigail stuck by Michal as if their tunics were woven together. Bird stayed near much of the time, disappearing only when Abigail dispatched her to instruct the kitchen staff. A generous buffet was laid out at serving points throughout the courtyard, and attendants circulated among the guests to offer food and drink from huge copper trays.

"Would you like to move away from this area where everyone is eating?" Abigail suggested after Michal refused several offers of food.

"Yes, thank you," Michal responded. "But you and Bird are not in mourning. Tell me where I may find a place away from the crowd. Then you can stay and have something to eat."

"If you insist." Bird eyed a tray of food as she spoke.

"We'll take you to the quiet part of the garden," Abigail said. Bird grabbed a cake and munched it as she followed Michal and Abigail to a corner separated from the main courtyard by a thick screen of trees.

"Would you like to sit?" Bird gestured toward several boulders arranged beside flowering plants beneath the generous shade of a massive tree.

"I need to walk. I'm an incurable stroller," Michal said. "But you two rest if you'd like. I'm still getting to know my new surroundings."

Bird immediately settled on a low stone. "It's hard to believe I was ever thin," she sighed. "I carry around more bulk now than when I was pregnant with Amnon."

Michal and Abigail ambled down a pathway. "Rose of Sharon." Michal touched the petals of a familiar flower. "We had a bush like this in our garden at home, not quite so full. That little house and its garden seem almost like a dream now."

"I can never remember the names of the plants," Abigail replied. "Bird says I don't pay enough attention in the garden. She may be right about that. After I take care of my household chores, and spend time with Daniel, there never seems to be time for anything else."

"Daniel. That's your son?"

"Yes." Abigail's face lit up. "He's the joy of my life."

"Was he born at Ziklag?"

"No. We weren't blessed with little ones until we left the hard life of Ziklag behind. David was away from home so much, and of course back then I was convinced I would never have a child."

"What changed your mind?" Michal asked.

"Not long after we came to Hebron, Bird discovered she was pregnant. Everyone was overjoyed, our husband most of all. Poor Bird had a difficult time. Some of the older women told us she would soon be past her morning sickness, but that didn't happen. And for her, it was all day sickness. I don't think she ate anything but roasted bird breast those last six months. She preferred pigeon, but dove would do. David built a bird pen and stocked it with fat pigeons. I would kill one each day and cook it for our little Bird. She was nothing but bones by the time Amnon was born."

Abigail's pretty face softened into a sweet smile. "In the midst of Bird's pregnancy there was a week or so when I felt ill, but I recovered and thought nothing of it. I recall thinking the soft city life was making me fat."

"You can't mean you were with child and didn't know it?" Michal was amazed, and more than a little envious.

"That is exactly what I am saying." Abigail nodded her head. "I was oblivious. One evening, about twilight, we were sitting in this part of the garden. I remember we were enjoying one of those rare nights when we had no guests at our table, and Bird was nursing Amnon. She and David kept looking at me, whispering, and laughing. I was somewhat offended, to be honest with you. At first I tried to believe they were playing with the baby. But I couldn't shake the sense they were talking about me, and I couldn't think why. Finally, I said, 'What has you two so amused?' David said, 'We are wondering if you're going to wait until you go into labor before you announce to us you're with child.' I stared at him, astonished by his impossible words. I started thinking how long it was since I bled. Now, my bleeding was always irregular. I had long since given up trying to predict when my periods would occur. I started to calculate and realized my last bleeding was months ago. And my belly was swelling!" Abigail patted her abdomen.

"The realization that there was a baby growing inside me leapt into my mind like a wild animal. I danced around the garden, singing God's praises. My singing made little Amnon cry, and Bird and David *really* laughed then. But I didn't care. I laughed with them, because for me to become pregnant was a miracle."

"I have heard it said that every baby is a miracle in its own way," Michal said. If God gave Abigail a child, why wouldn't He do the same for her? As they came to the break in the trees where Bird sat dozing, Michal observed, "We've been walking in a circle."

Bird opened her eyes, yawned, and smiled. Abigail sat beside her and continued her story, "My little Daniel was born just four months after Amnon. What a wonderful, blessed time that was. The people of Judah embraced David as their king, Bird and I each had a healthy baby boy, and our house was filled with joy."

"Yes." Bird sighed. "And then Maachah came to join us."

Abigail lifted her eyebrows and nodded her head. "Yes. Maachah."

All three women turned toward the sound of approaching footsteps. "Fasting, my ladies?" David's rich voice washed across them, catching Michal by surprise.

"Only Michal," Bird was quick to respond. "Abigail and I are just keeping her company."

"Of course." David sat on the ground next to Michal, across from Abigail and Bird. His back rested against a tree.

"And you also, my lord?" Abigail asked. "Are you fasting as well?"

"Yes, out of respect for Lord Abner." David looked up at Michal. "Your uncle taught me how to be a soldier. I will always be grateful to him for that." He gazed into the distance and continued speaking. "He walked a jagged pathway, trying to do what he thought was right without being disloyal to his king. Men with his strength of character are not easy to find."

"I regret he died the way he did," Michal said.

"I have seen many men die." David leaned forward, elbows on his knees. "There is no good way. There is only the question of speed. The faster the better, and Abner did not linger. Suppose the situation were reversed, Michal. Do you think Abner would hesitate to plunge a knife into *his* enemy?"

"No," Michal admitted. "He was old school, hard line. That much I know about him. If he thought he was entitled to extract revenge, he would do it. The part I don't understand—"

The sound of high-pitched laughter stopped her in mid-sentence. A naked little boy ran giggling through the break in the trees. As the child emerged into the secluded glade, a woman caught up with him.

"You nasty little foreigner! I'll teach you never to humiliate me this way again. When I get through with you, you'll be sorry you were ever born." The woman punctuated her words with a hard pinch on the shoulder that turned the little boy's peals of laughter into a shriek of pain.

In one swift motion, David was on his feet. He took the boy in one arm. With his free hand, he stayed the slap the woman was poised to deliver. "What has my son Absalom done to deserve such rough treatment, Maachah?" David demanded.

"My lord. I did not see you," the attractive woman replied with an instant, painted-on smile. Her face hardened as she glared at the little boy in David's arms. "Absalom stripped off his clothing and paraded himself around in front of our guests like the heathen he is."

"He is not even four years old," the king spoke sharply. "He's too young to know the difference in being clothed or naked." David released his grasp on Maachah's hand. "I can see this boy is no heathen. It's perfectly obvious to me that he has been circumcised." He tickled little Absalom's tummy and was rewarded with a giggle. "You have shown everyone you're a little Hebrew, haven't you, son?"

"Surely, my lord," Maachah said.

David ignored her. "Bird, you know how to handle children. Why don't you find my boy something to wear?"

"I have his clothing right here," Maachah persisted.

Without acknowledging Maachah, David handed Absalom to Bird.

"Let's go find some clothes, you brazen young warrior," Bird cooed to Absalom as she carried him away. The child looked back at his mother over Bird's shoulder, with an expression that Michal could only classify as a smirk.

Michal was searching for a way to break the tense silence when Abigail made the attempt for her. "My lord, your eulogy of Lord Abner was most touching. I was moved to tears, even though I did not know Michal's uncle well."

"Thank you, Abigail," David said without moving his eyes from Maachah. "The words came straight from my heart." He shifted to a harder tone. "Tell me, Maachah. Why would you call my son names like 'foreigner' and 'heathen'? Do you consider Absalom somehow tainted because you, his mother, are from Geshur? Or do you make reference to my great-grandmother?"

"Come now, husband." Maachah's tone suggested barely-controlled anger. "The prince has to understand that he must behave himself, especially at a public gathering. I used common expressions. My words have no hidden meaning."

"He's just a child," David countered. "You are much too harsh with him."

This was awkward for Michal, since it was the first time she'd ever seen Maachah. She wished she could be somewhere else at that moment.

Maachah did not give in readily. "You must admit Absalom was behaving badly. He humiliated me. Us."

"I am much more embarrassed for my wife to declare my son a heathen than I am by the sight of Absalom's perfect little body."

If Maachah is smart, Michal thought, she will not try to win this debate.

"My lord." Maachah's voice was metallic, with an edge like a dagger. "Absalom is old enough to know better than to strip off his clothing in public. When I didn't pay enough attention to his other antics, he did something outrageous to make me look foolish in front of everyone."

David's words were soft and low, which Michal knew to mean he was transitioning from irritation to anger. "Decent mothers do not call their sons names, Maachah. I forbid such behavior in this household. I never want to hear you call Absalom, or any of my children, a heathen or a foreigner again. Never. Do you understand what I am telling you?"

Maachah glared at David. She neither answered his question nor acknowledged his command. Her eyes swept over Michal before turning to Abigail.

"I feel suddenly tired." Maachah threw the edge of her scarf across her shoulder. "I believe I shall retire for the evening."

The king stood looking after the retreating Maachah until she disappeared through the trees. Michal studied her husband's handsome profile in the stillness of the dwindling daylight. David's father's grandmother was a foreigner from Moab, a woman with the peculiar name of Ruth. Michal wondered if Maachah knew how the people of Bethlehem looked down on David and his brothers because of their imperfect lineage.

CHAPTER TWENTY-TWO

"Who can find a virtuous woman? for her price is far above rubies. The heart of her husband doth safely trust in her, so that he shall have no need of spoil. She will do him good and not evil all the days of her life. She seeketh wool, and flax, and worketh willingly with her hands." Proverbs 31:10-13

ABIGAIL AND MICHAL sat cross-legged near each other on the floor of their workroom. Abigail's hands expertly passed a shuttle back and forth between the warp threads strung tightly around the pegs on the frame of her wooden loom. Meanwhile, Michal used her spindle to twist linen fibers into a fine twine. The heavy shutters were fully opened, and the shouts of children at play wafted through the room on a cooling breeze. Michal enjoyed Abigail's companionship, and trusted her somewhat.

The sound of Bird's voice occasionally mingled with the sounds of little boys playing war. "Bird is so good with the children," Michal commented.

"She is indeed," Abigail agreed without looking up from her weaving. "At first we tried to take turns with all of the chores. After a while, we laughed at our foolishness and divided labor along the lines of what each of us liked to do. That worked out much better."

"And as new wives came along, each one found her niche?" Michal half-questioned.

"Something like that," Abigail said. "Eglah looks after our animals and the gardens. Haggith oversees housekeeping. Bird, of course, takes care of the children. Abital was in charge of food, but she has been ailing for almost a year. So I manage the kitchen, do the purchasing, keep our accounts, and supervise the servants." She smoothed her hair with one hand, never interrupting the rhythm of her weaving. "Well, that is, I have been doing those things. I know you will want to redistribute the household responsibilities."

"What does Maachah do?" Michal worked at untying a knot in her twine.

Abigail's hands slowed their steady back and forth movements. "She always appears to be busy doing something or other. Yet she can never make time to take care of things I ask her to do." Abigail glanced toward the wide doorway, and then added, "Mostly Maachah causes trouble."

"I sensed some discord." Michal stretched her neck and continued her spinning.

"Maybe some of that will change now that you're here." Abigail returned to her normal weaving speed.

"What difference could I make?"

"Maachah never lets us forget she is the daughter of a king. I think she resents being a junior wife to someone like me, someone not of royal blood." A note of pride crept into Abigail's voice as she added, "She will have to be more cooperative when you take charge, since you too are a princess."

"Princess," Michal sighed. "It has been a long time since I've heard that said without scorn." She put down her spindle and looked out the window.

"You were unhappy at Gallim." Abigail's voice was quiet.

Through the open window, Michal watched Abigail's son, Daniel, peek over the edge of a low hedge. He dodged a clod of dirt, tossed his own dried mud ball, and yelled with laughter.

"More than unhappy," Michal was surprised to hear herself admit. "After Tirzah's little daughter died, I could find no reason to go on living." She began to wind the newly spun twine into a ball. "Many times I prayed for my life to end. Now I am so grateful God ignored my pleas."

"Who is Tirzah?" Abigail questioned as she wove a purple stripe into the blue fabric on her loom.

"Tirzah is my handmaid," Michal replied. "Phaltiel, the man my father forced me to marry—" She paused as an image of Phaltiel's fleshy face flashed through her unwilling mind. "He regarded me as nothing more than a chattel. Therefore, he felt he had every right to force my handmaid into his bed."

"Poor girl," Abigail said. "But she's not alone. It happens in many households."

"And not in ours?" Michal's curiosity overrode her fear of knowing.

"Of course not." Abigail laughed. "Concubines? David? Goodness, no."

Michal tried not to let her relief show. "As our husband, of course, he technically has the right to possess our servants."

"You were not married long before David went into exile," Abigail observed. "Do you not know what a godly man he is?"

"I know. Or I knew." Michal resented the idea that another woman could presume to know David better than she. "He was always a man of honor, but many years have passed. When we parted, he was one of my father's military commanders. Now he's a powerful king. I wondered if perhaps things had changed."

"I would not say David has changed at all in the time I've known him." Abigail stopped working and turned to face Michal. "You are still his most beloved wife, if that's what you are wondering."

"I didn't mean that, exactly," Michal stammered.

Abigail put her hand on Michal's arm. "I knew from the beginning that he would always yearn for you. He would not speak of you often, but when he did the pain was clearly evident. You may not believe this, Michal, but I thank God for the miracle of your return to this house. You please David, and that makes me happy."

"You love him that much?" Michal stared into Abigail's kind face.

"Yes." Abigail dropped her eyes. "I love him that much. And a thousand times more."

"I understand perfectly." Michal's words were barely audible. "So do I."

The women worked for a while in silence. "I've finished this batch of spinning," Michal said. "I believe I'll go and make fresh dye now. It's so beautiful outside. Do you want to come with me?"

"Thank you, no." Abigail turned back to her loom. "As fast as you spin, I may actually have thread to weave enough fabric for everyone in the household to have new clothing this year. If you choose to continue spinning, that is."

As Michal put her tools away, she asked, "Abigail, are you content with the household tasks you now do?"

"Yes, of course."

"Then why can't all of the wives continue with their current assignments? Our large household needs clothing. I love to spin and dye and knit. Why couldn't I do those things for the time being? If that plan doesn't work out, we can always change things later on."

"That would be wonderful." Abigail beamed. "I mean, well, it would be most efficient." After a pause, she added, "Aren't you concerned about asserting your authority? It may seem as if you are deferring to me if I continue to give instructions to the staff."

Michal laughed. "Maybe I should care, Abigail, but I don't. I am alive, and I am with David. Nothing else matters right now."

Michal was grateful when Abigail declined her invitation to go along. She wanted to be alone at the stream where clay pots sat on dry kindling, ready to be heated for dying wool yarn and linen twine. Out under the sky, with no one else around, she could bask in the information Abigail just revealed.

"He grieved for me," she whispered to the gurgling water. "He loves me," she cooed into a large pot. "I am his most beloved wife," she shouted as she tossed a ball of twine toward a passing cloud. "Abigail said so." She hummed a psalm of thanksgiving as she started the fires and stirred different colored powders made from crushed flower petals into each pot.

Some time later, Michal noticed Abigail's young son watching her from a short distance away. "Hello, Daniel," Michal called to the little boy. "Do you want to see how to make colors?" She laughed as the child ran away, knowing his curiosity would bring him to the stream again someday.

After the day's chores were done, Michal washed and dressed with more care than usual. A length of dark green linen tied about the waist of her lighter green tunic emphasized the slender curves of her figure. She smiled at her reflection in her mirror of polished brass. The color of her dress turned her eyes green, an effect that endlessly fascinated David years ago.

"You look lovely tonight, Michal," Abigail commented as they strolled across the courtyard toward the kitchen. "You have such beautiful eyes, so unusual."

"Thank you," Michal responded. She hoped with all her heart she still had the ability to captivate her husband. She'd made it her business to find out there would be no outside guests at this evening's dinner table.

CHAPTER TWENTY-THREE

"For the commandment is a lamp; and the law is light;...to keep thee from ...the flattery of the tongue of a strange woman." Proverbs 6:23-24

MICHAL CONCENTRATED ON sounding unconcerned as she quietly asked Abigail, "Does Maachah dance often?"

"Depends on her mood," Abigail murmured.

Bird leaned across Abigail and whispered, "Whenever it's a good time for her to conceive, she pushes herself into our husband's bed ahead of the other wives."

"Hush, Bird!" Abigail hissed.

"Do I not speak the truth?" Bird tossed her head angrily.

"We are a family. We must behave accordingly. Forgive me." Abigail turned to face Michal. "I forgot myself and spoke as the senior wife."

"There's nothing to forgive." Michal patted Abigail's upper arm. "I agree with you. Nothing brings a family more misery than a group of wives at war with each other." She thought briefly of the animosity that was always at work among Phaltiel's wives, but forced the image out of her mind.

"The only way to get along with Maachah is to act like she's better than everyone else." Bird helped herself to another portion of lamb, ignoring Abigail's disapproving look. "You have to kiss her toes three times a day, like Haggith and Eglah do. And, of course, you can never forget that she is the daughter of the king of Geshur."

Michal picked at her food as she watched Maachah move rhythmically to the beat of a drum and the wail of a shepherd's pipe. Maachah used her upper arms to push her breasts forward, while she tossed her hair over her face. Meanwhile, her hips never stopped gyrating. Michal stole a quick glance at David then quickly looked back at her food bowl, and took a deep breath. The king's full attention was locked on Maachah's writhing body. His face told Michal instantly that his response was everything Maachah would have expected.

Michal exhaled and turned her eyes back to her rival. She could barely resist the urge to throw her bowl of lamb stew at Maachah's undulating navel.

Michal realized Bird was staring at her. "Typical foreigner," Bird muttered, as if she read Michal's thoughts.

Michal's eyes were on the dancing Maachah, but the only image before her was the look of hot desire on David's face. How could she compete with this foreign princess's overt sexuality? Years ago she and Merab performed folk dances to entertain King Saul's guests. She did not know how to put on the kind of teasing, suggestive display Maachah performed, nor did she want to.

She let her eyes rest on David for another stolen moment. His handsome face glowed almost red in the reflected lamplight. His eyes were bright with excitement. She longed to kiss his full lips that were just now curved into a half-smile. His tunic was thrust back to show the rounded muscles of his arms. It looked as if his strong but gentle embrace would enfold Maachah before long. Michal wished Tirzah could be here, to help her plot and plan.

"That was an interesting dance," Abigail said. "I wonder if anyone else would like to entertain us?" After a long moment of silence, Abigail asked, "Princess Michal, do you want to favor us with a song?"

Michal hesitated. Much as she feared having her simple songs compared to Maachah's sophisticated dancing, she would not let someone else absorb all of her husband's attention without a fight. "I would need help." She gave David a sidelong look from beneath her eyelashes. "Perhaps our lord the king would be kind enough to accompany me on the harp?"

"I'm always ready to play a tune." David's smile melted Michal's heart. He looked directly at her, and she felt for an instant that he was hers exclusively.

A serving girl hastily fetched one of the king's harps. David put the instrument in his lap, leaning it against his shoulder then cocked his ear to check the tune of each individual string. When he had the feel of the harp, he motioned Michal toward him with a quick nod of his head.

Michal could not keep from smiling as she repositioned herself. She sat so close to David she could feel the warmth of his body. She longed to snuggle even closer. Instead she remained almost, but not quite, touching him.

"The Shepherd Psalm?" she suggested. His fingers immediately began to strum the melody of a song Michal knew to be one of her husband's favorites.

David set the beginning note perfectly for Michal's contralto range. "The Lord is my shepherd," she began. Michal looked at David as she sang and he gazed back into her eyes, only occasionally glancing down to pluck a string.

There was a moment of reverent quiet when the song was finished, followed by exclamations of delight. "Do you remember this one?" the king questioned as he transitioned from the sedate Shepherd Psalm into a livelier tune.

"Make a joyful noise unto the Lord." Michal paused. "All ye, all ye people?"

"All ye lands," David corrected her.

"I can't remember all of the words. Will you sing it?" Michal asked.

"If you will do the harmony," David agreed, "the way you used to sing with your sister."

Michal felt as if there was no one present other than her husband and herself as they sang the ancient hymns of praise and joy. She hummed through the words she could not remember, enjoying the vibrant sounds of David's melodious baritone. He slipped effortlessly from one tune to another.

Other voices joined in singing more familiar psalms. At one point, Michal caught a glimpse of Maachah studying her intently. There was hostility in Maachah's narrowed eyes, but perhaps a glimmer of respect for a worthy opponent as well.

While Bird attempted to cover a yawn with her hand, Abigail stood and smoothed the lines of her tunic. Her action signaled that the wives should bid good evening and withdraw to their own quarters. Maachah took her time wrapping a filmy shawl over her skimpy dance costume. After one last flirtatious look toward David, she shook her hair, set her jaw, and swept from the room.

"I'd forgotten what a wonderful treasure we have in our psalms," Michal commented as she drew herself to her full height.

David stood beside her and put his hand on her arm. "Don't go," he whispered.

Michal's pulse quickened at the thought of lingering alone with him. She stood perfectly still while Bird and Abigail disappeared, afraid any sound or movement might break the spell. Did her husband's words indicate what she hoped they meant?

David took Michal's hand in his. "Would you like to come and keep me company tonight, my darling wife?"

CHAPTER TWENTY-FOUR

"My beloved is white and ruddy, the chiefest among ten thousand. His...locks are bushy, and black as a raven. His eyes are as the eyes of doves...His cheeks are as a bed of spices, as sweet flowers: his lips like lilies, dropping sweet smelling myrrh. His hands are as gold rings set with the beryl: his belly is as bright ivory overlaid with sapphires. His legs are as pillars of marble...This is my beloved..." Song of Solomon 5: 10-16

MICHAL WAS SURPRISED to find David's sleeping chamber was no larger than her own. Brown and black cushions made from animal skins were tossed here and there, some with the furry exterior of a long-haired goat, others made from smoothly tanned leather. Larger skins were scattered across the stone floor.

"This room reminds me of a small, quiet cave," Michal commented.

"Do you think so?" David was obviously pleased. "That is precisely what I had in mind when I designed this place. I wanted to create a retreat like the caverns I explored as a boy around the Bethlehem countryside.

"Still a shepherd at heart, my husband?" she teased.

"Yes, I am, and always will be. I am a lowly commoner, amazed to be alone with the daughter of King Saul." David lightly brushed his lips across the back of her hand, never taking his eyes from her face. "You are even more beautiful than I remembered, Michal. Make yourself comfortable." He gestured toward the bank of cushions.

"You still know how to dress like a man who tends sheep." Michal giggled as she watched the king change into a short tunic much like one a simple working man would wear.

David settled next to her. "You look exactly like what you are, a princess royal." He grinned mischievously. "So why shouldn't I dress as what I am?"

"What you *were*," she said, longing for him to take her into his arms. "Now you are a great king."

David ducked his head and looked at Michal through narrowed eyes. "There's not that much difference between the work of a shepherd and that of a king."

Michal smiled as she thought how her proud father would have reacted to being likened to a humble shepherd. "That's a comparison I've never heard before."

"Think about it. A nation and a flock of sheep both need someone to look after them. And both resist the best of care. They get into mischief, and expect the shepherd, or the king, to realize they're in trouble and rescue them."

"At least sheep don't scheme or plot, or lie to you." Michal thought of the men who flattered her father to gain influence.

"Don't be so sure, palace-dweller." David curled a tendril of her hair around his finger. "While it is true sheep are not smart enough to carry out elaborate intrigues, they try to trick their shepherds by pretending to be obedient. If no one is watching, they go off exploring forbidden places and get themselves into all kinds of silly scrapes. When it starts to get dark, they cry for help. The good shepherd goes and saves them."

"And you thrive on the responsibility, the challenge." Michal thought again of her father. Being head of state pressed heavily on King Saul, but her husband wore his crown joyously.

"You know me too well." David smiled and touched her cheek. "Everyone can see I relish being king, but very few can understand why I love the job. It's the power, not the wealth or the fame. I don't mean in the raw sense of exercising authority, but the ability to do things that make life better for our people." His eyes glowed. "It's an honor to be God's partner in leading His flock."

"I don't know that my father would have described his role that way," Michal said, "but I wouldn't be surprised to learn Uncle Abner understood your point of view."

David nodded affirmatively. "Your insight into politics and people always amazes me." His hand grazed lightly across her forearm. "This shepherd boy will obey the princess's wishes," he said, "daring to do nothing except what my lady demands of me."

So, he remembered the game they played in their honeymoon home. Michal smiled and gave her husband a sidelong glance. "I would like to hear a song, shepherd. Afterward, if your tune pleases me, perhaps I will allow you to kiss my hand."

David took a lyre that hung on a nearby wooden peg and sang softly of a lovely lady with lustrous hair and mystifying eyes. The richness of his voice washed over Michal like a warm summer rain. As the last notes of his song died away, she was inflamed by her desire. Gold bangles clinked and sparkled as she extended her hand to him. "Never tell anyone I allowed you this liberty," she commanded.

With a sly smile he took her hand and kissed each finger, pulled her hand closer, and playfully flicked his tongue across her palm.

"You are an insolent fellow!" she said haughtily, one eyebrow raised. Then she smiled and added, "I've always admired boldness in a man. Tell me, shepherd, have you ever gone to war?"

"I have indeed," he dusted a row of light kisses from her wrist to the inside of her elbow. "I have been in a great many battles."

"I have heard that some soldiers use their swords to stab women." Michal slid her hand down his chest. "Have you ever done such a thing, shepherd?"

"I have." His voice was husky. "My magic sword cuts deeply but without lasting pain."

"I must taste this magic," she whispered.

"What will King Saul do if I plant his daughter with the seed of a child?"

"I promise you my father will never know."

MICHAL ROUSED FROM her sleep, startled by a strange noise.

David's hand rested on her shoulder. "What is it, Michal? Are you all right?"

She propped up on one elbow, still frightened. Embarrassed to realize the moaning sounds came from her, she mumbled, "Just a bad dream."

"Ah," David grunted. He pulled the bedcover to their shoulders. "It's over now."

Michal thought how blessed David was to be able to wake instantly and fall asleep with almost as much speed. She stared into the darkness and listened as her husband's breathing became deeper and more regular, content to lie awake in his embrace. A few hours of sleep were not worth the risk of another nightmare.

What brought the terrifying image of Phaltiel into her dream? She tried to blot every memory of him from her mind. If something reminded her of the Gallim years during the daytime, she quickly turned her thoughts to something else. But at night, evil scenes invaded her dreams. Oftentimes she awoke shaking, crying, sweating, or screaming, afraid to doze off again.

Maybe David's baby was growing inside her at this very moment. A son would be a source of great pride. Yet a daughter would be safer, less likely to be drawn into royal power struggles. She smiled and patted her stomach. Yes, a sunny little girl like Zora was her wish.

Michal shivered as another memory forced its way into her consciousness. *"Our Lord Phaltiel commands you to come to his bedchamber this evening."* Bida smirked. *"And bring Miss Tirzah with you. Our Master has heard your handmaiden claims to be a virgin. That will not be the case tomorrow."* Little Zora, the daughter of Tirzah and that putrid pig Phaltiel.

I must force myself to think of other things. Michal tried to picture her nephews, and wondered if she would ever know them. Did Jonathan's son survive? Did he have his father's skill with weapons of war? Had any of the children inherited their grandfather's height or their grandmother's cunning?

Was there any substance to her Uncle Abner's prediction that David would rule both Judea and Jerusalem? If that happened, she could ask David to find her young relatives. Perhaps the day would come when her own child would play with his cousins in the courtyard of King David's palace.

After a long while, Michal managed to stop trembling. Her acute hearing picked up sounds of the household awakening. A door opened and closed. Someone clattered pieces of pottery against each other. David's dark profile traced itself against the brightening promise of dawn. She nestled against his warm body and waited for daylight.

CHAPTER TWENTY-FIVE

"...the floods of ungodly men made me afraid;" II Samuel 22:5

A FAINT NOISE caused Michal to straighten from where she bent over her dye pots. She stretched her back and tried to locate the source of the sound. The top of a head bobbed up and down in the tall grass nearby. A little boy's shrill voice floated to her on the afternoon breeze. "They're coming!"

Who was coming? Michal rested her free hand on the handle of the knife stuck in her sash. She quickly considered various escape routes while scanning the meadow behind the boy to see if anyone followed him. How quickly could she get across the stream with the child? Was there a place nearby where the two of them could safely hide? There were heavy bags of freshly spun yarn to be dyed today. Why did she think that was reason enough to leave behind the pouch of emergency supplies she usually kept within reach?

"They're coming!" It was Amnon. "The people from Barim."

"Bahurim," Michal corrected in a whisper as she let go of her stirring rod. She felt a rush of relief when she realized Amnon was announcing the arrival of friends, not enemies. Michal ran to meet Bird's young son.

They found the courtyard crackling with anticipation. The little boys abandoned their daily game of war to watch preparations for a lavish feast. It was quite an occasion when travelers brought news from other places, particularly an Israeli military village such as Bahurim. Everyone seemed caught up in a spirit of excitement, except for Abigail. She remained serene, calmly listening to complaints, solving problems, and imposing order on the chaos.

At Abigail's request, Michal went to check Maachah's progress at turning the fabric working room into a place for the Bahurim women to sleep temporarily. A mountain of bedding occupied the middle of the long room where Michal and Abigail normally did their carding, spinning, and weaving. Maachah sat in a far corner, staring out a window.

"Working hard?" Michal asked.

Maachah started. "Why did you creep up on me?" she demanded in a manner that was both defensive and aggressive. "As you can see, I've been busy getting the sleeping mats from storage. It's exhausting work. I'm recovering for a moment before finishing my work. Abigail should have sent a servant instead of me."

"She thought you might need help." Michal was mildly amused by Maachah's discomfort, and considered her swipe at Abigail not worth discussing.

Maachah stood and smoothed her hair. "I suppose I am rested enough to do the mats now." The two of them unrolled mats and spread them with blankets. "You sing very well," Maachah commented.

She wants me to compliment her dancing, Michal thought. Instead she merely said, "Thank you."

"Perhaps we shall entertain our guests tonight." Maachah fluffed a blanket. "You could sing and I could dance. Some diversion would make everything more cordial for our visitors. And I'm certain David wants to demonstrate that King Saul's daughter is now at his side."

"I would be surprised if we are asked to perform." Michal realized her tone of voice revealed her shock. She thought there might be some singing this evening, but Maachah's suggestive dancing seemed to her to be entirely inappropriate for a gathering of men.

Maachah shrugged. "We had wonderful parties back in Geshur, in my father's kingdom."

Although Michal didn't want to make conversation, she knew Maachah was likely to find an excuse to leave. Interesting talk just might keep the younger woman engaged long enough to finish making the beds. Michal was anxious to go to the rooftop where she could see the mountain road that led into the city gates of Hebron.

"Did you dance often? In Geshur, I mean?" Michal cut a cord that resisted being untied, and unrolled another mat.

"All the time," Maachah said. "My father often said his daughters were skilled at singing, dancing, and appeasing enemies." She shook a blanket and let it settle onto a mat. "I guess he must have been right. He was always trading one of my sisters to seal an alliance with one country or another. He made shrewd bargains for my older sisters. I always knew my turn would come one day, and I would end up living away from Geshur, in some alien culture." She looked around. "And here I am. The king's fourth wife, mother of the third eldest son. In the backwater of Judea, a place most civilized people think of as something less than a kingdom." She sat back on her heels and smiled. "At least David is young and handsome. My sister Selima got a fat old man who wore bear skins and stank like a wild animal. Ate like one, too, she said. She told me getting sons with him was the most disgusting thing she ever did. Can you imagine sleeping with such a man?"

Michal was not quick enough to lock her mind against the image of the drunken Phaltiel on their wedding night. Like a sharp sword, remembered words sliced through the humid air of the workroom. *Tell me, Princess, what do you know of the pleasures of the lost cities of Sodom and Gomorrah?*

Michal fought the irrational impulse to run and find a place to hide. Feeling weak, she leaned against a nearby wall for support and said, "I am sorry for your sister's fate."

"Oh, no! Have no pity for Selima." Maachah's eyes grew wide. "Her oldest son now rules. As soon as he was old enough, Selima helped him kill her husband and take the throne. My sister now lives lavishly as the king's honored mother. She has twenty handmaidens." Maachah picked up a blanket and immediately tossed it aside. "And never has to do housework."

"She helped her son murder his father?"

Maachah shrugged and unrolled another mat. "So she says, although Selima was never known for her truthfulness. It could be she merely put the idea in her son Hogarth's head. That way, if the prince failed, she might be able to claim ignorance and escape the king's wrath. I do know that my sister's nasty husband was in good health until the arrival of soldiers my father sent at Selima's request. The next day, the old man was dead and my sister's son was declared king. The troops from Geshur kept order until King Hogarth was firmly in control."

"How horrible," Michal said.

"You truly think so?" Maachah knelt on the floor, patting air from beneath the blanket she'd just spread. "I think it's just the way things go sometimes. I wish our lives could be as exciting as Selima's, don't you?"

"No," Michal answered. "I've had my fill of danger and violence. I hope to grow old in David's house and live out my days in peace."

Maachah raised her eyebrows. "Peace? You almost remind me of Abigail. She talks like an old woman. You know, she's always fretting about the king getting hurt and says he should stay out of all battles. But you're a princess like me. Surely you know our safety depends on the strength of David's army. He dies the day his soldiers cannot defend his territory, and his wives and children die with him. Or we become slaves."

"There is some truth in what you say," Michal admitted. "Judea has no choice but to fight the enemies around us. That's not the same as killing within your own family. Murder is forbidden by the Law of Moses."

"Ah, yes. Your Law of Moses." Maachah sat back on her heels for a moment. "The special law that governs the people of God." Suddenly she jumped up and brushed debris from her clothes. "I almost forgot. I have to look in on Abital. She has been sick for months, ever since her little son was born. I must be sure her handmaiden has brought her fresh drinking water."

Maachah was gone before Michal remembered that fewer than half of the beds were prepared. She was aggravated with Maachah for leaving before the job was done, but equally annoyed at herself for failing to assert her rightful authority. Why didn't she simply demand Maachah's cooperation? However, the anticipation of seeing people from her homeland occupied all of her thoughts. She couldn't wait to sit and talk with her friend and servant Tirzah, the only living woman who'd known her since childhood.

With the temporary women's sleeping area neatly filled with makeshift beds, Michal decided to take a quick trip to the rooftop before returning to the courtyard. As she passed by the other wives' chambers on the way to her own, Michal was not surprised to see Maachah lounging in Abital's reception room.

"Abital is doing well," Maachah said quickly. "I was about to go back and see what else Abigail wants me to do. Is that where you are going?"

"I'm going to the rooftop." Michal thought briefly about chiding Maachah, but did not consider it worth the effort of listening to a series of dramatic excuses.

"I'll accompany you," Maachah said immediately.

Michal would have expected Maachah to ask permission to join her instead of boldly announcing she would go along, but again she said nothing as they ascended the stairs to the rooftop. A cloud of dust hung in the air outside the entrance of David's house. People, animals, and carts were crowding into the courtyard directly below them. "They're already here," Michal said. She raced down the stairs, not caring whether Maachah kept pace or followed.

In the crowded courtyard, Michal and Tirzah hugged as if their last meeting was years ago. "Tirzah!" Michal held her friend at arm's length. "Let me look at you." The women embraced each other again. "We thought you would be here long ago," Michal said. "No one knew what to think."

"Most of us walked the entire distance, and of course we made camp early each day to let the children rest. We did not dare to take a direct route because we knew to stay out of the sight of villages and other travelers." Tirzah stopped. "I am so sorry to hear the news about Lord Abner. His death saddens everyone in Bahurim."

"Thank you, Tirzah. Uncle Abner may have been the last member of my family I will ever know."

"Oh, no, my lady," Tirzah said. "Come and see the five fine sons of your dear sister, Merab."

CHAPTER TWENTY-SIX

"All these men of war, that could keep rank, came with a perfect heart to Hebron, to make David king over all Israel:..." I Chronicles 12:38

MOST OF THE men from Bahurim joined King David's army. The few who were not soldiers blended into Hebron or surrounding farms, finding places for their families to live and profitable work to do. Michal jumped at the chance to have her nephews reside in the palace under her watchful eye. Her brother-in-law, Adriel, readily accepted the offer, anxious to concentrate on adjusting to his military duties in the Judean army.

In addition to finally meeting Merab's sons, Michal could see Rizpah's boys were her illegitimate half-brothers. Both were tall for their age, and walked with the distinctive, purposeful stride typical of her family. The eldest boy inherited his grandfather's round head and half-moon eyes. King Saul's rugged features were clearly imprinted on the youthful face of the younger son, Armoni.

No doubt these adolescents could find subsistence work as apprentices to craftsmen or farmers. While they learned their trade, their earnings would consist only of their training and the meals they consumed at their master's table.

How should she deal with Rizpah, Michal asked herself. While she felt no responsibility for her father's former concubine, she knew the woman would face a difficult life with no adult male relative to provide her with protection. Rizpah might be able to eke out an existence by begging in the streets and gleaning leftover crops after farmers harvested their fields. Or she could take up the shameful occupation of prostitution.

Although Michal disliked the thought of the former handmaid's relationship with her father, she was realistic enough to know Rizpah could not refuse King Saul once he decided to have her. With some doubts still lingering, Michal approached Abigail and David with the possibility of allowing Rizpah to join their household to assist with caring for the children. With Michal's five nephews added to David's brood, everyone agreed Bird could use the help.

Arrangements were made without anyone openly acknowledging Rizpah's indirect family ties. Neither Michal nor Rizpah mentioned the name of King Saul in the other's presence.

As winter brought shorter, darker days to Judea, King David's household settled into a comfortable routine. Michal found a measure of welcome peace in her husband's home with her beloved Tirzah back at her side, serving as her confidant as much as her handmaid. Shortly after daylight, Michal ate breakfast with King David's other wives, children, and household servants. She spent the next few hours fussing over her nephews, and seeing to the boys' needs. The remainder of the morning and all afternoon were spent in the workroom. Through the winter, Abigail, Michal, and Tirzah would weave, knit, and sew the fibers that were carded, spun, and dyed during the previous summer and autumn. When springtime came again, flax would be harvested, the sheep would be sheared of their wooly coats, and the cycle would repeat.

After the evening meal, while servants put the children to bed, King David's wives lingered at the table, each hoping for an invitation to spend time alone with their husband. David asked Michal to stay behind with him more often than all of the other wives combined. There were also frequent occasions when the king dined apart from the women, entertaining his military staff and visitors from outside Judea. Michal took pride in the other wives' knowing how often a servant would walk down the corridor to her bedchamber after one of these state dinners. Holding an oil lamp aloft to light the way, the servant would escort Michal to the courtyard entrance of her husband's room. An occasional yawn was sure to bring one of Abigail's knowing looks or a hateful glance from Maachah.

Michal did not consider it strange that new barns and stables were hastily constructed across the stream where she dyed yarn. Nor was there anything unusual about the constant sound of metal workers pounding out spears, swords, and chariot wheels from dawn to dusk six days a week. Every standing army required workmen to keep their weapons in repair, and winter was the logical season to do this routine maintenance. Like everyone else, Michal noticed nothing remarkable until the visit from Armoni, Rizpah's youngest son.

Armoni was apprenticed to a bow and arrow maker who plied his trade in a forest southeast of Hebron. Late one afternoon, the boy drove a cart into King David's courtyard. The lad was clearly proud that his master allowed him to make the two-day trip to Hebron alone—armed only with a slingshot and a spear—to pick up a load of animal sinews. The Sabbath was about to begin when Armoni arrived. As his master instructed, he came to his mother for shelter during the day of rest. After the Sabbath, he would pick up the sinews and take them back to the forest.

In the flickering lamplight, Michal held Merab's youngest son, Joel, while he slept, and whispered a prayer Adriel would never take the children from her. Michal used her index finger to make ringlets of the damp hair around Joel's sweet face. She raised the sleeping baby's chubby hand to her lips and kissed each finger. Smiling to herself, she half-heartedly listened to Armoni parade his adolescent importance. "There are fifty other apprentices like me," he claimed. "We spend our days shredding animal sinews to make new bows for the army. And that's not all." Armoni seemed to be enjoying the rapt attention he received from the younger boys. "There are at least two hundred men who cut wood for arrows all day, every day."

"To hear him tell it, Armoni is making enough weapons to fight the biggest battle this world has ever seen, isn't he?" she whispered into Joel's closed fist.

Taking a deep breath, Michal looked around the room. No one appeared to have paid attention to the question she cooed softly to the baby, but her own words connected an array of observations that had seemed unrelated until this instant. How could she have been so blind? Had she not seen elders of Israel slipping into the palace late in the evening and leaving under cover of darkness the next night? Such men would come to Hebron only for pressing military or political missions.

Men were training war horses in the fields beyond the new barns. Abigail bargained for extra sheep and cattle, far beyond the needs of their immediate household. Weapons, animals, vehicles, and provisions were being made ready everywhere. The preparations were far too extensive merely to maintain Judah's borders. Before he was murdered, didn't Uncle Abner say her husband must rule the combined kingdom? King David was preparing Judea for a war—and from the looks of things, a big one.

The oil lamp threw its soft light on the faces of the boys. They were enthralled by Armoni's stories of how the sinew was shredded, then carefully glued to the outside of a new bow to improve its resilience. How sweet and innocent Little Tamar looked, nestled between Bird and Amnon. Although the tiny princess was sound asleep, she sat straight and tall, as Maachah so frequently instructed her.

Later that night in her bedchamber, Michal found sleep impossible. Her body was weary, but her thoughts would not quiet themselves. Was it possible her brother, King Ishbosheth, was negotiating with David?

She dismissed that idea immediately. The only communication Ishbosheth would accept from David would be an oath of allegiance, and Michal knew her husband would never offer him a false pledge. Michal paused to savor how her brother would be humbled if David took the crown from his arrogant head. Try as she might, she could feel no shred of loyalty to King Ishbosheth.

The annual season for wars was approaching. As soon as the spring lambs began to appear among the herds, the men traditionally began their military campaigns. The seasonal strategy would give them the longest stretch of days before the cold mountaintop winters forced even hardened soldiers to seek shelter.

Ever since Abner told her about Samuel's anointing of David, Michal knew the day would come when her husband would attempt to unite and rule the nation of the people of God. Yet she avoided thinking about the consequences of that destiny. She walked back and forth in her bedchamber. David would certainly lead his army into battle. He could be killed, even if his soldiers overpowered their enemy. If he lived, he risked being conquered. The humiliation of defeat would be an opportunity for power-hungry neighbors to test Judea's defenses.

Michal was concerned for the safety of her family, but she had confidence in David's military ability. She paced and thought, finally concluding defeat and physical danger were not her greatest fear. She decided the only possible outcome for David was for him to fulfill Samuel's prophesy. Yet a king's daughter knew only too well how a victory would hold its own unknown terrors. Being the king of Judea was one thing. King of Israel was quite another.

Michal mourned the innocent happiness she knew as David's first and only wife. Those days when he was hers alone were gone forever. Now he had other wives, and children of his body that he adored. Sharing her husband with other women was frustrating, but paled in comparison to the frightening competition of immense power, fame, and riches.

Michal remembered her father and the advisors who constantly surrounded him. Some had King Saul's best interests at heart. Yet there were also plenty of power-hungry jackals who would have sold their own mothers into slavery if some measure of profit could be found in the bargain. Would David be wise enough to distinguish good men from those who poured lies into his ears for their own gain?

It was almost dawn before Michal was able to calm her mind enough to sleep. She was irritated when Tirzah shook her awake after what seemed like only a few minutes.

"Go away," she mumbled. "I want to sleep."

"My lady," Tirzah persisted. "There are men here from Israel. The rumor is they bring startling news."

CHAPTER TWENTY-SEVEN

"And they brought the head of Ishbosheth unto David to Hebron, and said to the king, Behold the head of Ishbosheth the son of Saul thine enemy, which sought thy life;..." II Samuel 4:8

TIRZAH QUICKLY LED Michal to the balcony outside the bedroom. They stood behind a vine-covered trellis that allowed them to observe without being seen by the crowd below. Abigail and Haggith were positioned on a nearby balcony, screened from the courtyard's view by wooden filigree work. Abigail nodded a silent greeting to Michal, while men spilled into the center of the courtyard. The public chamber door stood open, indicating the haste with which the room was emptied. David sat on a large stone, flanked by Joab and Abashai, his top military advisors.

There was a rustle on the balcony adjacent to where Michal and Tirzah stood. Maachah hurried to Haggith's side, dragging her two children with her. "I hope we are not too late," Maachah commented to no one in particular.

From her vantage point, Michal could look over the back of the king's head. The administrators and advisors in the courtyard would normally be sitting in the public room discussing matters of state.

Soldiers dragged two men before the king and pushed them to a kneeling position.

David's voice rang out across the crowd. "Speak."

Michal could clearly see the young man's face as he lifted his eyes. "Great King, I am Baanah, the son of Rimmon. My brother Rechab and I"—he inclined his head toward his companion—"we are loyal men of Israel from the tribe of Benjamin. We have long been in hiding for fear of our lives." Baanah licked his lips and continued. "Yesterday, Rechab and I ended the life of an evil king who spent many men's lives in an attempt to kill you, Great One."

"Tell me how this happened," David demanded.

Baanah smiled. "We entered King Ishbosheth's house disguised as tradesmen come to deliver a cartload of wheat. We bribed a guard and made our way to the royal bedchamber. As the king lay in his bed I plunged my dagger under his fifth rib, as we hear was done to Lord Abner in this very city not long ago."

The young man paused, as if hoping for a response. When nothing but silence met him, he spoke again. "May it please your majesty, my brother Rechab and I know that before he was slain, King Saul was your sworn enemy. And so we have brought the head of his son, who also hated you, to lie at your feet. We trust you will look with favor on our vengeance, taken on your behalf."

Baanah nudged his brother. Rechab scampered to a spot near a large earthen jar. Grinning broadly, he reached into the jar, pulled out Ishbosheth's bloody head, and held it aloft by the hair. Michal wanted to turn away but could not. She felt as if she might throw up. Instead, she covered her mouth tightly with one hand, flattened herself against the wall, and held on to Tirzah.

Meanwhile, Maachah slapped her little daughter Tamar's hands away from the child's face. "Stop that! A princess never hides her eyes."

How can I have tears for Ishbosheth, Michal wondered. He was responsible for Merab's death, and who would ever know how many nieces and nephews he killed? Yet he was her brother, her blood and bone. How long would the sword of vengeance continue to strike down members of her family? She prayed for the safety of Merab's sons and even for Rizpah's two boys. The house of Saul must survive, she thought defiantly.

160

David leaned forward. "A man who claimed to have killed King Saul also came to me expecting a reward. Do you know what happened to him?"

Baanah shrugged as his brother returned to kneel beside him. "No, my lord."

"I had him executed, for the capital offense of murdering God's anointed ruler." David's voice rang with the hard edge of a sharpened sword.

"But, Great King..." Baanah stopped smiling.

"Silence!" Joab roared.

"Your guilt is much greater than the Amalekite's," David continued. "King Saul would have died that day without the foreigner's help. However, you, by your own admission, went into a Hebrew brother's house and killed him in his own bed. You know the Law of Moses demands the death penalty for such a crime."

"My lord—" Baanah began.

"Quiet!" Joab shouted again.

Baanah ignored Joab's command. "Surely, Great King, you would not punish men who acted in your interest."

"Have mercy!" Rechab begged.

"Mercy?" David leapt to his feet, stepping closer to the two kneeling men. "What mercy did you show King Ishbosheth? As for acting in what you claim to be *my* interest, am I not sworn to uphold the Law of Moses? Is the tribe of Benjamin somehow exempt from the Ten Commandments?"

The men did not reply. Perhaps they were too terrified by the young soldiers who sprang forward to let the tips of their swords rest on their chests.

Michal could not hear the quiet conversation that took place between David and Joab while everyone in the courtyard stood quiet and motionless. The king whirled away from the cowering men, nodded to Joab, and re-entered the public chamber.

"It makes a terrible mess when someone bleeds all over the place," Haggith complained. "At least they're outside this time."

Michal turned to go inside. "Don't you want to see the execution?" Tirzah asked.

"No. I already know the color of blood only too well."

"But those men killed your brother," the handmaid insisted.

The shouts of men's voices rose from below. As she walked away, Michal heard Maachah say to little Absalom, "Watch carefully, my son. This is what must happen to anyone who angers you when you are king."

Clenching her fist, Michal vowed Maachah's son must never be heir to King Saul's throne. As the only surviving member of the house of Kish, it was her duty to carry on the royal line. Her son, the one she would conceive with David, was entitled to rule Israel. The blood of her family purchased that right. And no one, especially not the foreigner Maachah, was going to take away that destiny without a fight.

Retreating to her bedchamber, Michal said, "Tirzah, please close the shutters." She drank a cup of water and took deep breaths to calm herself. There was no doubt now that her father's crown was available for the taking. David would have the support of the Israeli elders behind him, in addition to the considerable might of the emerging Judean army. If her husband's popularity was anything near what it was when King Saul reigned, David would be the people's choice as well. No one could stand in his way now.

Michal fretted over snide remarks recently made by Maachah, words that suggested David wanted his first wife back only because of her royal Israeli heritage. How she longed to be certain her husband wanted her for herself, and not because she was a princess.

As darkness descended, servants disappeared into the public chamber with trays of food. After a quiet meal with the other women, children, and household staff, Michal spent time with her nephews, telling them stories of their uncle's and grandfather's bravery before leaving the room where they and the little princes slept. As she passed through the antechamber where attendants slept near the children. Michal asked Rizpah, "Do you still have a makeup kit?"

"Why, yes," Rizpah answered. "Though there hasn't been much interest lately."

"I want you to help me decide on the best enhancement for me, and teach me how to apply it."

"With pleasure."

"And Rizpah," Michal added.

"Yes?"

"Do not speak of me as your reason, but do not help any of the other women with makeup."

Rizpah's lips started to curve into a smile. "Certainly." Her face resumed its lack of expression. "My lady."

CHAPTER TWENTY-EIGHT

"And the king and his men went to Jerusalem..." II Samuel 5:6

MICHAL TOOK CARE with her appearance the next evening. She hoped David would spend time with a wife before making his final preparations for going into battle. She planned to do everything she could to assure she would be the first, perhaps the only, woman to share King David's bed before he left Judea. She couldn't help but notice that Maachah was also carefully groomed.

"Why is there so much activity around here these days?" Abigail asked Michal as they stood in the courtyard one afternoon. "Do you think something is going on?" Michal held her tongue, speaking only with Tirzah about the coming war—and then only when she could be certain they would not be overheard. Whispering in the darkness when the rest of the household was asleep, they agreed Bird, Haggith, and Abital had no inkling everyone's life was about to change.

Two days later, Michal observed the public room standing empty in the middle of the afternoon. As she suspected, that evening's meal was a private affair among King David's immediate family. Michal wore a green linen tunic embellished with a wide gold band at the bottom of each sleeve and around the garment's hem. Light brown

164

embroidery criss-crossed the golden bands. After working for weeks to perfect the dyes for this tunic, she finally created colors that matched and complemented her eyes.

Maachah wore a red dancing costume, one that revealed more skin than anyone other than a foreigner would find appropriate. It did not escape Michal's attention that an ample portion of Maachah's perfectly-formed breasts kept slipping into view above the drape of her scarf.

The weary children were quieter than usual. Earlier in the day, Bird and Rizpah arranged for stable attendants to take the boys across the stream to visit the fields where horses were kept. The trip included going through the stables, observing equine training, and peppering their guides with dozens of questions. After eating a midday meal with the soldiers, the boys went for rides on gentle horses. Then archers demonstrated how a soldier could maintain his balance while firing arrows from a galloping horse. Today's outing was an introduction. Soon the princes would begin to study horsemanship and learn weaponry skills.

"Would you care to favor us with a song, husband?" Abigail asked after the date cakes were served.

"Not tonight, my dear," David answered.

Maachah instantly announced, "Then I must dance for you!" Without waiting for anyone's agreement, she moved to the opening around which the U-shaped table was arranged. The musicians beat their drums to the rhythm of Maachah's swaying hips. A horn player and piper played a tune in time with the drums.

Michal sat at King David's right hand. She spoke to him as if continuing a conversation. "So, will you attack Jerusalem earlier than you planned, now that King Ishbosheth is dead?"

David studied her face. "Who has told you of my plans?"

"No one," Michal said, happy to divert her husband's attention from Maachah's sensuous dance. "The natural time would be when the new lambs are born. Nevertheless, it is clear that Judea is preparing for war. Signs are everywhere. And now I think you will go sooner."

"What signs do you mean?" David seemed interested, and somewhat amused.

Michal did not want to bring trouble down on Rizpah's talkative son. "Where can you look and not see a Judean storing food, making weapons, building chariots, training animals—doing whatever it takes to prepare for war?"

"And how would your brother's death change anything?" David now completely ignored Maachah's performance.

"The legitimate heir anointed by the prophet Samuel must rule. Why wait for some upstart, or a foreigner, to take the kingdom? The time is now, before someone else acts." She knew she must work hard to keep her husband's eyes away from Maachah. The foreign princess tossed her head forward, causing her hair to fly over her face. How fortunate that the tidbit concerning the old prophet bubbled to the top of Michal's thoughts at this precise moment.

"I'm absolutely certain I never told you about Samuel."

"Uncle Abner told me of your anointing the day before he died. He said the information came from your brother Eliab."

"The story is true. But you must believe me, Michal. I had nothing to do with King Ishbosheth's assassination."

"I never thought you did," she replied. "And I saw how you dealt with the murderers who came to you expecting a bounty."

"You saw?"

"We watched from the balcony—Abigail, Maachah, Haggith, and I."

David glanced down and then looked back at her, questioningly.

"Yes," Michal said. "I saw that murdering dog pull my brother's head from the jar."

David rested his hand on her forearm. "I'm sorry you saw that. I had King Ishbosheth's head properly prepared and sealed in Abner's tomb."

"I have many confusing thoughts about my brother," Michal confessed honestly. "We are—were—of the same blood and bone. Yet, he was responsible for the death of my sister, and many other members of my family. I mourn not for Ishbosheth himself so much as for my father's house." She wanted to leave this line of discussion. Tears would not help her cause now. "I could not help thinking Ishbosheth's death affects the timing of your march on Jerusalem."

The music stopped. Maachah sat at the end of the table, dabbing at the beads of perspiration on her forehead.

"Thank you for entertaining us," David said, barely glancing away from Michal.

Maachah inclined her head in a slight bow. "My lord."

Abigail shifted her position at David's left side. "If our lord the king is tired—" she began.

David stopped her with the raised motion of his hand. A sense that something significant was about to happen seemed to grip everyone at the king's table. As the room became quiet, it was as if the family was carved from wood. From the head of the low table, David made eye contact with each wife, resting his eyes on one, then another, as he spoke.

"My beloved children and wives, in a few days I will be gone from you for a while." A low murmur passed through the room. "As some of you apparently know..." David paused to let his glance rest on Michal. "God has commissioned me to unite His people into one kingdom. I believe the time is now." *Ooohs* and *ahhhs* swelled, then died. "Most of the Judean army will go with me. A small force will fortify Hebron. As an example to my soldiers' families, it is important for you to carry on your daily routines as usual—the way you always do when I go to fight. God willing, I will be back before winter comes to the mountains."

A shocked silence followed the king's words. "Will you bring me a horse when you come home?" Little Absalom's question broke the tension, causing the adults to roar with laughter.

"If that is your wish, my son, you will have your own horse. Come to me, children." David held his arms open. The four children who were old enough to walk rushed to him.

"I want a horse, too," Amnon shouted.

"Me, too," Daniel chimed in.

"Me, too," Tamar said.

"You're a girl," Absalom admonished Tamar as he pushed his little sister aside to insinuate himself closer to their father. "Girls can't have horses."

David hugged the four children close to him. He held Amnon and Tamar with one arm, Absalom and Daniel with the other. "You will all have fine things when this is over," he told them.

"Tamar, too?" Amnon asked, clasping his little sister's hand.

"Yes." David kissed his shy little daughter. "Tamar, too. Boys, I want you to be good soldiers until we see each other again." The simultaneous responses of 'yes, Father' brought a broad smile to

167

David's face. "Do as your mothers tell you. Remember, all soldiers have to obey orders. No teasing Tamar. No war games inside the house. No slipping away to swim in the stream without permission. Do I have your solemn promise?"

"We promise," the three boys chorused.

David took each of the baby boys in his arms, kissed them, and handed them back to Haggith, Abital, and Eglah. He patted Michal's nephews on their heads and told them to take care of their aunt.

Bird ushered the children out with their attendants. The king embraced his wives, and spoke briefly but optimistically to each one. Meanwhile, Abigail deftly guided wives out the door after each one said goodbye to David.

When only Michal and Abigail remained, he took Abigail into his arms and told her not to worry. "This won't be another Ziklag," he assured her. "I'm leaving Eliab here to manage things. I'll send a messenger to him from the battlefield every evening, and he will dispatch a messenger to me each morning. If you need anything, go to Eliab."

"Be careful, my dear husband." Abigail's voice trembled. "God be with you."

Michal was thrilled to be alone with David. Her heart soared when, instead of embracing her, he took her by the hand and led her toward his chamber.

"If Eliab stays behind," she asked, "who will be your right hand?"

"Joab."

"I don't like him," Michal said without thinking.

"Naturally. Because of what he did to Abner." David used the small oil lamp he carried from the table to light a larger lamp in his chamber.

"It's more than that." She shook out her hair. "I don't trust Joab."

David chuckled. "To tell the truth, I don't much trust him, either. But he and his brother Abashai are two of the best soldiers I've ever seen. I can depend on their loyalty because of our blood ties. They are as cunning as Abner was in his prime, and almost as brave as your brother Jonathan. I need Joab, and so I tolerate him."

Michal did not want to talk about war or politics. She wanted David to give her a son. She looked at her husband from beneath her

168

eyelashes. "Please be careful, dear husband. I could not bear it if you were to be hurt."

David grinned and stroked her cheek with the back of his knuckles. "I used to count on having to get a son before I died. Now that I have six boys, I suppose I must be more cautious."

"I'm serious. Promise me you will take care of yourself." Michal wanted to beg him to name her son his heir, even though she was not sure what that would mean. But her first priority was to conceive David's male child.

CHAPTER TWENTY-NINE

"For by thee I have run through a troop: by my God have I leaped over a wall…He teacheth my hands to war; so that a bow of steel is broken by mine arms." II Samuel 22: 30, 35

A FEW DAYS after King David said his goodbyes to his family, Michal awoke before dawn. She was not sure if her own restlessness or the sounds of men talking in the courtyard roused her.

One look from the window told her the march to Jerusalem was beginning. David stood with Joab, Abashai, and other men Michal recognized as the military elite of Judea. Armor bearers were mounted nearby, each holding the reins of his master's war horse.

Michal drank in the sight of her husband dressed for battle. If ever a man looked like a king, it was David. Although not quite as tall as King Saul, David's regal bearing, handsome face, and muscular body combined to present the perfect image of a man born to rule. Soon he would stand once again in her homeland of Israel. She prayed no harm would come to him. Somehow, her husband's absolute fearlessness infused Michal with the same confidence.

Before long, the group in the courtyard began to disperse. The men who were dressed for battle swung themselves onto the backs of their waiting horses. As the first rays of dawn turned the Judean sky the color of a Rose of Sharon, Princess Michal watched King David ride toward his destiny in the city of Jerusalem. The king's brother Eliab stood silently in the courtyard with a domestic servant.

While the long column wound its way through the northern gate of Hebron and out of sight, Michal was comforted by the measured rhythm of her people's traditional blessing: *The Lord bless thee and keep thee: The Lord make his face shine upon thee, and be gracious unto thee: The Lord lift up his countenance upon thee, and give thee peace.*

"God be with you, my beloved husband," she whispered.

The awakening household buzzed with the news that the men were gone to war. Despite the presence of servants, children, and wives, a sense of emptiness hung over Hebron. It was as if David's departure stopped the heartbeat of the household. No one made extended plans. Everything was prefaced with "When the army returns", "After the men get back", or "When my husband comes home."

"I forgot how difficult this waiting is," Abigail said. She brushed back a stray lock of hair as she picked at her food.

"Can't be helped." Bird eyed Abigail's half-eaten portion of stew. "Men go and fight while the women sit and fret. That's the way it has always been. Always will be. Are you going to eat that?"

"Take what you want. I'm not hungry." Abigail pushed her bowl away.

"Thank you." Bird dug into Abigail's lentil broth. "Why are you so worried? David has won plenty of battles. This one won't be any different. They will surrender or he'll bash in their skulls. Maybe both. And then he'll come home, and bring us gifts, and make us laugh."

"I truly don't know why he must keep fighting." There was an unusual edge in Abigail's voice.

"That's what kings do," Maachah said. "They make war."

Abigail frowned. "Kings sit at the gate and dispense judgment. They care for their people. They do many things. Why must they also go off to war all the time?"

"They fight to hold onto the right to exercise their power to judge." Maachah looked around. "Am I not correct?"

"Of course," Haggith said immediately.

"Well said, my lady," Abital agreed without looking up from the face of the infant son in her arms.

"I can't help but worry about him," Abigail continued. "What if he's wounded, or..." She looked toward where the children sat playing. "I want him home with us. I don't know how much of this I can bear."

"Oh, come now, Abigail," Maachah reasoned, "David has only been gone for one day."

"And how many more days before he returns?"

"What would you have him do then?" Maachah shot back. "Sit quietly in Judea for the rest of our lives? Someday give his son a kingdom that's nothing more than what he himself started with?"

Michal kept her eyes down, while she followed the conversation with growing interest. The normally unflappable Abigail was agitated this evening. She was normally so able to meet any challenge flung in her path. With David out of the house and certainly in danger, Abigail seemed almost unable to cope.

Bird took the situation at face value. In her country-girl way, she went placidly about her business, concerned more about what to have for dinner than the nature of kings' obligations. Abital and Haggith didn't seem to know their thoughts until Maachah told them what they should be. As the senior wife, Michal felt she should step in. Yet why should the women listen to her, and what wisdom did she have to share anyway? Abigail's worries were well founded. On the other hand, Maachah was correct—war was sometimes necessary. However, her obvious ambition for Absalom undercut her logic.

As the bickering continued, Michal's attention drifted. She wondered how far the army traveled since this morning. Could they have reached Mount Zion? No, they would stop and camp somewhere south of there, as close as possible without being detected. Leaving some distance between themselves and Jerusalem would preserve the maximum amount of daylight to engage the enemy the next day. How strange it was to think of the Judeans as 'us' and her own people as 'the enemy.'

How different things might have been if Jonathan were alive. Michal was certain her favorite brother and her husband would never have fought against each other. She remembered David's words to the bounty hunters a few days ago. He said he executed an Amalekite who killed King Saul. Did that same man take Jonathan's life? When the time was right, she would ask David to tell her the story of her father's last battle. She hadn't wanted to speak of the king's death on the last night she and David were together.

The sound of her name pierced her reverie. "What do you think, Michal?" Abigail asked. "Is it right to make war against our own people?"

Michal was pleased to have her opinion sought, even though she knew Abigail was merely seeking an ally against Maachah. "David had to go," she answered.

"But why?" was Abigail's shocked question.

"David is carrying out God's will for him to rule Israel."

Maachah rolled her eyes. Abigail looked pensive.

No one is entirely satisfied by what I said, Michal thought. *But then no one completely disagrees, either. And one or two have no idea what I mean. I'm becoming my mother.*

When the silence dragged on, she asked no one in particular, "Has today's messenger arrived?"

"A soldier rode into the courtyard just a few moments ago," Amnon announced proudly. "He talked to Uncle Eliab."

"What did he say?" Bird asked her son.

Amnon's eyes were wide. "The soldier said, 'I bring greetings from your king, sir', and he jumped off his horse." Amnon hopped forward to emphasize his point.

"What else?" Maachah pressed.

"I don't know." Amnon grinned.

"Absalom," Maachah addressed her boy, "did you hear any of this?"

"Only what Amnon already said. After that, Uncle Eliab and the soldier went into the public chamber."

"You should have followed them inside, or listened at the door," Maachah said sharply. She glanced around at the other women and smiled. "So we could all know."

Michal drank the last swallow of her wine. So far, so good, she thought. It would have to be enough that the promised messenger arrived and no alarm was raised. Some day the struggle between Israel and Judea would be over, and she would make a pilgrimage to Jerusalem. There she could go to the Holy Mountain and tender an offering of thanksgiving to God for David's victory. Maybe she would also present a sacrifice to celebrate the birth of the son she prayed was growing inside her.

Later that evening, the sound of soft rain interrupted Michal's sleep. She listened to the raindrops falling on the rooftop and wondered if her husband was safe tonight. Was he slogging through a muddy field—hungry, wet and tired? Wherever David was, she hoped he would spare a thought now and then for her.

CHAPTER THIRTY

"...and they anointed David king over Israel. David was thirty years old when he began to reign,..." II Samuel 5:3,4

THE DAYS PASSED slowly. Michal was disappointed when, a few days after the men rode out to war, her monthly time of bleeding came upon her She comforted herself with the thought that Abigail was older than she when Daniel was born. She viewed her bleeding as a delay in her plans, not a change. She would have to bide her time and become pregnant when David returned home.

Michal understood the other women's apprehensions, but most of the time she did not share them. David's venture was ordained by God, and she was confident of the outcome. Occasionally, when she endured a bad dream or a sleepless night, she wavered. However, rest, daylight, and meditating on God's miracles restored her faith.

Abigail continued to be easily flustered, and occasionally short-tempered. She turned from her loom as she and Michal toiled in the fabric workroom. "I think I will slap Maachah if I hear her tell Absalom that he's going to be king just one more time," she fumed. "What makes her so sure our husband would favor her disobedient son over Amnon, or even Daniel?"

"It could be she has hopes her son could reign in Geshur." Michal glanced toward the doorway to make sure she and Abigail were alone. "I agree with you. She should not make so definite a promise to him. Still, each of David's sons must be brought up knowing he could be king someday."

"All six sons?" After a short pause, Abigail added, "And God willing many more yet to be born."

Michal did not look up from her knitting. "Of all my brothers, there was one everyone agreed would never reign, and that was Ishbosheth. Yet he became king. There was no doubt my brother Jonathan was the most worthy of my father's sons. But Jonathan never sat on the throne so much as one day. So, you see, we never know what will happen."

"Tell me, Michal. Do you truly believe the prophet Samuel foretold David's rule over Israel?"

"Yes, I believe prophets are sometimes given a vision of what lies ahead." Michal stopped knitting, looked at Abigail, and smiled. "Of course, Maachah is not exactly my idea of a prophet."

Both women laughed. Michal gazed unseeingly at the doorway. "It's a strange thing about prophesies being fulfilled. I don't completely understand how they work, and maybe no one does. People look ahead with what they think is knowledge. Then events unfold precisely as was said, and yet not at all as everyone expects. Do you know what I mean?"

"No." Abigail's shuttle worked back and forth between the cords on her loom. "I only know there are days when I don't think I can stand the sound of Maachah's voice. And Abital and Haggith make things worse, behaving as though every word that drops from Maachah's mouth is a precious jewel."

"What was that noise?" Michal tucked her work into her knitting bag.

Abigail sat still and cocked her head. "I hear nothing. What did it sound like?"

"A shout. In the distance. Maybe it was nothing," Michal said. She sat motionless for a moment. "Let's go and have a look from the rooftop."

The two women made their way through Michal's bedchamber. Michal led the way, driven by a feeling as much as by the peculiar noise she heard. Now there were only the normal sounds of workaday Hebron. Here and there a sheep bleated while merchants hawked their wares in the streets.

"In the distance, beyond the gates, there is dust. Look." Abigail pointed.

"Yes, you're right." Michal squinted in an attempt to see more clearly.

"Soldiers, perhaps?" Abigail's voice quavered slightly. "Our men cannot be coming home so soon. But, who could be approaching?"

Michal's mind raced. Could David's army have taken Jerusalem so quickly? If not... No, she must not allow herself to think of the alternative.

Abigail and Michal stood with their eyes fixed on the moving cloud of dust. After what seemed a long time, mounted soldiers became visible. A lone horseman rode ahead of the column.

"David," Abigail said, her hand at her throat.

Michal looked at the advancing soldiers. She could not see their faces at this distance, but they were not approaching at a gallop as if being pursued. No, they rode along at an easy trot. Men sat tall. They did not slump against their horses' necks. They wore the unmistakable air of a victorious army.

"He has done it!" Michal shouted. "David has taken Israel!"

"How can you tell?" Abigail received no answer to her question. Michal was already racing down the steps.

The courtyard was quiet when Michal arrived. Eliab stood talking with a gardener. Little boys flung dried mud balls at each other from behind two lines of low hedges. A baker was putting fresh bread into the outdoor oven made of stones and mortar.

"Someone's coming," Michal said breathlessly.

Eliab looked briefly in her direction, and then continued his discussion on the pruning of bushes.

David burst into the courtyard. "God has given us victory!" he shouted.

It seemed that everyone in the household suddenly appeared in the courtyard, along with a few townspeople and merchants. David slid from the back of his horse and tossed the reins to the gardener. He clapped Eliab on the back and embraced him. Michal stood as if rooted to the earth. She could not take her eyes from her husband's triumphant face. She wanted to run to him and fall into his arms. Such an open display of affection, even in this jubilant moment, was unthinkable. Only a harlot would lay hold of a man in public view. No decent wife could humiliate herself and her husband with such behavior.

As more and more people thronged into the courtyard, Michal retreated to her bedchamber's balcony. She found Tirzah standing behind the trellis, taking in the spontaneous celebration in the courtyard below. The other wives were congregating on adjacent balconies. "This is a great day!" Tirzah said.

Seeing Joab and Abashai ride into the courtyard to an approving roar barely dampened Michal's exultation. Shouts and cheers arose at random from the crowd. Armor bearers and stable attendants began to lead the horses away. Servants seemed to appear from nowhere with trays of food, hardly able to thread their way through the multitude that now packed the courtyard.

Sunset did not end the activities. Wine flowed, the food kept coming, and torches provided light. The women went inside, but the excitement in the courtyard was contagious. Bird put the princes to bed, although no one expected they would go to sleep.

The wives gravitated to Bird's bedchamber. Abigail's eyes glistened with tears. Little Tamar clung tightly to the tunic of her mother, Maachah. Even the deathly-pale Abital ventured from her bed, leaning on Haggith for support. "Eliab must have known the men were returning," Abigail said to Bird, "I don't know why he didn't tell me."

Jealousy, Michal thought. Eliab can now tell David how he alone obtained the wine and ordered food to be prepared. She knew that David's elder brother would use any device to bolster his own importance. Could it be that Eliab still deluded himself that he deserved to be anointed instead of David?

"Let's celebrate," Bird said. Not surprisingly, she had some food tucked away in her bedchamber. Maachah remembered a skin of wine that somehow found its way into her possession. When each woman returned with her donation to the festivities, they sat cross-legged against the array of brightly colored cushions in Bird's bedchamber, basking in the euphoria.

"How much territory does Israel possess?" Maachah asked.

"A great deal more than Judea," Michal answered.

Maachah's eyes shone. "Impressive. And taken in such a short time."

"I doubt there was much of a fight. No, thank you," Michal said, refusing the wine a servant offered. "The people of Israel love David. There has been talk of making him king for years, even when my father and brothers were alive."

"True enough," Bird said as she reached for a plump fig. "Even when we were at Ziklag, I heard rumors among the women."

"Did you?" Abigail seemed genuinely surprised.

"You have to talk about something when everybody's at the well drawing water," Bird replied with a shrug.

Maachah took a long drink of wine and motioned for a refill. "Our sons will now ride through the streets with their father in his chariot, while the conquered slaves walk behind them in chains."

Abigail looked stunned, while Michal and Bird broke out laughing. Abital suppressed a grin. Haggith did her best to disguise her giggle as a cough.

"What's so amusing?" Maachah demanded.

"The people of God have not become slaves," Abigail said.

Michal added, "When my father rode through the streets of Jerusalem, he was mounted on the royal donkey. I would expect David to follow that tradition."

"A donkey? The king on a donkey? That's ridiculous." Maachah waved a hand dismissively. "*My* father rides a great Arabian stallion through Geshur. And rest assured, his enemies put their faces on the ground when he approaches, not daring to move until after he has passed by."

"Israelis and Judeans are not enemies." Michal was tired of hearing about Geshur. "We are one nation. God is our master, and the king is the servant of both God and the people."

"Servant!" Maachah spat the word. "That's not how kings behave."

"Yes." Michal refused to give ground. "That is precisely the nature of our kings."

CHAPTER THIRTY-ONE

"So David dwelt in the fort, and called it the city of David. And David built round about from Millo and inward." II Samuel 5:9

"THE HOUSE I'M having built will sit in a high meadow above my new capital," David said as he ate the evening meal with his family.

"We're moving from Hebron?" Michal welcomed this news. As soon as David spoke, she realized that this small Judean city could not serve as the unified capital. Naturally, they would move to her homeland. Why did she not realize this before?

"Yes, as soon as possible," David replied. Turning to Abigail, he added, "I want my family in Israel for Passover." David arched an eyebrow and smiled at Abigail. "Do you think it's possible to have the household packed and ready to move in two weeks?"

"Yes, my lord," Abigail beamed. "Most certainly. We will begin making preparations at once. But if plans are just now being made for construction of a house..."

"We'll stay in tents while the house is being built," David said. "I'm having King Saul's old place torn down. The builders will reuse the materials, although I'll order new timbers from Tyre as well. I know Abigail will have the household move organized perfectly." His eyes rested on Maachah. "And that everyone will cooperate by doing what she asks. Eliab will conduct you safely to me."

"You will not travel with us, my lord?" Abigail was clearly disappointed.

David smiled. "No, my dear. Joab and I will leave tomorrow morning. I have urgent business in our new capital city."

After making the announcement that would change their lives, David took his leave of the women. A stunned silence followed the king's brisk departure. Then everyone spoke at once.

"Will we take everything with us, or just a few necessities?"

"What about our animals?"

"I need a new tunic."

"Where will we get enough carts?"

Michal was excited to realize she would again live in the land of her birth. When she had a son, she would take him to the places she knew as a child. Perhaps she would help him explore the little caves beyond the cool mountain stream, where Merab used to wet her feet. Michal was disappointed that David did not give her advance warning her girlhood home was to be destroyed. Perhaps he did not realize that razing the old house was, for her, symbolic of the continuing destruction of her family and everything reminiscent of King Saul's reign.

"What is this new country like, this Israel?" Maachah asked.

"You've never been to Jerusalem for Passover?" Bird looked almost amused.

"Of course not. Have you?"

"My father took us there when we were children," Bird replied.

"It is the most beautiful place on earth," Michal cut in. "The city of Jerusalem sits on a high plateau ringed by mountains. You'll love it."

The next day, Abigail set to work organizing the wives. "Let's stop all planting in the gardens. Then we'll see what seeds, cuttings, and plants we can take with us to our new home. Bird, would you figure out how many carts will be needed for the children, their clothes and bedding, and any other of their belongings we will take?"

"I'm on my way." Bird was already moving toward the children's bedchamber.

"What will we wear when we enter the city?" Maachah asked.

"We'll dress the children in their best garments. The same for us, I suppose. There's no time to worry about clothing."

"Something modest," Michal said, remembering Maachah's dance clothes. "I plan to wear a plain tunic and headdress. Then a shorter wrap, with a contrasting border." In truth, she already knew she wanted to wear the blue-green tunic the color of her eyes in the sunlight, along with a headdress of that same fabric. Her wrap would be her favorite—deep green with fine embroidery embellishments around its wide border.

Maachah cocked an eyebrow. "And your best jewelry?"

"Yes," Michal said. "The people will want to be proud of the way we look."

"Abital, do you feel strong enough to oversee packing in the kitchen?"

"I think so, my lady." Abital glanced toward Maachah as if to pick up a hint as to what she should do.

"Good," Abigail continued. "See what we need to take, and how many carts will be required. Remember, the cooks must have access to the things they need for our meals along the way." She paused and chewed her bottom lip. "I'm guessing we will leave early in the morning and arrive in the late afternoon or evening. We could be delayed along the way, so let's be prepared. "Haggith, my dear, please inventory the store rooms and household goods. Bird, you can use bedding to cushion carts for the babies. Michal and I will pack the workroom tools, our fabrics, dyes and pots, twine and yarn. Maachah, would you mind helping Abital in the kitchen? Oh, my! There's so much to be done."

The days passed quickly with the women busy from daybreak until well after dark every day except the Sabbath. Everyone seemed relieved when the household move was planned, packed, provisioned, and ready to make the journey to their new home.

Abital, still weak from her long illness, occupied space in a narrow cart with her baby. The other women and children who were old enough would walk most of the way. Anyone who grew tired could ride in one of the family carts, provided there was room. However, nursing mothers would have priority.

Eliab told Abigail to gather David's wives together the night before the move was to begin. "We will leave Hebron at tomorrow's first light," he said. "When we reach the vicinity of our destination, we will stop and make camp. I will send word to my lord the king that we are nearby. When he sends permission, we will enter the city of Jerusalem."

Permission? Michal wondered. *How formal.*

"At that time, I will announce the order in which the family will proceed into the city." Eliab pursed his lips and folded both hands over his rounded belly.

A brief murmur of surprise rippled among the women. Eliab droned on, reminding mothers to make sure their children did not fall behind the caravan, warning about the presence of wild animals that might attack stragglers, and cautioning them that any belongings lost along the way or left behind in Hebron would never be recovered.

"Good evening," he said finally.

"About the order of entering the city—" Maachah began.

"I'll discuss that when we make our final camp." Eliab's smug grin suggested he was enjoying exclusive possession of information.

Maachah continued boldly, "Would not the proper family order be sons first, followed by wives, daughters and finally household servants?"

"We all know what's proper," Eliab answered shortly. "We will be entering Jerusalem in a line two abreast, because of some narrow passages. When we are permitted to go in, I'll tell each of you who your partner will be, and who you will follow. There is no need for anyone to know that information in advance. Since I am sure there are no further questions, I'll bid you good evening. At daybreak. Be on time."

Michal and Tirzah went to Michal's bedchamber. In the morning, they would roll up their temporary sleeping mats and stow them in the designated cart.

Stretching out on her bedding, Tirzah whispered, "Your brother-in-law is impressed with his new station in life, is he not?"

"Eliab is just being Eliab," Michal sighed. "Always out to prove he deserves to be ranked above his little brother, David."

"Why is he making such a fuss about who walks in front of whom?" Tirzah continued.

"I cannot say. In truth, there is no decision to be made. The two eldest sons have to be first, the wives must go in rank order, and there's only one daughter. Eliab has a way of making something from nothing." Michal planned to walk all the way to the city. Riding in a cart was dusty, noisy, and reminded her of the long ride out of Gallim. She wished her five nephews could enter Jerusalem as royal sons, but she knew that was impossible. They would bring up the rear, in the vanguard of the household servants' group, accompanied by Rizpah.

CHAPTER THIRTY-TWO

"And David perceived that the Lord had established him king over Israel, and that he had exalted his kingdom for his people Israel's sake." II Samuel 5:12

MICHAL FOUND WALKING through the countryside most enjoyable. Although sometimes the road to Jerusalem seemed to go straight up, the cool weather and slow pace of the caravan made the walk easy for her. Her habit of taking long strolls proved to be good preparation for the journey. Her senses feasted on the sights and sounds of the birds, butterflies and wildflowers, while her mind was preoccupied with thoughts of home.

She thought of the wonderful events that happened to and around her in the past year. Against all odds, she was rescued from the bitterness of Gallim, and her husband welcomed her back to his house. Her nephews were safe in her care. She would live once again in the nation of her birth, and David would rule all of Israel. The land she loved to the very core of her being would now be her home for the rest of her days.

Just one more miracle, Lord, she prayed. *A healthy son is all I need. Two or three would be better, but I only ask for one.*

Michal's times of bleeding came and went while David was taking Israel. That was just as well. How fitting it would be to have her son born in her native land. She wondered how long it would take for the cedars and other building materials to arrive. If her son was born in a tent instead of a palace, so be it.

Several hours into the final day of their journey, the caravan stopped briefly at a cold pool of water to refresh the animals. The little boys begged to get into the water, but could not convince any of the adults to accept the delay they proposed.

"I'm worn out," Bird declared. She dipped the end of her scarf into the water and dabbed at her forehead. "My feet hurt, my back aches, and I have to ride a while in one of the carts."

"You can take my place with Abital," Abigail said. "I'm ready to stretch my legs again. Is everyone else doing all right?"

"I'm fine," Michal replied.

After Maachah nodded in agreement, Haggith and Eglah did the same.

Michal's excitement grew as time wore on. Tirzah brought her food and drink at regular intervals, but Michal resisted her handmaid's attempts at conversation. She maintained a brisk pace that left the other women unable to keep up with her. She wanted to capture every moment along the way to lock away in her memory. When I'm an old woman, she thought, I can tell my grandchildren about this great homecoming journey.

The countryside began to look more and more familiar. Michal thought a peak visible in the distance was sure to be the Holy Mountain, and her heart soared. They passed landmarks with names Michal recognized. When Eliab directed his horse to a watering place, Michal learned the well bore the name of one of her ancestors. At last, her weary feet were walking on ground once ruled by her father. Her happiness overflowed.

"The children are slowing us down," Eliab addressed the group of wives as they drew fresh water. "Put them in the carts."

Michal drank from a hollowed-out gourd and watched Eliab ride away. She did not especially like her husband's eldest brother, but she felt some sympathy for him. How demeaning it was for him to be in charge of the women, servants, and baggage while David reigned as king. If others had compassion for Eliab, Michal did not hear them express it. The wives grumbled about his high-handed attitude. They complied with his demands, but slowly enough to show as much resentment as they could afford to display for their arrogant brother-in-law.

Michal helped get four of her nephews settled among a load of copper cauldrons. However, they could not locate enough additional space for Rizpah and Joel. "If you can keep up the pace by yourself, I'll carry the baby," Michal said.

"Thank you, my lady," Rizpah said gratefully.

Michal nestled her youngest nephew into a sling she made by tying together the ends of her long scarf. She briefly considered putting her bag of emergency supplies into a cart, but decided to keep it with her. Slinging the bag over her free shoulder, she made her way back to the wives' group. Eliab rode by and gave her a critical look. Michal smiled and walked faster. Eliab looked in the other direction and rode on.

He can hardly claim I can't keep up, she told herself.

The road continued to incline upward. Michal started a psalm but soon discovered singing required too much of the breath she needed to keep moving. Climbing the steep grade with Joel in her arms was much more difficult than carrying only her small traveling bag. "Do you like this land where your grandfather was king?" she cooed to the baby.

Suddenly, people were yelling and running toward a cart that stopped the caravan's movement. Michal rushed to join the crowd. She was jostled by servants, wives, and the escorting soldiers. "What happened?" was the question on everyone's lips.

Even before she was able to make her way through the gathering crowd, Michal heard a woman's high-pitched scream over a child's cries of pain. *Was that Abigail's voice?* Her superior height allowed Michal to see a group of stunned servant girls who stood with hands clasped over their mouths. Then she saw Abigail kneeling in the dirt, cradling her weeping son.

Eliab dismounted and pushed his way to the center of the circle. "What is going on?" he asked.

Abigail looked up at him. She choked out the word "Daniel" before resuming her great, heaving sobs.

"Michal, what happened?" Eliab demanded.

Michal stepped forward through the now silent crowd. "I don't know," she replied. "I was walking ahead."

"Daniel fell out of the cart," Maachah said.

"How?" Eliab's eyes were now fixed on Maachah.

"How would I know?" Maachah shrugged. "The boys were playing together, and I suppose he just fell."

"Absalom pushed him," Amnon volunteered.

"That's impossible," Maachah snapped. "I was holding Absalom in my lap. If Daniel was pushed, then *you* must have done it, Amnon."

"We can argue about who's at fault later. We must take care of my baby," Abigail said. She wiped her tears on the same scarf she used to mop blood from Daniel's gashed forehead.

"I'm not a baby," Daniel whimpered.

"You're crying like one," Absalom said.

"Absalom!" his mother chided.

"Well, he is," Absalom insisted. "Listen to him."

Maachah quickly dragged her son behind her, narrowly preventing Bird from landing a slap across the boy's face. While Abigail and two healing servants attended to Daniel, Maachah maneuvered Absalom away from the crowd. Michal jiggled Joel, coolly surveying the cart. Its side would strike Daniel at mid-chest. It would be difficult to fall over such a barrier. Being pushed was no more likely. Perhaps Daniel stood on a tall object inside the cart and lost his balance. That was certainly possible. Michal was skeptical of everyone involved. Absalom obeyed no one except Maachah, who would do anything to advance her son's position. Likewise, Amnon's claim that Absalom pushed Daniel might or might not be true. In Michal's estimation, Bird's son lied as often as he told the truth.

It took time to rearrange loads to allow Abigail and a healing servant to ride with Daniel. Amnon protested against moving into a different cart where Bird was riding, particularly when he realized he would have to sit on his mother's lap. Bird was adamant, and Amnon reluctantly complied.

When the weary travelers made their final camp that evening, Michal learned that the cut on Daniel's head was not nearly as bad as the amount of blood made her think. The worst news was that bones were broken in his right arm and right leg. Unless the arm healed perfectly, Daniel would not be able to wield weapons with skill. If the broken leg caused him to limp, that visible physical defect would be devastating to any chance Daniel might have to succeed David as king.

Michal spent the night near her nephews and Rizpah, as if her mere presence would somehow protect them. She noticed all of the mothers seemed to be keeping a tighter rein on their children. Eliab walked around the camp, letting everyone know he blamed the wives—all of them—for Daniel's injury. No one argued, but Michal was certain David would hold his brother accountable for bringing a royal son to Jerusalem with bruises and broken bones.

Eliab is fortunate the injury did not occur to David's favorite son, Absalom, Michal thought.

The first streaks of dawn found Michal sitting on her bedding wide awake, washed, dressed, and ready to go home at long last. She woke her nephews, gathered them around her, and told them what an auspicious event they would be part of this day. She did not expect the three youngest of Merab's sons to grasp the significance of what she said, but she hoped the two older boys would remember both her words and this occasion for the rest of their lives.

As the sun climbed in the sky, everyone waited for Eliab's order to move forward. When it seemed to Michal as if she sat patiently on the grass for a lifetime, a rider approached. Eliab met him some distance from where the women waited, and the two men talked at length.

Finally, Eliab came to stand near where the wives sat. "The king's household will now enter the city." A cheer rose from every person within hearing distance. Eliab motioned for quiet. "Amnon and Absalom, sons of our lord King David, will lead the procession." Eliab continued, "My lady Ahinoam, mother of our lord the king's, eldest son, and Michal, King Saul's youngest daughter, will be first among the wives, then Maachah, Princess of Geshur, and my lady Haggith, carrying her infant son. My lady Abital will be next, walking beside Eglah."

There were no throngs waiting to greet King David's family as they walked into the city. People who happened to see the carefully arranged procession seemed surprised but friendly. Many shouted a warm 'Welcome', while others cheered spontaneously. Some of the old women wiped their eyes or raised their hands toward Heaven in praise. Michal's heart soared when she heard a woman shout, "Princess Michal".

They wound their way up the hill toward a high meadow, where red anemones were just beginning to appear. Michal thought again how this was one of the happiest days of her life, second only to her wedding day. She waited patiently while carts were unpacked. With Michal's help, Abigail mapped the arrangement of tents to minimize the confusion about who was to settle where.

Rizpah and Tirzah expressed confidence they would have Michal's nephews settled before nightfall. Michal walked around as if in a dream. She wandered through the kitchen tent where servants were already clanging pots together, putting some away and beginning an evening meal in others.

"The tents are not as large as I expected," Maachah said. She glanced up and added, "But I'm sure they will be adequate."

An adolescent girl Michal did not recognize lingered near the women's tents. "You can come over here, child. We don't bite," Bird said.

The girl approached slowly. She looked at Daniel and then at the women with obvious curiosity. "Who are you?" she asked.

"We are the wives of the king," Abigail said gently. "And who are you?"

"I am Kerah, daughter of the chief priest," the girl said. She cast her eyes downward. "I, too, am the wife of our lord King David."

CHAPTER THIRTY-THREE

"And David took him more concubines and wives out of Jerusalem, after he was come from Hebron: and there were yet sons and daughters born to David." II Samuel 5:13

MICHAL AGREED TO show Abigail and Bird the best place to do laundry. It was a swift, shallow bend in the stream behind the meadow.

"When I was a girl, I played in this very meadow," Michal said. "I've always loved it this time of year."

"Too bad the new house will take up most of this ground." Bird was breathing hard from the exertion of their short walk, pulling along bags of laundry.

"Yes. I'll miss the wildflowers," Michal said.

Without warning, Abigail changed the subject. "They did not have a decent betrothal period. How old do you suppose that girl is?"

"She's thirteen," Bird replied. "And she has been bleeding for over a year."

"Thirteen," Abigail repeated. "But how do you know?"

"Simple. I asked her."

"Bird, you didn't. You asked her how long she has bled?"

191

"No." Bird grinned. "I asked her age. She told me the rest on her own. Maachah was skulking around, trying to recruit another follower. So I figured if Maachah can ask the girl a bunch of questions, I can, too."

"Here's the spot." Michal pointed to the place where the stream curved toward the mountains. Several large, flat boulders were visible.

"Good rocks," Bird commented.

Michal was curious. "What kind of questions was Maachah asking?"

"Her usual. She wanted to know about Kerah's family, mostly."

"So what did you hear?" Abigail asked.

"Her father's a very important man, or at least Kerah thinks he is. Respected almost as much as the prophet Nathan in the religious community. She is very devout. She doesn't like Maachah."

"She said that, Bird? That she doesn't like Maachah?"

Bird snorted a laugh. "No, Abigail, she didn't say any such thing. She isn't rude or stupid. But I could tell. There was something about the way she looked at Maachah. I just have a feeling this little girl, Kerah, is not used to kissing anybody's toes."

The women waded into the cold stream. They plunged the garments and bedding into the water. "You were right, Michal. This is a good place. We don't have to bend over to reach the scrub rocks." Bird always appreciated anything that reduced physical labor.

"David should have told us he was taking another wife." Abigail slapped a tunic hard against a flat rock.

Michal agreed, but she could not bear to hear her husband criticized. "I'm sure he would have if we'd been here."

"True enough," Bird said. "I imagine the heathen Philistines didn't give him time to get his house in order before they decided to attack that border town the army has gone to defend."

Abigail pounded the same tunic against the rock several times. "He seems to have found time to take another wife."

"I wonder if Eliab knew," Michal said. "Is it possible he was supposed to tell us?" She liked this idea that just occurred to her.

"Eliab," Abigail said with obvious disgust. "He didn't do anything about Daniel getting pushed out of that cart." The tunic received another round of pounding. "And then he blamed me for letting it happen. He said I should have kept a closer eye on my son. I wasn't even in that cart. And he's the one who made the children get in the carts in the first place."

"That tunic is going to be worn out by the time you get through washing it." Bird took the garment from Abigail and handed her some blankets.

"I can't say that anyone's to blame for Daniel's accident," Michal said cautiously. "But Eliab was responsible for protecting us."

"Of course he was," Abigail agreed. "Daniel and the other boys would have been walking if Eliab wasn't in such a big hurry to arrive at the place where we sat and waited. I told him that. I told him it was *his* fault my little boy got hurt."

"I'm sure he didn't like that." Bird pressed water from an armload of clothing.

"That's when he said my punishment for being a bad mother would be that I would not walk in the group with the other wives, when we entered Jerusalem."

"No, Abigail!" Bird said.

Michal was shocked. "We thought you asked to stay in the cart with Daniel."

"Daniel was sleeping when we came into the city." Abigail hurled a wet blanket against the flat rock. "All Eliab's doing."

Michal mulled things over as she did her share of the laundry. Was Abigail jealous that yet another wife joined them, or merely angry that the marriage came as a surprise? Naturally, she was worried about Daniel's injury. Was that the only reason—the little boy's pain? Or could it be the realization his broken leg might eliminate him from consideration to succeed his father as king?

For Michal, Kerah represented a new rival for David's bed. She vowed to redouble her efforts to attract and hold the king's attention. Surely a child little more than half Michal's age would not know how to vie for a man's affection. At least that was Michal's hope. Between foreign wars and this new wife, she would have to work even harder to seize her opportunities to conceive a son.

"Abigail, it isn't like you to get all worked up. You're always so calm," Bird said as they crossed the meadow with their clean laundry.

"I can't be calm when Daniel's safety is involved," Abigail grumbled.

Michal tried not to dwell on the notion that Bird's optimistic outlook was due to the clear emergence of Amnon as the king's heir. Bird's son was, after all, the eldest of David's boys. Something else scratched at her thoughts. According to time-honored tradition, she was the senior wife. Yet Bird was announced first when they proceeded into Jerusalem. Michal heard Eliab's words again in her mind, "My lady Ahinoam, mother of our lord the king's eldest son, and Michal, King Saul's youngest daughter." Could the inverted order have been nothing more than Eliab showing no respect for protocol?

She soothed herself with the knowledge that she was King Saul's only living daughter. No one else could lay claim to being David's first wife. When she became a mother, bearing the king's son would solidify her position in the forefront of David's women.

They spread the laundry on bushes near the tents to dry. Michal stretched her arms and thought about unpacking her dye pots and fabric tools. A servant walked by, her arms full of pots, and nodded at Michal. "Someone is looking for you, my lady. He went to see your sons."

Michal smiled. Many of the servants in the household referred to her nephews as her sons. She never corrected them.

She knew something was wrong as soon as she saw Rizpah's face.

Adriel stood beside her tent. "Greetings, sister-in-law," he said in a brusque monotone.

"Hello, brother-in-law," Michal replied. "As you can see"—she swept her hand toward her nephews—"your children are thriving."

"Yes, they look well. I must thank you for caring for my sons. I've come now to fetch them home."

Michal's heart stopped. How she prayed this day would never come. Her first thought was to send a message to David asking him to forbid Adriel to reclaim his boys. Without asking, she knew what the king's decision would be. A father's rights clearly outweighed an aunt's. Her only chance to remain part of her nephews' lives was to curry favor with Adriel.

"Certainly, my lord. I trust you will remain with us this evening to give us time to prepare your sons for their journey. We arrived from Judea only this week." Michal smiled what she hoped was her sweetest smile.

"I do not wish to inconvenience you," Adriel replied. "But the king is even now at battle with the Philistines. I must hasten to get my affairs in order so I can join him and engage the enemy. I can send for the boys' belongings later if necessary."

"I understand. Surely we can offer you a meal before you take your leave." Anything to hold onto Merab's sons for another hour.

"Another time, perhaps. I fear we must begin our journey as soon as your servants have tended to my horses."

"Of course." She caught sight of Rizpah's worried face. "Rizpah has been your sons' nursemaid since our time at Hebron. No doubt you will want her to accompany you to tend to little Joel."

Adriel's flat "No" banished the expectant smile from Rizpah's face. "I have taken a new wife," he added.

"I see," Michal said. "Come and bid me farewell, children." She hugged and kissed each boy in turn. The two elder sons accepted her words of love with shame-filled glances toward their father, but the little boys clung to her.

"God be with you and your sons, brother-in-law Adriel," she said, still holding baby Joel in her arms.

"And also with you, dear sister-in-law." Adriel took his child from Michal. "God willing, I will bring my family to celebrate Passover in Jerusalem next year, and we will see you then."

From her vantage point at the top of the hill, Michal watched through tears as her nephews rode down the winding road from the meadow. Joel rested against his father's back in a sling. The two older sons expertly guided their own horses, each boy with a younger brother snuggled against him, holding on for dear life. The two oldest sons already exhibited the straight posture of the soldiers Adriel expected them to become.

Michal remained looking down the road long after her nephews and Adriel disappeared into Jerusalem. She knew it was a sin to hope her brother-in-law would die in battle. Instead, she tried to focus her thoughts on the hope Adriel's new wife would be kind and patient. Too late, she realized she'd neglected to ask the name of the woman who would now be mother to Merab's little boys.

CHAPTER THIRTY-FOUR

"And Hiram, king of Tyre sent messengers to David, and cedar trees, and carpenters, and masons: and they built David an house." II Samuel 5:11

AFTER MONTHS OF construction, King David's house was ready for occupancy. Everyone else seemed to be delighted to be moving to the elegant new dwelling, while a part of Michal mourned the destruction of her old home. Even she had to admit the new palace was magnificent, but it was so different from her father's old palace. David brought materials and craftsmen from near and far to make sure every detail met his exact specifications.

The women's quarters alone had fifty rooms, which Bird predicted was a sign of how many sister wives they would eventually have. Michal could only hope that was said in jest. In addition to bedchambers, there were spacious workrooms, nurseries, a special room for giving birth, and a retreat for the women who were unclean because of their time of bleeding. The rooftop view was impressive, looking up toward the mountains in the back and down on the city in the front.

King David personally designed his huge bedchamber. It was elevated a full story above the rest of the house. The rooftop over the space was accessible only through a staircase inside the king's bedchamber, and was enclosed by a low, notched wall.

The huge public hall took up half of the front section of the palace. The décor was lavish, intended to impress both citizens and visiting dignitaries with the wealth of the kingdom. The household servants who lived in the palace had rooms close to where their duties were performed, near the kitchen, or the stable area. Alcoves in the walls near the palace's elaborate main entrance could provide shelter to the few foreigners who did not have homes in the city.

The move progressed slowly, with each wife responsible for getting her possessions and servants relocated to the new living space. Abigail patiently listened to both sides of numerous disputes among the women over who should get their choice of bedchambers or children's rooms. Finally, Abigail advised the women to remove everything they wanted from the tents before the coming Sabbath.

Abigail gave Michal first choice among the women's rooms, and she selected a corner chamber on the second story at the rear of the palace. She loved the view of the mountains from her window. As a bonus, she had easy access both to the lower tier of the rooftop and to a downstairs back exit from the courtyard. The ante chamber provided ample space for Tirzah, and Rizpah too, if she insisted on tagging along. Abigail and Bird selected chambers not far from Michal's. Maachah was nearer the front of the palace, having expressed her preference for the city view. Abital and Haggith followed Maachah's example by choosing places near the front of the palace. Kerah's rooms were well away from Michal's, further away even than Maachah's. Beyond Kerah's chamber, more rooms awaited future rivals for the king's attention.

"Your bedchamber looks lovely, Michal." Abigail looked around. "You have such an eye for color."

"Thank you," Michal said. "Speaking of color, I want to experiment with some new berries next week. There's a particularly bright shade of blue I've never been able to make."

"You know you don't have to dye or even knit any more if you don't care to." Abigail walked to the window and gazed out. "We have more than enough wealth to buy everything we need in this household."

"Making colors fascinates me. And I like to keep busy. The need for me to work is like a disease."

Abigail laughed. "I understand. It appears that illness has not spread beyond you and me."

"I've noticed our sister wives do appear to enjoy their leisure." Michal took out her prized blue berries from Damascus, and began to separate them into bowls according to lighter or darker hues.

"And I suppose I shall do the same soon," Abigail said, her eyes still fixed on a far-away mountaintop.

It was clear to Michal that Abigail wanted to talk about something. She knew Abigail's way was to wait for questions rather than blurt out information. "What do you mean by that?" Michal continued to sort dried berries.

"I had a long talk with Eliab today," Abigail said. "Or, more accurately, he had a long talk with me."

Michal waited a moment. "And what did our dear brother-in-law have to say?"

"That he is taking over the management of our household, which has become too complex for a woman to handle." Abigail sighed deeply. "That I should stop forgetting to go to meetings and keep the wives from arguing with each other. That I should be more careful not to say 'David' but 'our lord the king,' when mentioning our husband."

Michal heard the pain in Abigail's voice and did not wish to see it reflected in her gentle face. She was happy her hands were occupied during the ensuing awkward silence. Eliab became more pompous and arrogant every day, but it would not be prudent to say so aloud.

"I've been thinking of asking permission to go on a pilgrimage to the Holy Mountain one day next week." Michal kept her eyes on the berries. "Would you like to go with me?"

"Thank you, but no. I have a special assignment I must attend to." Abigail turned away from the window and sank onto a cushion near Michal. "I have been told to get a bedchamber prepared for a new wife."

Michal's hands paused only a moment from the rhythmic tossing of berries into this bowl or that. *Another rival?* She took a deep breath. "Don't tell me he's tired of Kerah already. What's the story on this new wife?"

"I think she's from somewhere north of here." Abigail sounded tired. "Other than that, I don't know."

"I have to remind myself all the time that a king can take as many wives as he wishes," Michal said. "I don't like it any more than you do, but our opinions count for nothing."

Abigail picked up a berry Michal dropped and studied it intently. "And also as many concubines as he wishes?"

Michal stopped sorting and looked at Abigail. "David hasn't—" She could not complete her thought.

"Kerah's handmaiden, Leah."

"I know the girl you mean. Young, dark, very pretty," Michal said. "What makes you think she has become a concubine?"

"She's pregnant with his child." Abigail slumped against a cushion. "I knew Kerah was concerned when she did not conceive immediately. So apparently she invoked the old tribal custom and offered to send her handmaid in her place to the bed of our husband. I meant to say, our lord the king. It is obvious he accepted."

Michal set the berries aside. Making a new color no longer held her interest. "I don't know what to say."

"Nor do I." Abigail brushed her hair back with a hand. "I thought David was different from other men. More noble. I've always known that I cared more for him than he does for me. And I understood you were his favorite. Still, I never thought he would hurt me this way. I even dared to think..." A single tear escaped and rolled slowly down Abigail's cheek. She smiled weakly. "He has never said so directly, but I thought perhaps he loved me."

Michal patted Abigail's arm. She, too, felt like crying. Her trip to the Holy Mountain seemed even more urgent. She would cleanse herself, offer an animal for the priest to sacrifice, and ask God for a son. What could she say to comfort her friend, when her own heart was heavy with sadness?

"I saw Daniel running in the courtyard this morning," Michal said. "He must be completely healed."

Abigail dabbed her face with the end of her scarf. "Yes, it took a long time, but he walks and runs as if nothing ever happened to that leg." She paused. "His arm will never be straight, but he's alive and healthy. I am thankful for that."

"Perhaps he will learn to use a sword with his left hand," Michal said.

"Maybe." Abigail slowly drew herself to her feet. "Thank you for listening to me, Michal. It seems I cannot speak frankly to anyone else these days."

"You can always trust me," Michal assured her friend.

Abigail clapped a hand to her forehead. "Oh, dear. I forgot. I'm supposed to be at a meeting with Eliab and the cleaning staff!" She hurried away.

Michal resumed sorting berries. She knew Eliab disliked Abigail for maintaining he was responsible for Daniel's accident. Lately, there were whispers of a growing rift between Abigail and Bird as well. Did her old friend confide in her this evening to unburden herself about David's misbehavior? Or did she come to complain about Eliab? Or both? The atmosphere of animosity in the new palace was little better than Gallim.

Later that evening, Michal planned to discuss this conversation with Tirzah. They would have to avoid Rizpah, who followed Tirzah around and pretended to be Michal's second handmaid. Rizpah often annoyed Michal, though not quite enough to banish her. The aging Rizpah might starve if she became unemployed. With an abundance of food in the palace, Michal was content to let the poor woman sustain her life at the king's expense.

"Forgive me for my lateness, my lady," Tirzah said breathlessly.

"It's of no matter," Michal said as she began to crush the darkest of the dried berries.

"Rizpah asks your indulgence, also. She has gone to arrange lodging for"—Tirzah said the next two words with obvious pride—"my visitor."

"Visitor?" Michal looked up from the hollowed-out stone she used for making powder for use in dyes. Her curiosity was piqued. Who could this be?

"A woman from Shiloh named Mahlah."

"From Shiloh? How do you know this woman?" Michal felt an uneasiness brought on by her handmaid's bright smile.

"I don't know her, or didn't until today," Tirzah said. "She's a matchmaker. She has asked to speak with you."

"With *me*? But why?"

"I know it's not the way these things are normally done," Tirzah said. "But I have no family remaining. No one. The king is always busy. Mahlah might wait weeks to get to see him. So I thought perhaps..." Tirzah twisted the edge of her scarf in her hands.

"This woman, this Mahlah, is here to arrange a marriage for you?" Michal could hardly believe her ears. David had so many women he rarely invited her to his bedchamber. Adriel had taken her nephews away. Was she now to lose her trusted handmaid also?

Tirzah beamed. "You may remember Joash, the slave who tended the vineyards of Lord Phaltiel in Gallim? The man you helped to escape from that wretched place? His brother has a farm near Shiloh, and Joash works for him as a hireling."

"What do you know of this man?" Michal's thoughts were muddled. Her handmaid's announcement took her by surprise.

"Only that he was never mean-spirited like the other men of Gallim." Tirzah came to sit by Michal. "That he knows everything that occurred between Lord Phaltiel and me. Yet he wishes me to be his wife."

Michal took Tirzah's hand. "If Joash works for wages, he is poor and is likely to have no inheritance. You will be the only wife, and you will work like a slave all of your days."

"Yes," Tirzah replied. "I know what you say is true. If Joash and I can have children and raise them together, that will be worth more than all the treasures of the earth to me. Please, my lady, I beg you on the bones of my mother, Sarah, to allow this marriage to take place."

CHAPTER THIRTY-FIVE

*"My kinsfolk have failed, and my familiar friends have forgotten me." Job
19:14*

ELIAB FINALLY REPLIED to Michal's request for a short pilgrimage,
reluctantly assigning his youngest son, Obediah, to accompany Michal
and Rizpah to the place of worship. Michal avoided any discussion of
her intention to make a sacrificial offering. She planned to make her
own arrangements for the animals she would present to the priest. She
thought her brother-in-law acted out of spite when he set the date for
her pilgrimage on the very day Tirzah was to leave the palace forever.
However, she did not dare to ask for a different date for fear Eliab
would seize on that as an excuse not to let her go to the Holy
Mountain.

Michal entered the courtyard and saw Tirzah dressed in a
traveling cloak, standing quietly with Mahlah. The matchmaker held
the reins of two donkeys—Michal's wedding gift to her handmaid.

Tirzah and Michal held each other for a long time, each wiping
tears when the embrace was broken. "How can I ever thank you for
your generosity?" Tirzah asked.

Michal attempted to speak but could not. She could almost hear her own heart breaking. She removed two gold bangles from her left arm and slipped them onto Tirzah's wrist.

Tirzah stared at the expensive bracelets. "No, my lady, you cannot."

Michal stopped Tirzah's words with two fingers pressed against her lips. "You may need to sell these someday." She clasped Tirzah to her one last time. "God be with you, my sister. May He bless you with many children."

"Thank you." Tirzah brushed away more tears and blinked several times. "Perhaps we can afford to bring our family to Passover in Jerusalem someday, and you and I will talk and laugh with each other again."

"Yes." Michal nodded. "At Passover." The deepening pain in her heart told her she might never again see the woman with whom she had shared the best and worst times of her life.

Michal watched her best friend and the matchmaker walk away, down the road that led to the city gate, each leading a donkey. There were too many unspoken words, Michal thought. *I should have told Tirzah to thank God for the gift of poverty. She may not understand what a great blessing it is that Joash would never be able to support an additional wife. Will she know to cherish the knowledge her husband belongs to her alone?*

"Must you carry that bag with you even today, my lady?" Rizpah's voice broke into Michal's thoughts.

"Yes. I never go out without it." Michal clutched her emergency bag to her breast.

Rizpah shrugged. "The boy awaits us at the gate."

As they went to join Eliab's son, Obediah, Michal thought how she would miss Tirzah, now that her handmaid had walked down the same road of departure that took Merab's sons away. Everyone seemed to assume that Rizpah would now take Tirzah's place serving Michal. She considered searching for someone else, but eventually concluded Rizpah was the most convenient choice. No one could replace Tirzah as a friend, but Michal could depend on Rizpah's loyalty. She resigned herself to alternating between too much pointless conversation and hurt silence whenever she demanded that the talkative Rizpah give her peace.

Michal adjusted her bag over her shoulder, checked her head covering, and focused her thoughts on the place of worship. She chose to make the short trip on foot. It would be an enjoyable walk for her. "I'm ready," she said.

"You are weeping, my lady," Rizpah stated the obvious. When Michal made no reply, Rizpah went on. "Ah, but you had some fine times with Miss Tirzah, no? Do you remember when your brother Ishbosheth lost his pet snake in your mother's bedchamber? She screamed so loud we thought there was a Philistine in there. And then Jonathan, he went over to the woods and got that big rabbit. And he—"

Michal increased her pace. She had her own losses to mourn today without listening to Rizpah's memories. The tears seemed as if they would never stop. Tirzah was on her way to Shiloh. Adriel did not bring his sons to see her at Passover. He'd sent no word since the day he took the boys from Jerusalem. Michal's mother, father, brothers, and sister were all gone. All evidence they ever existed seemed to have been systematically wiped from the face of the earth. David made a concubine pregnant, while she herself had no son. Nothing in Michal's life was turning out the way she thought it should.

The morning was spent by the time they arrived at the Holy Mountain. Michal took comfort from the familiarity of the place. Although everything else in her life changed over the years, this spot remained unaltered from the first time she saw it as a girl.

Here and there, pilgrims pitched tents for temporary lodging. Among the tents, merchants had pens filled with animals suitable for sacrifice—bulls, oxen, red heifers, rams, and lambs. Crates of birds were displayed as well, for purchase by the poorer worshipers. Michal walked through the noisy, dusty market, searching for just the right vendor.

The area was not crowded. A few people wandered around, some striking deals, others passing the time of day in conversation. A group of small boys used sticks to bat rocks into a nearby meadow. After she looked over the entire area and concluded all of the merchandise was essentially identical, Michal and Obediah made their way to a vendor. The man stood by a pen of choice cattle. A woman sat nearby on a stump, engulfed by an oversized cloak. Michal assumed she must be nursing a baby.

"Greetings," Michal said.

"Good morning," the merchant answered.

An old woman started to pass by, but stopped and came to stand very near. "I would like a lamb for a sin offering and a bullock for a peace offering." Michal took out her favorite pair of earrings. "I have these to trade."

The merchant took the earrings and examined them. The old woman who stood near suddenly pushed ahead of Obediah. "Nice jewelry," she muttered. She looked up at Michal. "Surely your husband could purchase animals for you?"

Out of deference for the woman's age, Michal attempted to be polite. "I did not ask my husband to make provision for me." She turned back to the merchant. "These earrings are made from pure gold. The stones are garnets."

The man turned an earring over in his hand. He motioned for Michal to wait, and walked over to the woman and baby. He squatted and spoke in hushed tones with the young mother.

"Why not keep your jewels and ask your husband to get the animals?"

Michal was tempted to tell the old woman to go away and mind her own business. However, she did not want to risk having Obediah report to Eliab that she was rude to a citizen, an elderly one at that. "My husband is away, fighting the Philistines," she replied. "Besides, where is the sacrifice if someone else pays the price?"

The old woman narrowed her eyes and stared at Michal. "Ah, could it be you are a true worshiper? Not just another rich woman trying to buy a blessing from God?"

The merchant returned from his conference at the stump. "All right," he said.

"No!" The old woman seemed to think she could speak for Michal. "You're cheating her. For those earrings you should give her the bullock, the lamb, and eight birds."

The merchant and the old woman glared at each other for a long moment. "She didn't ask for birds. She offered me her earrings for a bullock and a lamb. And I agreed. What business is this of yours?" Then he said, "One pigeon. No more."

The old woman and the merchant ignored Michal and engaged each other in a loud, fast-paced negotiation they both appeared to enjoy. Obediah wandered away. Rizpah shrugged when Michal caught her eye. At last the bargain was settled. The nursing mother put on the earrings, never knowing King Saul had brought them home from some far-away battle. Michal discovered she now owned a bullock, a lamb, and four pigeons.

"I am Tozah. My tent is over there." The old woman gestured toward the valley. "You should stop by before you leave."

"Perhaps some other time," Michal said. "We must get home by nightfall." She was not in the mood to visit, and the words about trying to buy a blessing still rankled her. Nevertheless, the old woman did her a favor by forcing the merchant to strike a fair bargain.

"Next time, then. Anyone can direct you to my tent." Tozah grinned. "I am always here."

Michal and Rizpah followed Obediah to the entrance of the place of worship. Eliab's son was hardly old enough to grow a beard, but he was a male relative. Therefore, he would transact business with the priest on Michal's behalf.

CHAPTER THIRTY-SIX

"And as the ark of the Lord came into the city of David, Michal Saul's daughter looked through a window, and saw king David leaping and dancing before the Lord; and she despised him in her heart." II Samuel 6:16

MICHAL SAT ALONE in her dark bedchamber, looking out toward the mountains but not seeing them. Countless offerings did not produce the son she so fervently prayed for. Wearing face enhancement and less modest clothing did not bring her to David's bed often enough. Imitating Maachah's suggestive walk and flirtatious manner brought occasional success, but there were so many obstacles. David pushed Israel's borders ever outward. His increasing wealth, power, and military might came at the price of extended absences from home.

When the king was in residence, matters of government took most of his time and energy. He spent his mornings at the city gate, listening to citizens' pleas and dispensing judgment. Afternoons were consumed by meetings in the public room of the palace, conferences with military advisors, and visits from foreign kings or their emissaries. Michal could not remember the last time the wives and children enjoyed private time or even a meal with King David.

Wives and concubines competed fiercely for a summons to visit the royal bedchamber. Maachah's dancing was a thing of the past. There was no longer any opportunity to use song, dance, or interesting conversation to gain favor with the king. Flattery and flaunting were the weapons of choice. The clique of young wives led by Kerah would wait for days in a corridor or the courtyard for a glimpse of King David. They would bow, and scrape, and giggle with delight at his smile, all the while slyly seducing him with their eyes. As if that were not bad enough, an even younger group of wives and insolent concubines appeared on the palace rooftop in shocking attire.

How dared they display their shapely bodies, openly discussing how the king would take notice from the vantage point over his elevated bedchamber? Michal seethed each time she saw a servant escort one of the brazen women to the king's bedchamber.

The evening before, Michal returned from the stream at twilight. While mixing colors, she failed to notice the daylight slipping away. She put her pots into the storage alcove inside the courtyard. Although she did not intend to eavesdrop, the hushed voices of women opposite a cluster of bushes caught her attention.

"How old do you think she is?"

"At least thirty."

"Someone told me thirty-*five*."

"No! That old? You can't mean it. At her age she should give up, like those other old rags, and stop making a fool of herself."

"She can't, because she doesn't have any children."

"What? Not even a daughter? Well, then, she's barren. Cursed. She may as well wash that paint off and face facts."

"Maybe she thinks she's like our ancestor, Sarah, who conceived a son when she was ninety."

In the wake of the muffled giggles, Michal walked noisily through the courtyard. She turned to look directly into two stunned faces she vaguely recognized as belonging to concubines. At least they had the decency to drop their eyes.

"Good evening," Michal said evenly.

"Good evening, my lady," they replied in meek unison.

Michal fretted and fumed as she sought the comfort of her own room. This family has become as uncharitable as the house of Phaltiel, she told herself. *Will idol worship be next?* She ate some cheese in her bedchamber and shunned the community meal that evening. She knew it was a mistake to allow her humiliation to remind her of life at Gallim. The evil dreams came less often now than in Hebron, but they still held the power to haunt her.

"*Ah, my beloved wife Michal comes to me with her virginal handmaid. I will take delight from two beautiful women this evening.*" Phaltiel's slurred words flooded into her memory. "*Miss Tirzah, I will command your mistress to demonstrate what I have shown her of the lost arts of Sodom. Then I will repay her with the joy of ministering to you as I teach you what it means to be a woman. Tell me, Miss Tirzah, do you know of the mystical bond between pain and pleasure?*"

"My lady, awaken! It is only a dream."

Michal slowly became aware of Rizpah shaking her shoulder. She sat up in bed, and shuddered as if to chase away every memory.

"Shall I bring you something? You didn't eat enough to keep a squirrel alive this evening."

"No, I don't want anything." Michal was relieved to see shapes of familiar objects in the dark chamber. "Try to go back to sleep, Rizpah. I'm sorry I disturbed you. Thank you for awakening me."

She lay motionless for a long while, giving anyone who may have heard her moans time to resume their night's rest. Then Michal arose from her bed, and sat staring out the window.

In times past, Tirzah would have sat with her. The two of them would have talked about their childhood, or the beauty of the mountains reflecting starlight, or the curious way a beetle ambled across the floor. But Tirzah was gone, and Rizpah could never be an intimate friend.

On another night, Michal might have prayed that the man Joash would be kind, that he would not ask too many questions when the dreams came to terrorize Tirzah, that he would hold his wife close enough to hear his beating heart and whisper that she was safe with him. Now Michal was angry at the Living God who continued to deny her heart's desire for an heir to her father's throne. She would beg no more favors from Him.

Today, there would be a celebration such as the city had never seen. David recaptured the Ark of the Covenant from the heathens. This very morning, the king would bring this most sacred national treasure into Jerusalem. Michal knew she should be elated, but she could find no trace of happiness within herself.

"Ah, my lady, you are up early. You must be as eager as everyone else for the big day to begin." Rizpah bustled about, tidying Michal's already immaculate bedchamber. "The other ladies are already gathering on the rooftop. There's a fine view of the city gate from there. We shall be able to see everything. Will you have some breakfast?"

"No. No, thank you, Rizpah. I'm not hungry."

"It's no wonder you are so thin. You never take enough nourishment. Not at all like your mother. She enjoyed a good meal, even when she was ill." How could this former concubine of King Saul dare to speak of Queen Ahinoam with such familiarity?

"Well, then, shall we go to the rooftop?" Rizpah prattled on. "I have chosen the perfect place for us. It's right near the corner. You should see the finery the lady Kerah is wearing this morning—"

"Go on without me," Michal interrupted.

Rizpah stopped and stared at her mistress. "Surely, you would not chance missing the sight of the Ark coming into the city?"

"No. I will go and sit with Abigail. I can see the gates from her window."

"The other handmaids say my lady Abigail is more confused every day," Rizpah said. "Shall I accompany you?"

"No. Go to the rooftop. And take note of all that happens, in case I miss something."

"Certainly. I shall take care to report everything to you." Rizpah fairly ran out the door.

Michal took a deep breath and forced a bright smile. There was a good chance she would encounter other women in the corridor on her way to Abigail's chamber. They must not see the weight of a heavy heart reflected on the face of King Saul's daughter.

"Good morning, Abigail," Michal said as she entered her friend's bedchamber.

"Good morning, mother," Abigail replied. "Are my brothers all right?"

"Yes, my dear." Michal fluffed the cushions behind Abigail. "Everyone is doing fine."

"My sisters also?"

"Our entire family is in good health and fine spirits. Have you had breakfast?" Michal asked.

"I don't know." Abigail turned to a young woman dressed as a healing servant who stood near her bed. "Have I had breakfast?"

The woman spoke with a strange accent. "Yes. You ate quite well this morning."

Abigail smiled. "I ate quite well. I must be getting better."

Michal nodded and patted Abigail's bony hand. "There's going to be a big celebration at the city gate. Would you like to get out of bed and watch?"

"Oh, yes. But I'll wait for father to come and lift me."

Michal looked toward the healing servant, who shook her head to indicate *no*.

"Yes, of course." Michal kissed Abigail's forehead and walked to the window. "I'll stay with her," she told the healing servant. "You can go to the rooftop with everyone else."

"Thank you, but I am to remain by my lady Abigail's side every moment. King's orders."

Michal wondered why the healing servant did not approach the window. There was plenty of room for both of them to watch the celebration. Before she could ask, the city gates burst open. Trumpets announced the beginning of the historic event. Musicians came through the gates, playing trumpets, drums, harps, and cymbals. They were followed by a choir singing psalms of praise and victory.

After the singers there were dancers who moved in rhythmic abandon to the chant, "We are the People of God". Michal frowned slightly. It annoyed her to know the younger wives whispered that she was old-fashioned. Still, she could not stop herself from thinking the clothing of the dancers could be more modest. The fabric of the women's tunics seemed light and airy. It swayed with their cadenced movements, and swirled up around their calves. She was surprised to see that a man was dancing along with the women in front of the Ark. The male dancer leapt and twirled in garments Michal considered as inappropriate as that of the females. He wore a short, white robe over a shepherd-length wrap around his loins. The robe gaped open, showing the dancer's broad, muscular chest.

Michal froze. She could not speak or even breathe. The male dancer was King David himself, dancing with a troupe of commoners in the street. She was both embarrassed and outraged.

As the Ark moved forward, the people thronging the city gate closed ranks behind it, many of them clapping in time with the music. It seemed as if everyone in Jerusalem was caught up in the jubilation of the moment. King David ripped off his robe and continued to dance with farmers, merchants, children—anyone who happened to be there—wearing nothing but his wrap. Women brushed against her husband's half-naked body, and no one stopped them. Some of those women could be harlots, possibly even foreigners.

Humiliation, jealousy, and rage welled up within Michal. Wasn't it enough that other women infringed on her right to be King David's wife? That concubines sat in the garden of her own home and ridiculed her? That women half her age now suckled their beloved sons while she had none? Unable to bear the scene in the street any longer, Michal ran for the solitude of her bedchamber.

She was too late. Her route was blocked by the crowd moving from the rooftop into the corridor. The press of bodies took her where she did not want to go. In the courtyard, Michal tried to fight her way to a stairway. Just as the railing was close enough to touch, a throng of servants poured down the stairwell, and her opportunity was lost. She was carried along helplessly, through the entrance to the palace, into the street to merge with the mob she saw from Abigail's window.

Michal could not hear over the roar of people shouting. Everything seemed to slow down. She observed herself with detachment. I've been here before, she thought. *When was it?* The sounds of praise faded into drunken curses.

In the darkness, Phaltiel grabbed her by the throat. "Tell me, woman, do you want to know what it is to die?"

From somewhere a voice intruded, "*Run, Michal. Run. Hide. Hurry.*"

I should have been the one found dead the next morning.

Oh, God, forgive me. Why didn't You make me stay and help her? Why do You permit men to do such vile things? Why did You allow me to be such a coward? Why didn't You let me die instead of Sarah?

David stood before her, sweating and smiling. *Or was it Phaltiel?* "How could you disgrace yourself, dancing half-naked with those…those street dancers?" Michal heard herself shout. "My father would never have made a fool of himself like that."

King David's face fell. "In case you haven't noticed, your father is no longer the king. God chose me to be king over His people, and I will worship Him however I please. The rule of the House of Saul is done."

"No. King Saul's grandson will rule. My son will be king after you."

"You have no son. And I don't believe you ever will."

"How can I when my husband spends his seed on concubines instead of wives who deserve to bear sons? Will you take one of those dancers next? Will I see one of those street women lounging on your rooftop tomorrow?" Michal was vaguely aware that people around them were suddenly silent.

"Maybe you will." David's voice grew louder. "And do you know why? Those women think I'm someone special. Do you see the way they look at me? With the same eyes you once had for me, before you were obsessed with producing a royal heir. You care nothing for me now. You have no time to be the lady to my shepherd. No, you must make haste to conceive."

"Liar! You have cast me aside to play with girls younger than your own sons," Michal spat.

David pulled her into an alcove. Michal knew their words could still be heard, but now they were shielded from the stares of the crowd.

"You say I lie?" His voice took on the low, slow quality she knew indicated a cold fury. "Think about it. There used to be poetry in our union. There was a time when thoughts of each other filled our hearts. I knew you wanted me. Me, not what you could get from me. Now you are just like the others. You see a king who may be useful, not a man who gives you pleasure. You use your devices to attack me the way I assault a walled city, thinking only how you can force King Saul's grandson onto the throne."

"You have no right to presume what I think or feel." She wanted to wound him as deeply as he hurt her. "If you knew anything about a woman's heart, Abigail would still be in her right mind."

"How dare you blame me for Abigail?"

"My king." Eliab stood at the edge of the enclosure. He cleared his throat. "It's time for your speech."

CHAPTER THIRTY-SEVEN

"Then king David sent, and fetched him...And Mephibosheth had a young son, whose name was Micha..." II Samuel 9: 5, 12

"RIZPAH? IS THAT you?" Michal cowered in the corner of her bedchamber.

"Yes, my lady. It is I."

The sadness in Rizpah's voice told Michal her handmaid knew what happened. "I suppose you've heard how I disgraced myself by shouting at the king in public."

"The news swept through the palace like a fire."

"Where will you go?"

Rizpah shrugged. "I'll stay in the palace if possible. I've done some favors for the baker's helper. She will keep me in food for a few days. Maybe I can serve a concubine, or perhaps a group of them. If not, I will try to make my way back to Judea and impose myself on my sons. What about you?"

"I'm hoping the king will not have time to issue a divorce decree for another day. With good fortune, maybe a bit longer because of the continuing celebration over the Ark. I think I will be able to spend tonight here."

"And then?" Rizpah put a hand on her mistress's shoulder.

Michal patted the hand. "The only family I have are Merab's little sons and my brother-in-law. I don't know where Adriel lives, and I doubt he would give a divorced woman so much as a cup of water." Michal willed herself not to cry. "There's an old woman named Tozah who lives near the tabernacle and fears no man. She may give me lodging for a night or two. If David allows me to keep my jewelry, I can live for a while by selling things carefully. I'm sorry I spoiled everything for you as well as myself, Rizpah."

"I've had hard times before. I know how to get along on almost nothing. But you, my lady…"

Michal sighed. "Have you ever been divorced?"

"Indeed so," Rizpah said. "When I was a bride of six weeks, I made my husband a raisin pie for his evening meal. Turned out he hated raisins. Who knew? We argued. He tossed me out into the street that night."

"How dreadful." For the first time, Michal felt sympathy instead of resentment for Rizpah.

"Maybe I deserved it for arguing. Anyway, I learned." Rizpah held an instructive finger in the air. "I have never made another raisin pie."

Michal tried unsuccessfully to force a smile. "There are caves on the other side of the stream where I dye yarn. Used to dye yarn. If Tozah refuses me, I could go there for shelter."

"Perhaps," Rizpah agreed. "Caves are nice and cool in the summer. You do have to be cautious about wild animals, though."

"You don't have to wait until…" Michal closed her eyes. "…until the king puts me away. If an opportunity arises, you must go ahead and take it."

"Thank you, Lady Michal." Rizpah began to gather her makeup cases. "If you would not be offended, I may go down and visit with the young concubines for a while. Perhaps I will show them what a skilled maid can do to enhance faces."

"Go. I wish you success."

Michal was relieved to be alone, although she liked Rizpah more this evening than ever before. She remembered how incensed she was to see her husband mingling with common harlots. Now she herself might soon be one of them. She suspected Rizpah resorted to prostitution more than once. Somehow, the occupation that was offensive before seemed tragic now.

For the first time, Michal was glad her parents and brothers were dead. They would have been shamed beyond words by her behavior. A subject who publicly scorned the king could be stoned to death, even if that subject was a member of the king's family. Furthermore, a decent woman did not speak to her husband in private as she had in public. She would have given anything to go back to yesterday, live that day again, and do everything differently. The worst part would not be the divorce. It was the nagging suspicion the hurtful words David spoke to her were true.

Michal stayed in her bedchamber and wept for the next two days. On the third day, with no handmaid to care for her needs, hunger forced her to join the other women during the evening meal. She went late and sat with the concubines, eyes downcast. No one spoke to her, but she was not refused food.

The next day, she ventured to Abigail's chamber.

"Good morning," Abigail said brightly. "Who are you?"

"Good morning. I am Michal." She smoothed Abigail's hair and swallowed a sigh. *The only friend I have left doesn't know my name.* "I trust you are feeling well."

"Please tell them to be quiet," Abigail said in the direction of her attendant.

"Who?" the healing servant asked.

Abigail pointed to an empty spot. "Those little boys playing there. One of them is my son. I forget his name."

"Daniel," Michal said, even though there were no children in sight.

"No," Abigail corrected her. "I think my son is called Nabal. I have seven sons. And five lovely daughters."

The sadness of Abigail's mental condition did nothing to lift Michal's mood. When she emerged from Abigail's bedchamber, she saw Bird and Maachah in the corridor. The two women looked at Michal and stopped talking. Bird turned and walked quickly in the other direction. *My old friend's coldness has now turned to outright rejection,* she thought.

"Good morning," Michal mumbled as she passed Maachah.

Maachah nodded a noncommittal greeting.

The celebration of the return of the Ark of the Covenant ended. The Sabbath came and went. A week after the public argument, Rizpah returned to Michal's ante chamber. When no one objected to Rizpah's presence, she resumed her duties as Michal's handmaid.

Bird, who now insisted on being called Ahinoam, distanced herself even further from Michal. Instead of the previous curt greetings, Bird refused to acknowledge Michal at all—conveniently looking in the other direction when they encountered each other. In the context of palace logic, that made sense to Michal. The mother of the heir apparent would naturally avoid fraternizing with a shamed wife. Even though she understood Bird's position, she found her old friend's snubs painful.

"Don't you know you shouldn't sing to me?" Michal asked the chirpy bird who sat on her window ledge one morning. The bird turned his head this way and that before he flew away. She watched the creature soar into the bright sunlight of a cool, crisp day and wished she could grow wings to carry her away. Bored with her inactivity, Michal wondered what prevented her from dyeing yarns. She could think of no obstacles other than those inside herself.

Donning a stained old tunic, Michal gathered her supplies, and walked to the stream. The dyes did not understand that she had done something terrible. They mixed and reacted exactly as they did before she was disgraced. The living waters of the stream did not dry up because of her shame. The squirrels and rabbits treated her with the same wariness they always displayed.

Animals are not people, she reminded herself. Still, they were God's creatures. And they did not shun her.

God, she thought, peering into the Heavens. How did Her Creator regard her? Everything that was dear to her was lost, even her husband. The Almighty One refused to answer her prayers for a son, and she refused to speak to Him.

"If You cared for me at all," she said, gazing into the clouds, "You would not have left me so alone. Even outcasts need someone to love them."

It occurred to Michal if she could walk out the back gate of the palace to the stream and return unchallenged, she might also be able to walk out the front gate and go to the place of worship. But for what purpose?

Two weeks after her outburst, Michal sat knitting in her bedchamber when a chilling summons came. She heard an unfamiliar messenger speaking with Rizpah. "The Princess Michal, daughter of King Saul, is commanded to report immediately to the south public chamber anteroom, by order of King David."

So formal. Michal breathed deeply and composed herself, waiting for Rizpah to come to her.

"My lady," Rizpah said sorrowfully.

"I know." Michal picked up her emergency bag, expecting she would not return to the women's quarters. "I heard." She took one last look around her room. Would someone dye the waiting yarns? She could not carry her knitting supplies, let alone dye pots or extra clothing. "I will never forget your faithfulness, Rizpah. Thank you."

"Shall I go with you?"

"No, you've done enough. Goodbye." They embraced, and Michal followed the messenger girl to the designated chamber.

A young man sat at the far end of the room. So, she thought, my husband assigned some poor unknown government official to deliver the divorce decree. Perhaps he thinks I will become hysterical, or lash out at him again. She regretted there was no opportunity for an undeserved chance to apologize.

As she walked to where the official sat, Michal thought he looked familiar somehow. *What kind eyes.* For a moment, she was overwhelmed with the sensation she was about to receive judgment from her brother.

No, if Jonathan were alive, he would be twice this man's age. Besides, the hair was wrong, too dark. She clutched at her throat, afraid she was descending into the pit of madness to join Abigail.

"Forgive me for not rising to greet you." He smiled, but sounded nervous.

I am the one about to be divorced, Michal thought. *No need for your voice to break, young man.* Nevertheless, she appreciated any glimmer of compassion. *Why was the situation difficult for him? Perhaps this was his first divorce decree.*

She knelt before the official. "Good evening. I am Princess Michal of Israel, daughter of King Saul, wife of my lord King David."

Unshed tears filled the young man's eyes. His mouth moved, but no words came out. Michal waited, calmly observing her judge. She saw crutches leaning against the wall behind him. Perhaps he could not walk without them. *Lame. Fortunate to be employed. Otherwise, he would live on what he could beg in the street.* Finally he cleared his throat and spoke. "I am Mephibosheth. My son, Micha." He gestured toward a solemn little boy.

How odd to see a little boy sitting nearby. A child of perhaps three years, she thought.

It was not appropriate for this man to introduce himself, much less his child. He was obviously a novice. However, if this civil servant wanted to prolong the proceeding for some unknown reason, why not accommodate him? If he had a soft heart, he might allow her to wait until morning before departing the palace.

She turned to the child. "Micha. That's a very nice name. Unusual. Sounds just like my name without the 'l' on the end."

"Yes, of course," Mephibosheth said. "I shouldn't have named him for a living person, but when he was born I thought you were dead."

Michal attempted to make sense of what she heard. "My namesake? This darling little boy?"

"Micha, for my father's favorite sister Michal. I am your nephew, Jonathan's son. No one told you?"

Michal adjusted her position from kneeling to sitting. "No. I thought—" She stopped herself. He didn't need to know she came here expecting to be divorced. She scooped up little Micha and wrapped him and his father in a heartfelt embrace.

CHAPTER THIRTY-EIGHT

"Now when Mephibosheth, the son of Jonathan, the son of Saul, was come unto David...David said unto him,...Fear not: for I will surely shew thee kindness for Jonathan thy father's sake, and will restore thee all the land of Saul...As for Mephibosheth, said the king, he shall eat at my table, as one of the king's sons." II Samuel 9: 6-11

KING SAUL'S FORMER landholdings were turned over to Mephibosheth, free and clear. David all but adopted Michal's nephew. The fifteen sons of Saul's old servant Ziba pledged their allegiance to Mephibosheth and took over management of his farms.

King David's generosity to Mephibosheth was the talk of the palace. It overtook the scandal caused by Maachah's teenaged daughter Tamar going out with four finger-widths of hair showing outside her headdress, twice the customary two-finger maximum.

Michal was not surprised to find her treatment by the other women improved because of her association with Mephibosheth. Her nephew might be lame, but he dined nightly at the king's table, seated among the princes. Rizpah reported whispers continued within the women's quarters that Michal should have been divorced or stoned or both. Yet no one dared to speak against her openly. Maachah suggested Michal was spared because she was the daughter of a king. Kerah said Maachah merely wanted to make herself seem important, that being a princess was no more impressive than being the daughter of the chief priest. Michal kept the other wives and the concubines at arm's length. She could not forget that Rizpah was the only member of the household who gave her comfort when she was out of favor with the king.

Mephibosheth began to come to the palace each afternoon, visiting with Michal in the shaded courtyard until time for the evening meal. Although he moved slowly and could not mount a donkey without assistance, his mind was exceptionally nimble. He seemed to delight in making people laugh, especially his aunt. On the occasion of his first visit, Michal's heart ached to see how useless her nephew's legs were. He leaned on crutches, each made from a smoothed sapling, cut to the correct length for the intersection of two main branches to fit his hands.

"Why did you decide to come to Jerusalem?" she asked him.

"The decision was made for me," he replied as he maneuvered himself to a sitting position on the shady bench beside Michal. "King David's emissaries searched Israel and Judea from one end to the other, looking for any remnant of King Saul's family. Naturally," Mephibosheth said with raised eyebrows, "I assumed his objective was to kill me. I say naturally. What else would I think, given our family history?"

"It was absolute chaos when we got the word of the defeat of Israel's army at Gilboa. People were yelling that the city would come under siege, the palace would be raided, and we would all be hacked to death. I remember those words specifically—'hacked to death.' I heard someone say my father and grandfather were dead. It was all terrifying for a four-year-old." Mephibosheth took a sip of cool water and glanced to the spot where Micha sat happily pouring dirt into and out of broken pieces of kitchen pots. "May God protect my son from such horrors."

Michal remembered how King Saul's palace seemed impregnable when she lived there as a girl. "It must have been terrible for you."

"For everyone. I never saw another member of our family again from that day until the night I met you. A man ran through the courtyard yelling, 'They are leaving. Go now.' My nurse grabbed me and ran for the carts, which were already on the road. The men had them hitched to horse teams, but they were designed to be ox carts. So they were out of control on the steep downhill slope." He indicated the angle of the road with his hand. "I don't know exactly how it happened. Maybe there were loose rocks by the roadside, or maybe my nursemaid misjudged the speed. I only remember I hit the ground hard and it felt as if someone had chopped my legs off at the ankles."

Micha held up a fat beetle and opened his mouth wide. "No, don't eat that!" Mephibosheth exclaimed. Michal sprang up and took the beetle. "Thank you. He'd have swallowed it by the time I got there. He's eaten insects before. So maybe they're not all that harmful." He spread his hands wide. "To continue with my story, someone dumped me in a cart and I started screaming. But everybody was screaming. I don't know if I passed out or just went to sleep. When I woke up, I was at a farmhouse with a stable boy and the farmer's family. I thought I would die from the pain in my legs."

"I'm so sorry." Michal dabbed at the tears that flowed at the thought of Jonathan's little boy, hurt and abandoned. What was she doing in Gallim the day he was injured?

"Don't be sorry," Mephibosheth said heartily. He gestured toward his feet. "These curled up ankles probably saved my life. As far as I know, I was the only male member of our family in that caravan who survived. All of the others were hunted down and killed, either by foreigners or by Uncle Ishbosheth's men." He shifted his weight to one side, resting a hand on one knee.

"The stable boy who took care of me was incredible. At the time I thought he was a man, but he was only eleven himself. He carried me around on his back, until I was able to walk again with the help of the sticks he'd talked some kind-hearted carpenter into making for me. Smart, too. Ep knew we were in danger. Every few weeks, he'd say, 'Time to move on,' and we would. I've seen more of this country than any wandering merchant you know." Mephibosheth tapped Michal on the arm. "The stable boy told people I was his little brother. My name was 'Bo', never Mephibosheth, and his was Ep. If somebody questioned him, Ep told them we were too poor to afford longer names. What an imagination! In one town we'd be orphans going to Damascus. Next place, we were headed to Jericho to join our parents. He was my protector and my best friend. Friendship was all I could give back to him then." Mephibosheth raised a finger. "Now he's a rich

222

man. Anything I have is his for the asking. Including what he talked about from Megiddo to Beer-Sheba and back—that fast Arabian stallion."

After wincing and shifting his weight, Mephibosheth continued. "Eventually, we began to stay in one place for months, then years at a time. Ep found a young widow and wanted to get married, but first he made her agree I could live with them. By then we had learned to make tents. We went east, mostly stayed in desert country, where there was a greater demand for our work. I never expected to get married. One day Ep met a fellow who offered to sell him his blind daughter. Ep asked if I wanted her. I said 'Yes, provided she is a Hebrew woman,' and between us we came up with enough shekels to buy me a wife."

"Micha's mother?" Michal asked.

"Yes. Norah. I think she had no eyes because extra room was needed to accommodate her huge heart. I loved her, and you may not believe this, but I know she loved me. She died giving our son life. I was constantly frightened for Micha. A king might not look on a lame man as a challenger, but my healthy son was in danger. When I tried to get Ep to move again, his wife wouldn't hear of it. He found a place for me to go with Micha, and helped me get there. Then one day, two men came to the house where I was staying and asked me to come with them, saying King David wanted to see me." Mephibosheth slapped an insect away from his face.

"Once again, being lame was an unknown advantage. I would have taken Micha and run away. But I knew we had no chance, so I surrendered. My best hope was for a merciful, private execution." Mephibosheth pried open a pistachio shell and popped the nut into his mouth. "It took weeks to get here from Lodebar. I have to admit, I slowed us down as much as I could. I kept praying for a chance to escape, or for Ep to come and rescue us. But we kept pressing on."

"You believe in prayer?" Michal asked.

"Most certainly. Another advantage of lameness. My weakness is undeniable, and so I have learned to depend on the One who is strong. You do not believe?"

"God hates me," Michal said angrily. "He never listens to my prayers. He has singled me out for harsh treatment, and I don't know why."

"Ah, I see now. You have told Him, perhaps many times, how your life should be arranged. Yet He fails to follow your instructions. Why would anyone pray to such a disobedient God?"

"You mock me, Nephew."

"Not at all. I have been through my own valleys of doubt and anger. I thought God was a fine master when I lived in the palace as the favored grandson of the mighty King Saul. When I woke up in that farmhouse, I asked God why He let my feet get crushed. He could have no reason for that, except to make me lame for the rest of my life. Why did my family abandon me? I was just a boy. Why did so many dreadful things happen to me?"

Mephibosheth drank from his water jar again. "So, now, would it be better to be lying dead in my tomb with two good legs? Is it not better to be sitting here, reunited with you, blessed by the sight of Micha sifting dirt and eating bugs?"

"Tell me this, then. Why has He not given me a son?"

"Tell me why he should."

Michal realized the insufficiency of her reason for the first time. "Because that's the one thing I want most."

"Forgive me." Mephibosheth removed the hull from another pistachio. "My religious education must be incomplete. I missed the part where God is supposed to comply with our wishes. That priest we lived with in Jericho told Ep and me we were supposed to obey God's will. That stupid wretch got the whole thing backward. I should go beat him senseless with my crutch."

"Seriously, now." Michal put her hand on her nephew's arm. "Why should it not be God's will to give me my heart's desire? It would be so easy for Him. What is one more boy baby to Him?"

Mephibosheth popped his open palm against his forehead. "You're right, of course. Some people are slow-witted. But you and I are much smarter than God. Why doesn't He realize we know what we need so much better than He does? Heal my feet. Give you a son. If He doesn't hear from us, He can carry on in His own wisdom. When He makes a mistake we'll let Him know, and He must repair things as we direct."

"You know God doesn't make mistakes," Michal interjected.

"Yet you are childless. So what is the inevitable conclusion?"

"I don't know."

"Yes, you do."

"You are too much like Jonathan. You don't know when you've said enough."

"And you are just like Grandfather. You can't admit you're wrong. I'm not trying to win a debate, Aunt Michal. This is crucial to your peace of mind. So I ask again. If God could give you a son but He does it not, and He never makes mistakes, what does that mean?"

"I'm going inside." She began to stuff her knitting into a bag.

"Face it."

"I won't."

"Say it."

"All right. God has chosen to make me barren." Michal stood and collected her things. "Are you satisfied?"

"And He chose for me to be lame. Since the all-wise God has made these decisions, who are we to question them?"

CHAPTER THIRTY-NINE

"And it came to pass in an eveningtide, that David arose from off his bed, and walked upon the roof of the king's house: and from the roof he saw a woman washing herself; and the woman was very beautiful to look upon." II Samuel 11:2

MICHAL WANTED TO thank her husband for his extraordinary kindness to Mephibosheth. First, of course, she would have to beg his forgiveness for embarrassing him in public and hope his anger was abated. By the time she gathered her courage, King David was on an extended campaign fighting the Syrians. After his victory, she considered trying to catch his eye. She could not interrupt him in the gardens where he spoke with a foreign king paying tribute.

Determined wives and ambitious concubines descended upon the king if he entered the courtyard alone, before the day's business began or after it was done. Michal was afraid she would be rudely shoved aside if she tried to break through the crowd and speak with her husband. Would he ignore her greeting? In any case, the daughter of a king could never say what was in her heart in front of those flirting, fawning, impertinent girls. Gone were the days when she could speak with her husband privately, basking in the warmth of a smile meant only for her.

David fought other wars in other places, extending the borders of Israel further every year. Despite occasional times of scarcity and infrequent plagues, there was no military threat. The People of God were safe and secure, ruled by a benevolent, beloved king.

Within the palace, life and death continued. More children were born, eleven royal sons and eight daughters in all. Abigail went to sleep one evening and never awakened. Abital's weakness went into the wasting disease and she, too, rested in the family tomb. Michal even missed Rizpah, who returned to Judea to be near her sons.

Bird and Maachah fought constantly. Each did her utmost to influence the other wives and concubines to join her faction. The younger wives either did not know how to avoid the strife or did not want to. Kerah sided first with one then the other, always scheming to gain some personal advantage. Michal kept to herself to escape the gossip, bickering, and backbiting that never let up in the women's quarters.

She taught little Micha to be an expert in mixing colors and dyeing. When the boy was old enough, Mephibosheth engaged a respected teacher to instruct his son how to read and interpret the law.

Michal no longer worried about occasions requiring a male relative to escort her in public. Mephibosheth never refused to take her places, nor did he complain about how often she chose to go out. His servants loaded him into his specially-made donkey cart, and away they went. He and Michal became well known for their regular attendance at the place of worship.

One Passover, Michal received an unexpected message saying Joash and Tirzah were in Jerusalem. Mephibosheth took Michal to a place where poor pilgrims stayed in tents. Joash and Tirzah proudly presented their children, Abimilech, Jonathan, Sarah, Abraham, and Ahinoam. "I hope you don't mind that we used some of your family names," Tirzah said shyly as they shared the meal Michal brought with her.

The men and children stayed in the tent while Michal and Tirzah strolled among the pilgrims' tents. How sad it was to realize how little she and her old friend had to discuss.

Joash's hair was white, but he retained the strength of an ox. After lifting Mephibosheth into the cart, he turned to Michal. "I would have died in Gallim but for you, my lady. If you or anyone in your family ever needs refuge, come to Shiloh. Our farm is east of the well named Ben Amir."

Michal thanked Joash, certain she would never again have occasion to travel outside the city.

Michal's bleeding became more irregular than ever, and eventually stopped. Yet she was content. She enjoyed the pleasant afternoons spent discussing life, philosophy, family, and the great mystery of God with her nephew. One warm spring day, they sipped from water jars while Michal knitted in a quiet corner of the garden. "This will sound like something my mother would say," she warned Mephibosheth. "I want to know what has happened to moral standards in this palace."

"Any answer of mine would be wasted, dear aunt, because you are about to tell me."

Michal smiled. "Yes, I am. This morning I awoke very early. Since I could not sleep, I decided to go to the stream and experiment with the new indigo plants you bought for me at the coastal ship market. There was a woman sneaking out the back gate of the courtyard just before dawn. Now what do you suppose that little foreigner was up to?"

"Let me think. She got lost on her way to the city gate. She confused the palace for an inn. I hope you didn't talk to her."

Michal recoiled. "No, I most certainly did not speak to her, and you are impertinent for even suggesting such a thing. I don't think she saw me. I was in the alcove, gathering my pots when she raced by putting on her head covering."

"Then how do you know she was a foreigner? Or do you use that term to mean she was where she should not have been?"

"Both. You should have seen her. Her hair was like a campfire, a curly crown of bright red with golden highlights shooting out like flames. It's a difficult color to make. You must mix three parts of strong, true red with one part of yellow. When she turned to look behind her, I saw her eyes were the color of the sky on a summer morning. No daughter of Jacob ever looked as this woman does."

"She sounds pretty."

Michal thought for a moment. "No, Nephew. Pretty is far too weak a word. Beautiful is not enough either. No words describe her. She was breathtaking, in the way of a snow-covered mountaintop in the moonlight. Her face shone like the stars did on those clear, cool evenings when I was a bride. She was so lovely it almost hurt my eyes to behold her."

"Aunt Michal," Mephibosheth said, lowering his voice, "you must tell no one of this encounter. Promise me."

"I see you know more of this than I do. Are this woman's comings and goings common knowledge in the palace then? I would not suspect Daniel to be her lover. So is it Amnon or Absalom who is carrying on this clandestine affair?"

Mephibosheth grabbed her arm tightly. "Speak not of this. I beg you."

"You are afraid for me." Michal studied her nephew's face for a long moment. "That can only mean..." She took a deep breath. "It is *him. He* calls this exotically beautiful woman to his bed in the dark of night."

Mephibosheth nodded and released his grip on her arm. "You understand why this must be kept secret."

"Other than you or Micha, who is too young to know such things, there is no one in this house I would tell anything." She sighed. "Again, he disappoints me."

"Everyone does, sooner or later. Only God is always faithful. The rest of us may try, but we fail."

"I have never told this to anyone," Michal began. "Years ago, your grandfather, King Saul, was out to kill David. I helped him escape."

Mephibosheth laughed. "I heard that story at my father's knee. It has become a legend throughout the nation, not just in our family."

"Not this part. He wanted me to go with him. I refused, and do you know why?" She waited for a response. Receiving none, she continued. "Because I was barefoot. How many nights have I sat sleepless in the dark, wondering why I didn't go anyway? How different could things have been? If I had gone with him, he might not have taken another wife. I'll never know." She put down her knitting and stared at her hands. "And my sandals were there. Right there in our kitchen. An extra pair I forgot about. I saw them later. And I wondered, did he see them that night and think I made an excuse because I didn't want to face hardships with him?"

"Did you ever ask him?"

"No. It was seven, eight years before I saw him again." Michal gazed into the distance. She resumed knitting. "Surely you know this secret affair with the foreign woman will come out. I give you my word I will say nothing. Nevertheless someone else will see her, or she will slip on a stair, or a jealous rival will expose them. They will be found out."

CHAPTER FORTY

"And...David sent and fetched her to his house, and she became his wife,..." II Samuel 11:27

FROM THE OTHER side of the courtyard, Michal was certain the man who squatted near Mephibosheth was King David. She was disappointed when her husband sprang up, clapped her nephew on the shoulder and disappeared into the public chamber before she was within speaking distance.

How splendidly men age in comparison to women, she thought. *We get fat or wrinkle like raisins. They get a dusting of silver in their hair, which only makes them more beautiful.*

"Good afternoon." Michal settled next to her nephew on their favorite shaded bench. "You did not bring Micha? He's not ill, is he?"

"Greetings, Aunt. Micha is as healthy as a bull. He eats like an ox. I must check his head when I get home, to make sure he is not sprouting horns." Mephibosheth furrowed his brow. "Our lord the king just asked me to do something for him. A personal favor."

Michal stared at Mephibosheth. "A king has no need to ask for favors. He is surrounded by people whose lives consist of obeying his commands. Don't you see? This means he thinks of you as a friend. And he trusts you. It is a deep honor. Did he ask something difficult?"

"No, it's simple and easy. I'm thinking about it."

"Thinking about it?" Michal was incredulous. "You don't think about your king's request. You give him anything he wants. If it costs your life, you owe him no less. How can you 'think about' obeying your sovereign? What did he ask of you?"

Mephibosheth smiled. "He wants me to deliver a message. To relay another request, really. To someone else."

"That's *all*? Shall I ask for your cart?"

"No, not just yet. You see, he will never know if I fail to do as he wishes."

"King Saul will not sleep well in his tomb this night, my nephew. His spirit will weep at the words his grandson speaks. And when I think what compassion King David has shown you. For the first time ever, you bring shame on our house."

"You would feel otherwise if *you* were the one commissioned to do the king's bidding."

"Am I not his subject, just as you are?" Michal protested. "I would be most pleased to carry out a request that came from the lips of our king. As it happens, the business of a kingdom is conducted by its men. And so it falls to you."

"Is this truly how you feel, Aunt?" Mephibosheth's eyes were fixed on her. "You are not simply saying what you think is expected, but what you recommend?"

"Mouthing words is not my way. I speak the truth."

"Good," he said. "That is good. Because you are the person to whom I am to relay the king's request."

"Me? I don't understand."

Mephibosheth fixed his eyes on the ground between his twisted feet. "King David is taking another wife. She will be coming this evening to make the palace her home. The beautiful foreign woman with hair like fire, the one you saw in the courtyard one morning. Her name is Bathsheba. She is a Hittite." He took a long breath and went on without moving his gaze. "The king asked me to ask you to help her feel welcome. To befriend her among the women."

"How dare he ask me?" she growled.

"Perhaps he thinks of you as a friend. And he trusts you."

"You know I don't like having my own words thrown back at me."

"It is a deep honor to comply with a request that comes from the lips of our king."

"She is a whore, a foreigner. She's everything I hate. You are dogs, both you and him, to think I would ever—"

"He is your sovereign lord." Mephibosheth continued to stare at the ground and speak calmly. "You must give him anything he wants. If it costs your life, you owe him no less."

"You don't understand. Forget that he is the king. He is my *husband*. I have served him more than half my life. And how does he repay me? He—"

"I wonder if King Saul will rest well in his tomb tonight."

"You tricked me into saying those things, Nephew."

"No, you are always truthful. It is not your way to mouth words."

"If I had another living relative I would never speak to you again. It's only for your father's sake—"

"And when I think what compassion King David has shown to you."

"I'll find her a place to sleep. Nothing more." She stood and glared at Mephibosheth.

"That is most charitable of you."

"It certainly is, you conniving little jackal. Send this Bethsheeda to me."

"Bathsheba."

"I will show her to a bedchamber." She bent and put her face near his. "After that, she is on her own." Michal shook a finger at him. "And you can tell my husband—"

Mephibosheth held his palms outward against her words. "No, Aunt Michal. Take pity on a poor lame man. I do not have the strength to deliver another message today."

"Lame indeed." She began to walk rapidly toward the women's quarters. "I ought to take one of your crutches and beat you with it. And use the other one on him. Is there any other message from my lord, the king? Any other dirty work he wants me to do?" Not waiting for an answer, Michal stalked up the stairway. She stopped at the landing and turned toward Mephibosheth. "Bring Micha with you tomorrow. If you come alone I'll have you thrown out." Michal stomped into her bedchamber and flung her knitting against a wall.

"May I get you anything, my lady?" her handmaid Ballah asked in a frightened voice. Why did I let this girl take Rizpah's place, Michal asked herself for the hundredth time. A gnat could make the silly girl tremble. Oh, to have Tirzah here for this one day!

Michal stared at her servant for a long moment, thinking through the arrangement of the women's rooms. "Who has claimed Lady Abigail's bedchamber?" she asked at last.

"A concubine by the name of Salomeha, my lady."

A concubine in her dead friend's bed? "Take some cleaning materials and go to that room. I will meet you there." Michal swept down the corridor, thinking how mortified Abigail would be if she knew. She stalked into the center of Abigail's room. A comely girl was sprawled across the bed, talking and laughing. Four others lounged on floor cushions.

"A new wife will occupy this bedchamber," Michal announced. "Remove yourselves and your belongings at once."

No one moved. "Where do you want us to go?" a girl resting against a bright floor cushion asked sarcastically.

Michal scorched the girl with her eyes. "I am preparing this chamber for Lady Bathsheba. Finding a place for you is not my concern."

"Salomeha was told this could be her room," another girl whined.

"Whoever said that made a mistake. Take your things and go. Now."

"Who are you?" the girl persisted.

"I believe you know perfectly well who I am." Michal glanced around the room, making eye contact with each young woman. "If you do not know me, you have no business in this area of the palace." She stepped near a shelf and rested her hand on a wooden box. "Abigail never wore makeup. This does not belong in this room."

The girl on the bed sat up. "That's mine!"

Michal hurled the makeup box through the open window. The whacking sound of breaking wood mingled with the concubines' shrieks. "Those aren't Abigail's." Michal pointed to several garments hanging on pegs.

"Wait! Please, not my clothes." The previously immobile bodies whirled into action. "Girls, help me get my things."

"Don't forget my cloak."

"Is she crazy?"

"Where are my sandals?"

"Put down the vase. That was Abigail's." Michal stood in the middle of the room, arms folded.

Women congregated in the corridor.

"What's happening?"

"Princess Michal has gone mad, just like old Abigail."

"Is Salomeha going somewhere?"

"Who does she think she is?"

"Didn't I tell you the king should put her away?"

Michal heard Haggith's voice in the corridor. "I would like to know exactly what is going on here." She came to stand a few feet from Michal.

Michal looked down at Haggith from her superior height. *Hello, my old friend from Hebron. How nice that you've decided to speak to me after all this time.* "Good afternoon, Haggith. These ladies are removing their belongings from this chamber. We will be welcoming a new wife this evening. I have decided she will sleep here."

"I know nothing of a new wife," Haggith said uncertainly.

"Nevertheless, she will be here soon. I have asked my handmaid Ballah to prepare the chamber." Michal glanced around. "And I must say it needs cleansing. Since you are here, you can oversee the cleaning maids while they take over that task. Immediately, if you don't mind. I know you wouldn't want the new wife to arrive and find an unfit chamber any more than I would."

Michal smiled as she heard familiar voices amidst the growing crowd in the corridor. *Come and challenge me. Do you imagine a few harsh words from you will make me tremble? I have faced angry kings alone.*

Kerah came to stand beside Haggith. "By whose authority is this being done?"

"I am the senior wife in this household," Michal said. *I should have taken this stand sooner.*

"Someone fetch Lady Ahinoam."

"The old hag has gone mad."

"Michal is not really senior, is she?"

235

The room fell silent as Maachah entered with Bird waddling behind her.

"Michal, I haven't given this room to anyone," Bird said. "And what's this about a new wife?"

"My son has told me no such thing." Maachah added.

Look at them, Michal thought as she surveyed the angry faces. *They look just like Phaltiel's women, when they gathered to give me a rude initiation to Gallim. No one here has the courage to tell our husband he has done wrong. Yet they stand ready to peck out the eyes of some helpless woman who may not even wish to be among us.*

Michal stood tall and crossed her arms. "Since we have assembled, I'll take this opportunity to make an announcement. Our Lord King David has taken another wife. I am confident everyone will obey the king's *command* to welcome her warmly and help her settle comfortably into our family. She will be here this evening. This will be her bedchamber. Her name is Bathsheba. She is a Hittite. I hope to receive no reports of anyone failing to carry out the wishes of our lord the king in this matter."

Michal made her way through the stunned gathering. As she walked sedately to her own room, she smiled at the sounds of noisy confusion erupting behind her.

At twilight, Bird appeared at the door of Michal's bedchamber.

"Good evening," Michal said. "Come and join me."

Bird remained standing in the doorway. "Granted, you are the senior wife," she said coldly, "but someday my son Amnon will be king." She turned and slowly walked away.

CHAPTER FORTY-ONE

"And David comforted Bathsheba his wife...and she bare a son, and he called his name Solomon: and the Lord loved him." II Samuel 12:24

"YOU'RE LATER THAN usual," Mephibosheth said. "Most days, you walk down the steps just as the baker begins to make fire in the ovens."

Michal smiled. "Do you think my age slows me down? No, Solomon made colors for the first time today. He had to try every combination. I don't understand how the women of this house can be so cruel to such a sweet little boy."

"He's half Hittite." Mephibosheth grinned broadly. "I've heard it said there's some doubt foreigners have souls."

"Someday, my nephew, you will throw my own words in my face once too often, and I will set the palace guards on you."

"The guards like me." He directed a salute to the back of the sentry at the gate. "I treat them like brothers. I have good news, Aunt Michal. The betrothal between Micha and Rachel was sealed today. When Solomon gets too old to play in the stream, perhaps Micha's child will come and learn to make colors."

"That's wonderful, Mephibosheth. I wish you many grandchildren. I pray your son will raise his family in a home filled with peace. He must never take a second wife."

"Peace is boring. Life is more interesting when the household engages in civil war."

"You wouldn't joke about such a thing if you lived in the midst of it. I often think I will pretend to be deaf to avoid listening to their backbiting."

Mephibosheth patted her arm. "Have you noticed what a fine day this is? How would you like to take a ride in my cart?"

Michal knew by now her nephew's request to ride together was a way to have a conversation away from the palace. "That sounds most pleasant," she answered, already starting to wonder what news he brought.

Mephibosheth wasted no time. As soon as his donkey cleared the palace gates, he asked, "How are things between the king's wives?"

"Bird is determined the king must name Amnon as his successor." Michal sighed. "Maachah campaigns constantly for Absalom. They trade sly insults when they meet and whisper vicious lies about each other when they are apart."

"I grant that David may be a difficult husband, but he is the greatest king this world has ever seen. No disrespect to Grandfather. Mighty rulers tremble with fear when our king mobilizes his army. I pray he will wear the royal bracelet for many years to come. But you need to be prepared for the day when the king sleeps with his fathers, God forbid."

"My husband no longer rides out to war. He walks strong and straight. Why do you think of his death, Nephew?"

"Look to your right, and tell me who you see."

"How would I know those men who do business at the city gate?" Nevertheless, Michal noticed a familiar face. "Absalom? What is he doing there?"

"Don't stare. The prince spends many hours near the judgment seat. He cunningly guesses what someone wants to hear, and that is what he says. If a man complains he should have an orchard the king awarded to his brother, Absalom listens soberly and then agrees. Since he has no authority to make decisions, nothing is binding. Yet he curries favor with the people at the expense of the king's reputation."

"Absalom has David's fine looks, coupled with his mother Maachah's base ambition," Michal observed. "But Amnon is the elder son. He has administrative skills Absalom will never possess."

"True enough, my clever aunt. In my opinion, Amnon is a self-indulgent, dishonest rascal. As long as he gets everything he wants for himself, the nation would be welcome to whatever remains. However, you're right. He might possibly hold the kingdom together for a while. And there are other contenders. Daniel openly acknowledges he will never be king, but Haggith's son Adonijah has high hopes."

Mephibosheth stopped the cart at the crest of a hill. "Look at that view. This is the most beautiful city I've ever seen." He relaxed his grip on the reins and leaned back. "My point is this, if something happens to David, Israel is in for a rough transition. Anyone could be in danger, especially us. You and me. Micha. Micha's children, when and if he has them."

"I know you're right." Michal put her hand on Mephibosheth's shoulder. "Whatever happens to me happens. I should have been dead several times over already. In a desperate situation, I could hide in one of the caves behind the palace. There are places back there where no one would ever find me. Then I suppose I could walk over the old, hidden pass to Bahurim. The most important thing is to know you and Micha are safe."

"A lame man may not be worth killing. I worry for Micha, though. Few people think in terms of my royal grandfather now, but who knows? Ep's family would hide my son, but that's the first place they would go looking for him."

"You have given this some thought," Michal said.

"I have."

"I know you too well, Mephibosheth. There is something you want from me."

"The woman who used to be your handmaid, Tirzah? She and her husband are good, honest people. I heard him say once he would give you refuge if you needed it. Do you think they would hide Micha for your sake? No one in Jerusalem knows them, let alone where they live."

Michal looked toward the Holy Mountain. "Thank you," she whispered.

"What?" Mephibosheth looked puzzled.

"I was again thanking the Living God for His superior wisdom. It seems only right, since I berated Him for separating me from Tirzah. Now I see that the distance between her home and ours could be a great blessing. Yes, I am certain Joash and Tirzah would provide Micha a place to hide. May God grant that he never needs it. Going back to what I said, the king is healthy and strong. Has something set your thoughts in this direction, Nephew?"

"Nothing in particular, just looks and whispers I sometimes hear at the king's table. I will make some preparations against the day we may need them." Mephibosheth took up the reins to his donkey cart.

"And now I will ask something of you," Michal said.

Mephibosheth grinned. "Why would I grant a wish to my father's favorite sister, who may have just saved my son's life?"

"Be serious. If something happens, and if you can do this without putting Micha in danger, take care of Bathsheba and her little boy. They have no one to look after them."

"You care that much for this child, Solomon, my aunt?"

"I do. You know I have a weakness for smart little boys."

"And you ask for Bathsheba's safety as well?"

"I never planned to have anything to do with her, as you, of all people, should know. She irritated me by clinging to me when she first came to the palace. Then she drove me mad asking so many questions about our God. After she became a believer, she shamed me by her simple faith."

"Interesting information, but not a motive to protect her," Mephibosheth said.

Michal regarded the city for a long time. "I have my reasons for the things I do. Reasons you have no need to know. And even if you knew, you would not be able to understand."

"No?" Mephibosheth asked. "My legs are lame, but my heart knows something about the power of love."

"Take me home," Michal snapped.

CHAPTER FORTY-TWO

"And she answered him, Nay, my brother, do not force me; for no such thing ought to be done in Israel: do not thou this folly. Howbeit he would not hearken unto her voice: but, being stronger than she, forced her, and lay with her." II Samuel 13: 12, 14

THE MESSENGER STOOD in the doorway of Michal's bedchamber. "My lady, Lord Eliab must see you at once in the stable. He says it is urgent."

Michal thought for the hundredth time that the inconvenience of assuming her rightful position as head wife far outweighed the benefits. *Why the stable?* Did Eliab want to complain again that a wife broke a cart wheel? Or was another groomsman caught trying to steal a kiss from a servant girl?

She stopped inside the stable, allowing her eyes to adjust to the darkness. Eliab sat on a stool, his head buried in his hands. In a dark corner, a girl sobbed quietly. *Maachah's daughter, Tamar? With a soldier's cloak wrapped around her?*

"What—"

The word was barely out of Michal's mouth when Eliab said, "Tamar has been violated."

"Violated?" She looked at the trembling teenager and realized the girl's hair was disheveled. "Oh, poor child!" She ran to wrap the frightened Tamar in an embrace.

"I'm ruined," Tamar moaned. "Ruined."

Michal looked over Tamar's shoulder. "Who dares do this to the daughter of the king?"

"She accuses Prince Amnon." Eliab rubbed the back of his neck. "King David will discern guilt or innocence. Meanwhile, you must take her to her mother."

Prince Amnon? Bird's son raped Maachah's daughter? Michal fought to comprehend how such a double tragedy could be possible. "Come, child."

Michal kept one arm wrapped around the shivering Tamar and waved away curious servants with the other. Fortunately, they found Maachah alone in her bedchamber.

"Your face is dirty and your hair is a mess, Daughter," Maachah said crossly.

"Tamar has been raped," Michal said.

All hope of keeping the matter quiet vanished as Maachah screamed. "Tamar! My daughter! Ruined! In the bloom of your youth! Soiled! How shall I bear this evil? The king must know of this at once! He will cut off the head of the dog that dared to touch our daughter."

While Maachah continued to shriek, women streamed into the room. Michal washed Tamar's face. Bathsheba began to comb the weeping girl's hair while wives and concubines started speaking.

"A girl isn't safe on the streets of Jerusalem anymore."

"Who did it?"

"She asked for it, the way she dresses."

"I'll bet it was some foreigner."

"Tamar? Raped? No!"

Haggith took the comb from Bathsheba's hand. "Let me do that."

Maachah, who had thrown herself across her bed, looked around the room as if checking attendance. Her glance flickered past Bird. She wailed, "Speak, Tamar. Who did this horrible thing to you? Who would dare to violate the king's own beloved daughter?"

The shaken girl looked at her mother with the eyes of a trapped animal, and breathed one barely-audible word, "Amnon."

"Amnon?" Maachah screamed. "The prince? Your own brother raped you? He is mad! Prince Amnon is an evil madman."

Bird stood as if she were rooted to the floor of Maachah's bedchamber. The color drained from her face. "No," she whispered.

Maachah's supporters clustered around her and Tamar. Kerah and her group stood back, clucking about the whole situation being an embarrassment to the royal family. The women who routinely kissed Bird's toes stood looking at each other with uncertainty. Bathsheba put a tentative arm around Bird, who shook it off.

As the crowd dwindled, Maachah rose. "I must be alone with my poor, desolate daughter," she sighed. "She wants only my comfort."

Michal led Bird to her chamber. Bathsheba followed at a distance. "Tamar is lying," Bird said without conviction. "Amnon has been ill. He couldn't..." Her voice trailed away.

Bird's distraught handmaid fetched cool water. Michal dipped a rag into the bowl and dabbed at Bird's forehead. "The king will find out the truth of this matter."

"Is there anything I can do?" Bathsheba asked in her slightly accented way.

Michal gestured there was nothing and waved Bathsheba away. Her flaming curls shimmered as she strolled down the corridor.

Within days, Bird acted as if nothing happened. Nevertheless, her private war with Maachah burned hot with fresh fuel. Gossip that Tamar seduced her brother circulated through the women's quarters. On the heels of that story, a rumor claimed Absalom used his sister as bait to discredit Amnon. Maachah was accused of plotting the incident beforehand, as evidenced by her hysterics when told of the rape. "She screamed," one wag said, "but I never saw a tear."

One group maintained the rape never happened, that Tamar never went near Amnon's house. A bold concubine theorized Maachah or Tamar fabricated everything. Someone suggested Haggith bribed Amnon, or Tamar, or both in an effort to improve her son Adonijah's standing ahead of King David's older sons.

Maachah noisily arranged to have Tamar moved into Absalom's house. "For protection from Amnon," she claimed.

There was agreement on one thing only. King David must take action. The situation demanded fact-finding, judgment, and closure. At least one member of the royal family was guilty of a grievous wrong, but the king remained silent on the matter.

"COULD YOU POSSIBLY convince your husband to deal with his children?" Mephibosheth asked as he drove Michal to the palace after visiting the place of worship.

"I have no influence. He never speaks with me," Michal replied, waving gnats away from her eyes. "Where do these pests come from?"

"I believe they hatch from eggs. We might be better off if people did the same."

"I hope *you* haven't tried to talk to the king," Michal said.

"No one seeks the advice of a lame man. Not even his aunt."

"Good. It is dangerous to speak against his children to David. He will always take their side, even if they're wrong. He is totally blind to the faults of his offspring."

Mephibosheth dismissed her statement with the lifting of his eyebrows. "Is there no one?"

"No. David will never stand for criticism of his sons. They are all perfect."

"And his daughters?"

"They have far less value."

When they'd left for the place of worship, the usual sentry stood in front of the palace gate. Now there was a group of four armed soldiers barring entrance to the courtyard. "Interesting," Mephibosheth muttered softly, before speaking up to say, "Good day, gentlemen."

A familiar-looking soldier looked at Mephibosheth, then Michal. He peered into the back of the donkey cart. "Sorry to trouble you, sir." Another soldier swung open the gates.

"What do you suppose that's all about?" Michal looked back over her shoulder.

There was no one in the courtyard. Even the lazy goats that hung around the kitchen were nowhere in sight. Michal helped her nephew transfer his weight from the cart to his crutches. She led the donkey out a side gate toward the animal shelter. "Where is everyone?" she asked the lone stable boy.

"You have not heard?"

"Heard what?"

"Prince Amnon is dead." The young man took the reins of the donkey.

"Dead? Was there an accident? What happened?"

The young man glanced left and right. "I am not certain, my lady."

Michal ran back to the courtyard. "I have to go to Bird," she told Mephibosheth. "A stable boy just told me Amnon is dead."

Michal found Bathsheba cowering in her bedchamber. "Prince Amnon," she blurted.

"I just heard," Michal said. "What happened?"

"Absalom has murdered his brother, Amnon. It is said he did this to avenge the rape of Tamar."

CHAPTER FORTY-THREE

"But Absalom sent spies throughout all the tribes of Israel, saying, As soon as ye hear the sound of the trumpet, then ye shall say, Absalom reigneth in Hebron. And there came a messenger to David, saying, The hearts of the men of Israel are after Absalom." II Samuel 15:10, 13

MICHAL WAS DISMAYED but not surprised when Absalom returned to Israel after two years of self-imposed exile in the land of Geshur, where Maachah's father was king. David did not challenge Absalom's return, but banished his son from the palace for a short while. A rumor passed through the women's quarters that Prince Absalom was pressuring the military commander Joab to intercede for him. Later, Michal heard from Mephibosheth that Joab brought the prince into the king's presence at a public gathering. David chose to embrace his son, and Absalom was back in favor with the king. Most occupants of the palace acted as if Amnon's murder never occurred

During Absalom's absence, Haggith assured the women her son Adonijah was the heir apparent. The relationship between Haggith and Maachah cooled noticeably, and their followers split into two camps. The women who were previously friendly with Bird distanced themselves from her and aligned themselves with Maachah, Haggith, or Kerah. Bird seemed to become invisible to the other wives, only occasionally associating with Michal and Bathsheba. Most of the time she kept to herself.

During this time, Maachah's father died, and she received permission to travel to Geshur. She did not expect to arrive in time for the old king's funeral, but she would participate in the celebration of her brother's coronation. She radiated excitement, submitting endless requests for extra clothing, jewelry, and attendants.

"You'd think she was the one being crowned," Michal grumbled to Bathsheba.

After Maachah's departure, the atmosphere in the women's quarters was noticeably less acrimonious. Haggith made a futile attempt to hold court, but she was as uninspiring as her son Adonijah. Neither seemed able to assemble a following.

Three days after Maachah left for Geshur, Mephibosheth offered to take Michal and Bathsheba to the city market. Solomon would have to go along, since Bathsheba would never leave the palace without her son in tow. They were wedging themselves into the cart when a bee stung Michal on the arm. She felt faint, then nauseated. With considerable disappointment, she decided to stay behind.

"We should be back early this afternoon," Mephibosheth reassured Michal as he guided his donkey out of the courtyard.

Michal went to her bedchamber and dabbed cool water on the reddening sting. She thought about asking a healing servant for a poultice, but decided to rest a bit first. The bed felt especially comfortable, and she drifted into a long restful sleep.

Upon awakening, she spent some time carding wool. Later, she took her handwork to the courtyard to enjoy the sunlight. The trees and flowers were unusually beautiful on this warm, peaceful day. Michal dozed, and her knitting did not progress.

As the late afternoon sun sifted through the leaves of the trees into the quiet courtyard, Mephibosheth unexpectedly appeared alone in his fast-moving cart. "Come!" was all he said. Michal was surprised. Her nephew was seldom in a hurry, nor did he ever speak to her in such a curt manner.

She climbed into the cart immediately. "What's wrong? Where are we going?"

He held up a hand in a signal to wait. Michal felt a surge of unexplained dread. Not far outside the gate, Mephibosheth turned his donkey from the road. He stopped behind a screen of trees. Michal dug her hand into her nephew's arm. "Did something happen to Solomon? What is it?"

Mephibosheth mopped his brow. "Rebellion. Absalom has raised an army and he is advancing on Jerusalem. The palace may be under siege before morning."

"How dare he? That son of Maachah. But Solomon?" She was afraid of the answer.

"Micha is taking the boy and his mother to...the agreed-upon place. You remember. They will not use the main roads." He looked at the sun. "God willing they are already well on their way."

"How did you find out about the rebellion?"

"It was the talk of the market. We left and went immediately to my farm, where I always keep a cart and traveling provisions ready for an emergency. Let us pray no one saw Micha harness the donkeys. I warned Bathsheba to make sure her hair was completely covered and to keep her eyes downcast. That's why I've been gone so long. I thought you would be worried. Now you must go home with me and hide."

"No, thank you, Nephew. God bless you for looking after the boy. And her. David is in the palace. I'm going to him."

"That's the most dangerous thing you could do, Aunt Michal."

"Don't worry about me. I'm an old woman. I'd rather die with my husband than live without him."

"You said you hated him," Mephibosheth said.

"Who I decide to hate or not hate is none of your business. Hurry and go home. The city will be a dangerous place for you. I will walk back to the palace. I know this pathway well."

"You should let me drive you. You can use the extra time to gather a few necessities."

"No need. I can walk the legs off every young woman in the palace," Michal answered. She held up her emergency bag. "And I have what I need with me. Food, silver, my knife, everything."

"Is there nothing I can do for you?"

"No, dear Nephew, nothing more than you have already done." She patted his hand. May God be with you in this troubled time."

"And also with you, my beloved aunt."

After Mephibosheth and Michal embraced each other, Michal climbed to the ground. She walked through the woods, and crossed the meadow to the rear gate of the palace. On the way, she tried to count how many times she had left her home without knowing if she would ever see it again.

A concubine stood at the gate. "Good evening," Michal said. She wished she could remember the young woman's name.

"No, my lady, it is a sad evening. Everyone is gone, except ten of us concubines. We remained behind to keep the palace open."

"Where did everyone else go?"

The concubine shrugged. "Most of the servants went home. A few soldiers deserted. The rest of the household went that way." She pointed toward the stream where Michal used her dye pots.

"If I were you, I would go home to my family," Michal said.

The girl looked down. "I cannot do that."

"Have courage then." Michal smoothed the lovely young woman's headdress. "And God be with you."

"Thank you, my lady."

Michal walked quickly across the stream to the largest of the well-known caves. She was not surprised to find it filled with soldiers and servants of the royal household. "I am looking for King David," Michal said to the nearest foot soldier. When he gave her a questioning look, she added, "He is my husband."

"I'll take you to him."

David looked up when Michal entered the small cave where he sat alone. "Michal," he said with obvious relief. "Eliab said he couldn't find you."

She sat down beside him. "You look tired, husband."

"Absalom. My own son." He rested his head on his knees.

"You will defeat him."

"Not if I do not fight. How can I try to destroy the son of my body?"

"Have you eaten anything?" she asked.

"There was no time for that. And I am not hungry."

Michal took out some meal cakes and handed him one. "You used to like these. I have some grapes, too. They may be bruised, but they're still good."

249

"So that's what you have in that bag you always carry." David took a bite of the cake. "I can't find Bathsheba or Solomon."

"They are safe. Micha is taking them to Joash and Tirzah at Shiloh."

David closed his eyes. "Thank God. Why didn't you go with them?"

She handed him another cake. "My place is with you."

"That's the worst place you could choose," David said. He leaned his head against the cave's wall then accepted the grape Michal pressed to his lips.

"No, the worst choice is being separated from you. I did that once, and I've never stopped regretting it. This time I have my shoes on, and extra sandals in my bag."

"That was a long time ago. Two kingdoms and half a lifetime." He took the stem of grapes from her hand and stared as if grapes were something he'd never seen before. "We all make mistakes, Michal. But I have made so many. So many."

"If God can forgive anything, why should we not do the same? As you say, we have all sinned. Your wrongdoings are always on public display because you are the king."

"The king," he repeated. "I have let being the king overshadow being a father. A husband. God's forgiveness, and my family's, may ease the pain. The human penalties must still be paid. I fear the sword will never leave my house."

"Perhaps that's the price of wearing the royal bracelet. All of my brothers and my sister died violent deaths. Who knows? I may yet carry on the family tradition."

"Brave Princess Michal." David put his hand over hers. "You deserved a better husband than me."

"I never wanted anyone but you, David. Ever. That has not changed."

"You were right about Abigail. I broke her heart. I've ruined everything. I can't even afford to feed my army."

"Everything will look brighter in the morning, after you've had some sleep," Michal said. "God will provide. The people will support you. And there is a full treasure chest in a little cave not far from where we now sit."

"What do you mean? There's no treasure here."

"I started hiding jewels and shekels of silver in my little private cave when I thought you were going to divorce me. I've kept up the habit over the years. Just in case I ever needed something."

David pulled Michal closer to him. "You're cold," he said, wrapping his military cloak around both of them. "How could you ever believe I would divorce you, Michal? You have always been precious to me. You saved my life."

And so the two of them slept in the same place for the first time in years. No longer passionate lovers in a luxurious palace, they were two old friends giving each other what comfort they could in the darkness of the cave.

The soldiers were up and moving before dawn. The bee sting on Michal's arm was red and swollen, but did not pain her nearly as much as the day before.

"It's a long walk to Bahurim," David warned her.

"Yes," she agreed with a smile. "I hope you can keep up."

David led the men forward. Michal hung back and joined the soldiers' women. A young mother hummed a psalm as she walked along and nursed her baby.

"It has been many years since I've heard that song," Michal said. She began to hum along with the young mother.

"That's the psalm we sang while Ziklag burned," an older woman said.

A soprano with a voice as strong as Merab's supplied the words. Soon, all of the women were singing. The men's heads stopped drooping. They walked faster, and most joined in the song.

"The Lord is my light and my salvation;
whom shall I fear?
The Lord is the strength of my life;
of whom shall I be afraid?"

"Good morning, Princess Michal," someone called out.

"Good morning," she replied.

"Your husband is the greatest king ever seen," another voice called out.

"Well said," Michal agreed. "But another, greater One will come from the House of David. And of His Kingdom there shall be no end."

AUTHOR BIO

Carlene Havel writes Christian-themed romances and historical novels set in Biblical times. She's lived in Turkey, Republic of the Philippines, and all over the southern half of the United States, from Florida to California. Carlene has worked for a banana importer, a software development company, and everything in between. She attended several colleges and universities, including one that surprised everyone by granting her a diploma. She enjoys reading, writing, and almost every variety of needlework. Carlene and her husband, Glenn, live in San Antonio, Texas, surrounded by their family. Read more about Carlene on her blog at:

http://www.goodreads.com/author/show/6440085.Carlene_Havel/blog.

Sharon Faucheux was born in New Orleans, LA. Raised in Austin, Texas, she graduated from the University of Texas with a degree in Psychology. After living in several other states and countries, she now resides in San Antonio, TX. Sharon's favorite activity is traveling with her always-entertaining family.

16500913R00136

Made in the USA
Charleston, SC
23 December 2012